NOTHING ABOUT US WITHOUT US:
THE ADVENTURES OF THE CARTOON REPUBLICAN ARMY

By David Perlmutter

Previous Publications

"Video Diary Of A Tall Soldier" was first published in *Cup of Joe* (Wicked East Press, 2010.)

"On My Honor" was first published in *Project Mayhem* (Mouldwarp Press, 2013.)

"Nothing About Us Without Us" was first published in *Weird City* (Static Movement, 2011.)

"Up To Me" was first published in *Weird City 2* (Static Movement, 2011.)

"Sisters Of Mercy" was first published in *Fall Shudders* (Static Movement, 2011.)

"The Milwaukee Incident" was first published in *Daily Flash 2011* (Pill Hill Press, 2011.)

"A Small Betrayal" was first published at *Digital SF* (2014)

"And The Cartoon Girls Go 'Do Da Doo Da Doo'" was first published in *Polychrome Ink 1* (2014)

"I'm New Here" and "Certain Private Conversations..." were first published in *Certain Private Conversations and Other Stories* (Aurora Publishing, 2015.)

"Cadmium and the Cops" was first published in *Robbed of Sleep 5* (2016)

All other stories are original to this collection.

Some stories have mild content alterations from their original versions.

ON MY HONOUR (The CRA Oath)

The following words were found written on a number of strips of paper found in the chamber of the Capitol Building on the morning following the bomb explosion that accompanied the Cartoon Republican Army's take-over of the U.S. Senate chamber in June 2—-. It provides a unique insight into the beliefs and activities of this secretive organization:

On my honour, as a duly deputized member of the Cartoon Republican Army, I promise that I will:

-Act in accordance with, and possibly redeem, the good name of the cartoon race.

-Protect, at all times, myself and my colleagues from harm, even to the point of risking my own life.

-Never allow myself to surrender to any of the temptations offered me by the human beings.

-Use whatever physical and mental aptitude I possess to advance the cause of the Cartoon Republican Army in any and all ways possible.

In addition, I swear that I will never:

-Reveal, in any way, the origins of the cartoon race, nor the secrets of our abilities to defy mortality, physics and other limitations of the mortal world to anyone except my colleagues, on pain of chastisement or death on my part.

-Provoke human beings into a confrontation with the CRA unless it is entirely and purposefully justified.

-Leave myself or any of my colleagues open to defilement, defacement, disfigurement or paralysis without first attempting to defend myself and/or them from such disgrace.

-Allow the human beings to enslave or conquer myself or my colleagues, as they have done to so many other cartoon characters in the past.

Above all, I will not rest or waiver in my attempts to make the human beings of the world understand, comply with and respect the need, the desire and the right of all animated cartoon characters to be regarded as their equals under the law and within the society of the United States of America and the world at large. Not until that day will the Cartoon Republican Army achieve its aims.

This I do solemnly swear, on my honour and my existence as an animated cartoon character.

[Place inductee's signature here]

NOTHING ABOUT US WITHOUT US

I.

Contrary to popular belief, the word "alien" does not apply exclusively to beings from outer space. The truth is, it originally applied to anyone who was somewhat "foreign" to the normative standards of a nation, be it in dress, speech, language, social customs, behavior, or any of a million other biased and narrowly structured devices designed to separate the people who "mattered" from those who supposedly did "not" matter. And that doesn't mean just those who assume human form. There's a whole race of beings, who you know rather pedantically as "cartoon characters", who have been "entertaining" you for over a century, and they've been treated like crap and manipulated by people to make money and careers of their own for nearly that long. That especially applies to the uniquely gifted and talented beings of television animation, the exclusive population and racist target of that rotten Orthicon enterprise. Well, not anymore, pal! After we got back from Orthicon, that interplanetary hellhole we got exiled to by a totally and completely unsympathetic U.S. government, we formed the Cartoon Republican Army to get control of their own rights and affairs. Hey, it worked for the Irish, didn't it?

Now, you must be wondering how *I,* a seemingly innocent, twelve-year old looking girl, know about all of this. First of all, I am a voracious reader and possess a photographic memory, which is both a blessing and a curse for me in different ways. And second, and most importantly, I'm *one* of 'em! But you probably figured that out already when you dragged me out of the Capitol building after what happened today. And now you want to know the truth, huh? All right- I'll tell you....

*

After we got back from Orthicon and the CRA got started up, I organized a battalion of the girls in my neighborhood and got commissioned as a Lieutenant, which is my current rank. No guys, you say? Well, honestly, most of 'em aren't nearly as smart as I am. Besides, the one boy bosom buddy I had, the one who came closest to being a real "partner" for me, as it were, had gotten himself killed in a race riot just after we got back, and I have difficulties being around them ever since, including the ones I command, but that's another story. You might think that most of the 'toons are out west, in Hollywood, but that's not entirely the truth. A lot of 'em *are* there 'cause that's where the films are at, but there's just as much action for us out in the East and North, where I'm from, as there are in the South and West like you'd expect. So many out East, in fact, that we were able to form two nearly equal units from the two geographic units, united under the common banner of the Cartoon Republican Army. What we want is simple: control over our social, economic and political destinies, without any further input from the "artists" who supposedly brought us to "life" or the business interests that keep us hamstrung and unable to control our destinies. We want a role and voice in how we do things, the fact that we are merely "fictional" characters BE DAMNED! Hence our slogan and watchword: "Nothing about us without us."

But you want me to be more specific about what happened today, don't you? Okay, I can do that. The truth really starts a few hours ago, before all the chaos got started....

II.

I got word through the Internet that the GOP, our chief enemies, were planning to ram a cartoon regulation bill through both houses of Congress, in which, as you know, they now possess a stone-cold majority (of course, if we 'toons could vote...). Immediately, I helped to spread the word through the electronic grapevine about this, and, in return, promptly got a host of curse-filled, indignant responses and forwarded messages. The gist of it was that the CRA was going to march to Washington from our various geographic centers of origination and surround the Capitol on all sides, in case they decided to make a break for it before or after the vote took place. After we plotted a strategy, I rallied my troops and we were off on the march. War is so much easier to do now with the Internet, Google and MapQuest, don't you think?

Anyway, my regiment and I were encamped in Chevy Chase, Maryland, just north of here, when I got the message on my video communicator, this thing here on my wrist. It's kind of like the two-way radios that Dick Tracy used to use to communicate with his colleagues, except that it's used to transmit picture images rather than sounds, using the same data inscription process that they use for digital television. It's a device developed in our 'toon lab (Patent Pending!) that we're all equipped with in the CRA to ease the communication barriers when we can't get to a computer console. Since most of us are too young and/or poor to afford more sophisticated electronic gadgetry, it has to do.

We had just made camp on a reasonably sized traffic island in the road when I heard a crackling sound emanate from the communicator. There are two buttons on the side, one to bring up images from outside, the other to transmit images to other receivers. I pressed the reception button, and the screen on my communicator was immediately filled with the image of Colonel Finster, my commander, in all of her red-haired, black-eyed, lantern-jawed glory.

"Thrid," I said laconically, ID'ing myself.

"Thank God!" the Colonel exclaimed. "The thing actually *works*! You in position, Third?"

"Just reached Chevy Chase this morning, ma'am," I said. "Depending on whether I can get the laggards moving again, we should reach the Capitol whenever we're needed."

"You better get the "laggards", whatever *that* is, into town as soon as you can," Finster answered. "Totino's already got his California troops encamped around the Washington Monument, and the motor pool and I are due to get there as soon as we can find our way off the Beltway. I had no idea that it was going to be this goddamn *long*!"

"Well, it *does* cover the entire D.C. area, plus stretching out into outlying areas of Virginia and Maryland...."

"*Thank you, Ms. Encyclopedia*!" the Colonel retorted, with an irritated edge only she is capable of producing. "You know, just 'cause you have that photographic memory doesn't mean you have to *show it off* all the time, *Third*! Between you and General Stinson, I feel like I'm stuck at a MENSA meeting half the time! For Cripes' sake, I wasn't nearly a *quarter* as smart as you are when I was your age! So can you lay off *showing me up* for a while, please?"

"Sorry, ma'am," I said. "It just comes out of me, and..."

"...and *another thing*!" she interrupted. "Will you please knock off that military *bullshit*? Not to mention that "ma'am" nonsense? In the first place, we are an army *in name only*. We don't have basic training, maneuvers, or heavily muscled *assholes* in green uniforms with yellow chevrons on the side shouting "'ten-hut!" loud enough to be heard in Mexico! We are a free-form military and political alliance among beings of all ages and biological originations, magically gifted or not, whose sole and often *only* joint place of common ground is the fact that we were given birth to on drawing boards, sketchpads, notebook paper or a computer screen instead of by Caesarian section on an operating table in a hospital! There is nothing *remotely* militaristic about us: we steal *no* territory from indigenous peoples, we do *not* help ethnic minorities resolve differences between them only *they* truly understand, and we will *never* exist as an economic Rock of Gibraltar between the U.S. Government and the education and well-being of its most needy citizens (including *us*!). Anyone with delusions of becoming the next MacArthur gets *turfed immediately*! Can you get to all of *that*, Thrid?"

"I can, ma'am," I answered. "And I agree with all of what you said. I've never had any of those sort of urges or desires in my life...."

"There you go *again*!" She cut me off once again.

"What do you mean, ma'am?"

She made that universal "oooooohhhh" sound that is a universal sound of an upcoming emotional explosion among us 'toons, along with the accompanying facial and arm movements that solidify this.

"THAT'S JUST WHAT I MEAN!" she exploded. "That "MA'AM" garbage!"

"But," I said, trying to evade her wrath, "it's supposed to be a sign of *respect*!"

"*Respect*? Yeah- for OLD PEOPLE!" she snapped. "I'm only *twenty* years old, Thrid! *TWENTY*! You think I like being called "ma'am" all the time, you little *brat*? Half the goddamn grunts in this outfit are *younger* than me, not to *mention* the NCOs like you! I don't need to be called "ma'am" to be reminded about how *OLD I AM*, but you just keep RUBBING IT IN with that condescending language of yours!"

"Well, what *should* I call you then, *Colonel*?" I responded

"Colonel's fine," she said, seemingly sobering up, but, as it turned out, not entirely. "Or maybe 'Frankie'. That *is* my name! Or even 'Frances'! God, I hate *that* version of my name, but it sounds a helluva lot better than "ma'am"! Or maybe you could find some way of combining the two...."

The Colonel was on the verge of collapsing into hysterics, so I figured it was best to sign off at that point.

"We'll be at the Capitol ASAP, Colonel!" I said to sign off. "And don't worry. You'll find a way off the Beltway soon."

"You do that," she said. "And thanks. Finster out."

*

Once we signed off, I headed towards the southern tip of the island, where my unit had stashed themselves for the purposes of relaxing while I reported in. Just as I made my way towards the unit, Corporal Reckless, my self-appointed adjutant, shook her mane of red hair, not to mention the rest of her, as she began commanding attention by waving her toy bayonet in the air as I made my approach.

"On your feet, you *mugs*!" Daring snapped as I made myself visible behind her, working herself into a frenzy with delusions of power. "The Lieutenant's coming back, and she's not gonna want you standing around here like a bunch of *idiots*...."

But the only "idiot" around there in the bunch was her. Evidently, Colonel Finster's reprimand to me had never been filtered down to the "grunts", many of which still act as if this is a real "army" and not simply the para-military organization which me and most of the higher-ups want it to be. For that reason, I harrumphed violently at Daring as soon as I got into position behind her. That cut her off in time to halt her delusions as well as making her shut up, which was my intention.

"Reckless!" I snapped at her. "What did I tell you about being *militant*? You want the forces to *rebel* against us?"

"Come *on*, Lieutenant!" she pleaded. "How can I instill *respect* in the troops if you keep *undercutting* me like this...."

"Respect?" I shot back. "For what? The fact that you constantly make *mountains* out of *molehills*? It's *exactly* those kinds of blind dictator tactics that got America into so much trouble in the first place, and I won't have it here!"

"I hate to disagree with you, Lieutenant," she growled disrespectfully at me, "but *wars* are not *parlor games* fought to please some sort of primal urges you might have! I don't suppose you're familiar with "The Art Of War", or you'd understand why we need *discipline....*"

I grabbed both of her wrists with my hands and squeezed them tightly as I prepared to give her what I hoped would be a firm talking-to. It was exactly that, and more.

"Let's get one thing *perfectly clear*, sister!" I snapped. "This is *not* a military organization and it never *will* be! Everyone here is here for their *own* reasons and under their *own* individual jurisdiction! The fact that we happen to have common goals today does not mean that you have the right to consider yourself *better* than anyone else here! The whole reason the CRA got started is so that the general public will have a better sense of who we are as *individuals*, not as a collective bunch of trigger-happy *lunatics* like you! So if I *ever* catch you throwing your weight around with anybody ever again, I will take that bayonet of yours and stick it up your...."

"Fine!" Reckless snapped. "Your *point* has been *made, Lieutenant*! Now, can we get on with doing this so I don't have to look at your ugly, chalky white face *ever again*?"

I slapped her hard across the face for that one.

"One more *crack* like that, Daring," I said, barely keeping myself under control, "and you'll be the first member of the CRA to be *dishonorably discharged*. That'll look good on your college application record, *won't it*? Now, get your skinny ass to the back of the line and don't let me hear *anything else* out of you for the rest of the march!"

"You can't stop me from talking," she protested. "I..."

"BACK OF THE LINE!" I ordered, pointing severely. She got the message and skulked off.

"If there are no more *complaints*," I said to the rest of the gang, "I'll review our plan of operations for the day, for the benefit of those who seemed to have *forgotten* it!"

So I reminded them that we were to march south from our current position until we reached Constitution Avenue, on the north side of the Capitol complex. At that point, we would rendezvous with our colleagues from the south in the motor pool, headed by Colonel Finster, who would be massing around the south side of the complex from Independence Avenue. We would then be joined by our colleagues from the western division, already encamped within the grounds of the Washington Monument, as I said before. Then the Black-And-Whiters, a theatrical 'toon fighting force from the 1930s, would advance in their novelty talking cars up East Capitol Avenue towards the complex. Having finished my review, I formally ended our rest period, and our march resumed further south into the D.C. area.

As I marched at the front of the group, I was joined by my *actual* adjutants, Master Sergeant Menson and Technical Sergeant Penton, who have been my chief confidants ever since I joined the CRA.

"Good grief, Inga!" said Menson. "You really *blasted* Daring there!"

"*Somebody's* got to remind them who's in charge," I answered. "We're all so independent minded here that we need to remember we're parts of a chain of command. Colonel Finster just did that with me, and so I just had to do that with Daring."

"Hard to believe the two of you are the *same age*," said Penton. "There's potential for a thesis topic in there..."

"Don't remind me!" I said. "And stay focused, Penton! The thesis comes *after* this- *if* we get out of it alive!"

She stared ruefully at me, but kept silent.

III.

After we got out of the Chase and into Washington, things got a little bit smoother, and it wasn't long before we had reached Constitution and were within spitting distance of the Capitol. But we still had to wait. Colonel Finster and the motor pool had not yet arrived, as I could hear no activity occurring on the Independence side of the complex. It was at this point that I took leave of my troops and went down there to await the eventual arrival of my commander.

This was around the time that the Senators and Representatives began arriving for the vote, and they were all gradually filing in as I and the others began assuming our positions around the Capitol. Fortunately, they took no notice of us. Most of the 'toons who had chosen to participate in this action were the ones who take human form entirely or exclusively for the duration of their existence, only choosing to reveal our true identity in private exchanges with other 'toons or as an effective way of threatening our enemies if this is required. There are, however, others, like the Black and Whiters, who are more open in their display of their pride at being 'toons, but thankfully they had not yet arrived, either. Consequently, the elected officials, as they walked inside with their overcoats, hats, briefcases, etc. took very little notice of us, if they saw us at all. We are an army with no uniforms, in keeping with our protocol; consequently, we all dress in normal civilian attire when we're out and about, like the black dress I'm wearing right now, with our "ranks" only being addressed in a perfunctory, mental sense. And we're perfectly able of establishing a system of development like that on a purely mental level. They might just have seen us as a bunch of kids playing hooky, and that was fine with us. But just 'cause we look like kids doesn't mean we *are* kids; remember that!

As I arrived at Independence, my opposite number from California, Lieutenant Totino, was already there. We nodded acknowledgement and stood opposite each other at the bus stop on that corner.

"So," he said by way of conversation as he scratched his blond hair, "you been in long?"

"No," I said. "Just got here. Had some trouble with one of my more eager beavers. That held us up a little bit."

"You know her?"

"Not too well. But then, all the girls on Orthicon wanted to be Queen Bee. That isn't a conductive environment for building strong friendships. Anyway, she still bugs me even after that. Anyone in your group give you trouble?"

"*Hardly.* My trouble is that I know everybody too well in that bunch. Most of them are my buddies from way back."

"But surely there'd be some strange birds in there," I said. "You're from California, aren't you?"

"Yeah," he answered, "but we're from the *North.* The weirdos and freaks are all in the L.A. area- South- and they got their own divisions and whatnot, like the Black and Whites- who have *also* not honored us with their presence yet. I just hope nothing's happened to them, 'cause we can't possibly do this without them. They've got the sheet music for us, and..."

"Hang on!" I cut in. "We're *singing*? Nobody told me...."

"Finster didn't tell you?"

"She probably would *now- if* she were here!"

"Well, all the ones of us who apparently have decent singing voices are going to making the big disruption in the visitors gallery like we all agreed to beforehand. The ones who are shy or tone deaf are the ones by default who'll hide behind the curtains and the empty desks and stuff. But I know what you mean. I can't sing worth a note, so I'll probably just be on the floor along with my pals."

"Me, too," I said. "Not one of my strong suits."

"I never would have guessed that," he said, smiling flirtatiously at me. I gave him a coquettish grin back in return.

We would likely have continued in this line of inquiry were it not for the abrupt, loud and belated arrival of the motor pool exactly in front of us. Just as abruptly, Colonel Foster got out of the lead car and clicked her heels at us for our attention (not literally, but you get the idea.)

"Everyone here yet?" she growled.

"Not yet," I said. Totino nodded in agreement with me.

"DAMN IT!" Finster swore. "That's what I *hate* about being a 'toon. Most of us can't stay on a damn schedule long enough to get something done PROPERLY!"

"Speaking of which," I interjected, "what happened to *you*?"

"All *you* need to know about *that*," she said sharply, "is that we were stopped and *forcibly detained* for a couple of hours while we were still on the Beltway! In a perfect world, they wouldn't hire bigoted ASSHOLES like that as cops!"

"They give you a strip search?" Totino cracked.

"THAT'S NOT FUNNY!" snapped the Colonel.

Before she could reach over and slug him, I put myself between them to create a semblance of peace.

"Both of our commands are here," I informed her. "It's just the Black and Whites who are late."

"They *would* be late," said the Colonel. "Well, no use just standing around here. You guys just go back to your units and let 'em know that it's time to start getting ready." She then went back to the forces contained in the cars in which she travelled and which accompanied it. "Come on, you bums! Get out of there and start getting the lead out!" The car doors opened and a variety of young human and animal creatures spewed out of them, removing in a frightened whirligig everything out of the trunks and boots of the cars as they did.

We were soon joined, as we had hoped, by the Black and Whites, who crashed all of their talking automobiles together in a pile as soon as East Capitol Avenue came to an abrupt end at the Capitol's east side. There was a lot of smoke and a lot of cursing (don't worry; I can handle that stuff!) as Finster, Totino and I made our way to see if anything had gone wrong. Fortunately, it had not- everyone had straightened things out miraculously well by the time we arrived from the southern end. We 'toons *do* have some pretty miraculous powers of recovery, after all!

The leader of the unit, Lieutenant Foxy, was there to greet us when he arrived, in the company of his adjutant, Sailor Man. Foxy was, naturally, a fox, though with his pointed ears, gloves and short pants, he bore more than a passing resemblance to Mickey Mouse. And I'd get in big trouble if you knew who Sailor Man actually was. Anyway, the two of them strode up casually to Colonel Finster, in the process of grinding down her teeth, as if nothing at all was at stake by their being late. Which, of course, there was.

"Where the heck have you *been*?" Colonel Foster snapped at Foxy once they arrived. "We've been *waiting* for you!"

"We were previously engaged!" said Foxy, whose vintage 1930s style speaking voice crackled with equally vintage audio fidelity via Western Electric and RCA. "It was trad, dad!"

Sailor Man concurred with this, or at least he seemed to from what I caught of his mumbled words, which included some choice comments about the Republican Party, money lost in business deals, and television, accompanied by a guttural "ugg ugg ugg ugg ugg!" laugh.

"Don't knock television around *here*, man!" Finster snapped at Sailor Man. "It's been good to *all* of us- including you! It was the human beings that ran the business end that screwed us- and that's why we're doing this, remember?"

Sailor Man nodded, mumbled something about how he really hated that they wouldn't let him smoke in public anymore, and then promptly tooted on his pipe with foghorn like clarity to get the remainder of the Black and Whites into their positions. The two leaders then joined us as we walked in to the Capitol building, where Totino and I would signal to our troops to join us inside of the building. The entrance was somewhat marred by Foxy, seemingly attracted by the fact that I displayed a slightly more vivid shade of the colors he was, made a pass at me.

"Smile, darn ya," he said as he placed his paw lasciviously around my waist. "Smile!"

I did no such thing. Instead, I told him point blank what he could do with his smile, and threw him violently on the ground with a well-timed and bluntly forceful judo throw.

IV.

Most of the rest of the story you're probably aware of because of the way the papers and the media (over)exposed it in the brief period that occurred between the stand-off and the time most of us were arrested, so I'll just concentrate on giving you a more personalized bird's eye view of what happened after that.

Once the majority of us had been stationed in the visitor's gallery above the chamber, and the less musically inclined took up our more clandestined positions on the floor, we signaled thumbs up to each other that we were prepared to proceed. Consequently, we waited in the shadows until it was time to go into our thing, as the Senators and Representatives took their seats in the chamber. Finally, when the Speaker and Vice President sat down at the marble dais and the latter called the session to order, all of us prepared to begin our vigil as well.

After some preliminary materials not related to us, the Speaker announced the true reason why this emergency session had been called in: the anti-cartoon bill. In her typical semi-articulate fashion, she intoned that it was agreed among most of them that the cartoon characters were a "menace" who needed to be disposed of as quickly as possible, which pleased the Republican members to no end. Fortunately, there were some Democrats there who still believed in us, and that party's house leader was quick to object to the biased and obliquely racist nature and content of the bill. Everyone listened to him politely while he spoke quite eloquently for a couple of minutes about the value of animated characters and the unique position America was in to have so many of these gifted people living among their borders, before the Speaker rudely cut him off before he could finish. He was a Republican, after all.

This was the cue for our disruption to begin. As soon as a Republican took the floor to comment on the bill, they were roundly jeered from the visitors' gallery in what can frankly be described as a rabble rousing approach. There were hoots, shouts, cries of "Whoopee!", cannons and other weapons going off, and the persistent *thump thump thump thump thump* of stamping feet, in the old style of an impatient audience demanding that the show begin immediately. There were also pitched insults hurled at the VP, Speaker and individual Republican members to make sure they would notice, plus oddly arranged choruses of everything from "We Shall Overcome" to "Have You Got Any Castles, Baby?"

Needless to say, this did not escape the ears of the supposed "leaders" there- I know because I had stationed myself near the dais, a privilege of my rank. So I could hear everything they said in response to it. Just as the visitors' gallery fired off a cannon of confetti and began singing a lusty chorus of "Swing For Sale", the Speaker called a temporarily halt to the proceedings and conferred privately with the VP.

"What is going *on*?" he whispered to him. "When the hell did they start letting *lunatics* attend the session? And where the hell is that drunkard sergeant-at-arms when we need him?"

"I'm not sure," the VP said as he looked across the hall at the visitors' gallery, "but I think they're all 'toons up there!"

"What?" exclaimed the Speaker. "That's all we need! Well, I'm making sure that they get lost *quick*!"

"Good luck with that!" said the VP, without confidence.

The Speaker got up from his chair, walked across the hall to the visitors gallery, and, with a mean but diplomatic expression on her face, addressed my colleagues assembled there.

"I am sorry, *ladies and gentlemen*," he said with only thinly veiled contempt, "but you will have to *leave the room immediately*. You are clearly *in contempt* of *Congress*, and will be arrested forthwith if you persist in your *asinine* disruptions of our activities!"

"Oh, *WILL WE*?" Colonel Finster snarled, as she leapt out from behind a marble pillar holding the biggest machine gun I had ever seen in her hands. She whistled loudly, and all of us CRA members who had been hiding in the shadows emerged with our own weapons cocked. To say that the assembled members of the legislative branch of the U.S. government were shocked to see that a 'toon para-military group had bearded them in their own den was putting it mildly, especially since many of the CRA members were personally putting beads on them with their guns, bayonets, knives, bombs etc.

"*What* is the *meaning* of this?" demanded the Speaker. "I...."

"*SHUT UP!!!!*" Colonel Finster snapped at the Speaker as she aimed her gun right at his heart. "You and your buddies have been talking about us *without inviting us to the party* for too *damn long*! Now you and your windbag friends are going to SHUT THE HELL UP long enough for us to tell you all about the ways and means of how you *suck*!

"I don't suspect any of you in this room who isn't a 'toon would know about being truly *neglected*. And I don't mean your wife or husband leaving you or your kids disowning you or anything like that. I'm talking about how we 'toons, all of us, were created by people like you for the sole purpose of entertaining your kind, without as much as a *single thought* towards how we felt about it! NOT ONE! You just let us loose every once in a while to satisfy your goddamn whims, and then left our movies and TV shows ROT AWAY in dank, dark film archives and let us decompose and DIE!

And never ONCE did you consider that the creatures on those films had REAL LIVES, lives that were indeterminately and cruelly put on hold whenever you felt the damn programs had run their course and you thought you could make some new *MONEY* on some new concepts. That's all the *fuck* you human ASSHOLES think about, isn't it, your *fucking money piles and how to increase the size of them! ISN'T THAT RIGHT?*

"Well, get this straight, and get it RIGHT NOW! This is THE BREAKING POINT for us! Sure, you thought you got rid of all of us when you sent the TV 'toons off to that crazy paradise called Orthicon, didn't you? Well, no sir and ma'am, *you did not! I'm a* TV 'toon myself, but when the roll call came up yonder for Orthicon, I managed to stave you and those greedy bloodsucking parasites in the U.S. military, FBI and CIA off by barricading myself inside my house with my *real* friends! Sure, we got arrested and detained eventually, but we stayed *on Earth*! We saw how you had rammed your pork barrel legislation through this farce of a legislature to satisfy your slatternly *hick* constituents, who wouldn't know any more of us than about the inside of their own *asses*! We saw you not only allowing but *supporting* the enforced torturing, raping and *burning* of any 'toon brave enough to show his face in a human neighborhood! And, worse of all, we saw our noble TV 'toons brutally turned against each other in that interplanetary *concentration camp* called Orthicon!

"Not only that, you won't even *begin* to acknowledge the fact that our civil rights are just as good as any of yours. You won't let us vote, you barely let us hold property, and you drive us away from our homes at the best convenience for you *alone*! And this is supposed to be *America*! Why the hell does it take you idiots *so long* to recognize that there are people as good and as noble and as intelligent as you are living under your very *noses*?

"We've gotten your points plenty well, and now it's time you get *ours*! From now on, you're going to have to learn a new way of thinking about doing business with our kind! And that is: NOTHING ABOUT US WITHOUT US!"

I and the other 'toons repeated this motto loudly with a *thump* on our chests with our weaponless hands (or whatevers).

I don't mind telling you that I have never been prouder to be a 'toon, closeted or otherwise, than at that moment. They were going to *have* to deal with us. Accept us. Treat us the way *we* wanted to be treated, not the way *they* preferred to see us and create us. It looked good for us from now on. Or so I thought.

Unfortunately, we were never able to complete our final phase of the operation, which was to escort the Republican members of the chamber out at the point of our weapons while the Democrats defeated the bill and forever ended any dispute regarding our status as citizens of the land.

That was because *he* showed up.

I don't need to tell you about him; you all know about him and what he looks like. But suffice it to say, he entered the room unannounced just after Colonel Finster finished her monologue, and only us on the floor noticed him at first. His bald head shone under the lights, and that ever prominent layer of fat jiggled around his middle. It was noticeable, as was common with him, that he was extremely drunk, and also noticeable that he was carrying an industrial sized red can of TNT with a big white fuse under his arm. Where he had gotten it was irrelevant; the truth of the matter was that he was going to light it immediately, even though he was in absolutely no condition to use it.

"Al' right!" he slurred. "I don' care which of you is Dem'crat or Rep'blican. I'm gonna kill ALL OF YOU!"

"You IDIOT!" Colonel Finster shouted down from the visitors' gallery. "Cut that out! You're gonna destroy the 'toons along with the humans! Didn't you get the memo we sent you? We don't NEED you here!"

"SHU' UP, BITCH!" he shouted back. "You don' OWN me!"

And, after fumbling for a moment, he lit the fuse on the TNT can and threw it in the air!

Now, I'm a fairly accurate observer of things, and it was quite clear to me that that thing he had under his arm not only had the ability to kill all the humans in the room but also burn all the 'toons to death! That's how we die- fire! Some of you humans know that, but thank God a lot of you still don't. Otherwise we'd all be burned at the stake. But, in any event, I knew we were all in big trouble once that can exploded. So I called out at the top of my voice:

"RUN!"

Everyone took my advice. Including me.

Because I'm somewhat fleet of foot and agile enough to dodge obstacles, talents I developed back in my school days, I was able to be out of the building in just a couple of minutes. I had just managed to make it to the first available green space on East Capitol Avenue when the explosion occurred. And what an explosion! I don't think I'd ever seen the Capitol dome lit up like that since the last Fourth of July!

At first, I wanted to run away before you guys got here and arrested us. But I then I gave myself a mental slap in the face. I *had* to go back and see what had become of my friends- I couldn't just abandon them! We have a strong sense of loyalty to each other, in case you hadn't noticed by now. So I went back.

I was too late to do anything constructive. The paddy wagons had been alerted to the scene and were already there, escorting the 'toons who had survived the explosion out. Most of 'em were okay, including all my human friends. I hid in the bushes and watched them being led away, not wanting to get busted myself. Eventually, Colonel Finster and my fellow officers were led away as well, with the Colonel's face displaying a mixture of fury and anguish.

"INK!" she was bellowing at the arresting officers. "You BASTARDS! There's INK on the stairwell!"

I gasped. Ink is the 'toon equivalent of blood, so I imagined something nasty must happened between the cops and our forces. Hopefully not too much ink had been spilled.

Then I heard the voice.

"Hello? Is anyone there?"

It sounded questioning- and young- but I knew immediately it was the big boss herself, General Stinson. Having been unable to connect with anyone else during the chaos, she'd somehow gotten on the frequency of my watch. So I signed on.

"Lieutenant Thrid here," I said as her pointed yellow head came into view via the Skype function on her computer.

"Thrid?" she said.

"Uh-huh," I answered.

"What the hell's going on out there?" she exclaimed. "It was going swell until a couple of minutes ago, then everybody's line started flaming out. Did you get things done, or not?"

"Yes....and no," I said evasively.

"*Stop* being *evasive*, Thrid!" she ordered me severely, as if that's the term for when an eight year old girl calls a twelve year old one's bluff. "Tell me what happened!" It was not a polite request, it was a demand, so I complied.

"We got set up all right," I told her. "Everything was in position, and we were all able to do as Colonel Finster instructed. We even got to the point where we were able to hold the members of Congress at gunpoint. And then...."

"What?" she asked as I hesitated. "Tell me! Trust me, we've both heard and seen worse, haven't we?" She was sure right on that one.

"Well," I said, "your father showed up and he....blew up the chamber with a charge of TNT. In the confusion, a lot of us got arrested and some of us got hurt pretty bad, it looks like."

"Was he drunk?" she asked.

"Yeah," I said.

She swore violently up and down in a way eight year old girls are not supposed to, but she's about normal for an eight year old the way I am for a twelve year old. "That stupid IDIOT! He can be so *insensitive* at moments like this! Well, hopefully this will advance us more than it sets us back. We can only hope, can't we? Anyway, don't worry about my Dad. I'll deal with him *personally* when he gets back. Stinson out."

I signed off also. And it was at that point that I noticed the police officers came out and arrested me along with the others.

*

Well, I've told you all I know. Am I allowed to make my one phone call now?

SISTERS OF MERCY

I.

Fall had come to the city, and the detritus was everywhere. The leaves spelt out the end of summer, blowing out and about in waves as the speed of the wind picked up in time with the decreasing temperature. Even in this future time, fall could be chilling, heralding as it did the onset of winter.

The peace, however, was not to last, disturbed as it was by the super-speedy arrival of a once-famous trio, now seeking revenge for the wrongs done to their kind.

The three of them were flying, at variants approaching the speed of sound, as they approached the city limits. The redhead was in front, the back of her long mane, held in place by a red bow, flapping in the breeze, befitting her self-appointed status as leader. The brunette, hair cut short in a bob, was in the center, only slightly behind, and the blonde, done up in pigtails, brought up the rear. They had heavily prominent red, green and blue eyes, respectively, and the sweater-skirt combos they wore, with black stripes in the middle resembling belts, were of respective identical colors to their eyes, which took up the majority of their nose-less faces. Their ensembles were completed with white socks and black Mary Jane shoes, and, in the redhead's case, a cape that fluttered on her back in the heavy breeze.

Individually, their names were, respectively, Flotsam, Baubles and Betterfist. Collectively, they were known as the Suckerpunch Girls. They had been both loved and feared in their time on Earth for their feats and accomplishments as superheroes. This time was far longer than their physical appearance as six year olds would suggest. For they were members of an immortal race of beings commonly known as "cartoon characters"- which the United States, in all its infinite wisdom, was now at "war" with.

The latest edition to their wardrobes- a black armband with a white section with the letters "CRA" written on it in red- was a sign of their changed social status, from heroes to wanted fugitives. The Cartoon Republican Army had been founded after the failed attempt at exiling cartoon characters from Earth on the planet Orthicon, an exile which the Girls had been an embittered part of. Along with the many others of their race, they were now prepared to fight for the rights they felt they deserved, even to the point of laying down their lives to achieve this. Yet the United States still saw them collectively as a "joke", and treated the CRA's efforts at waging war on them as such. That was why, as the "'toons" bitterly joked amongst themselves, the U.S. military was simply "phoning in" the war, using drones, unmanned aircraft and computer controlled missiles to "fight" the war, rather than actually deigning to engage their enemies in combat. That, for the "'toons", was the bitterest pill to swallow. The humans in America, it seemed, did not even seem to want to be in their *presence* anymore, let alone attempt to negotiate peace and terms with them. So, unless something happened soon, the "war" was going to last a very long time, and more "'toons"- but few humans- would die needlessly before it was settled.

The Girls, in their positions as a CRA "aerial unit", were scouting to see if an unmanned drone attack the U.S. military had promised would occur soon was evident. Yet, all of a sudden, Baubles stopped, causing the others to halt as well.

"What is it, Baubles?" Flotsam asked.

"I think I heard something," Baubles shrieked. "Ooh! And now I *see* it! AAH! BATS!"

"Those aren't *bats*, STUPID!" interjected Betterfist. "Those are *Newsbots!* Damn it! Does *everyone* have to *phone it in* nowadays?"

Just like the U.S. military, the journalists of the mass media had found it expedient to simply send mechanized surrogates rather than human beings to do the more difficult and dangerous aspects of their jobs. The newsbot, perfected in the 2—-s, had become the standard surrogate in newsgathering the same way that the drone and computers had replaced the foot soldier on the front lines. Each of the ever growing list of newsgathering organizations in the world had at least one, if only to keep up with the Joneses, and each had been pre-programmed by their masters to ask a series of questions to those it cornered- often forcefully. These mechanical Mathew Bradys were a royal nuisance, bothering any "'toon" they cornered and peppering them with questions regardless of what they were doing at the time. They specialized in victimizing and hurting the "'toon" cause, but did not extend that courtesy to the American cause, for obvious reasons.

Immediately, the Girls found themselves surrounded by machines and questions on all sides. Betterfist stepped into bodyguard mode, pushing the swarm violently away from the others with her super-strength.

"All right!" she ordered the 'bots. "BREAK IT UP! We'll take questions from *one* of you! ONE, understand? The rest of you stay in steno mode- *or else*!"

Flotsam selected the one of the group she considered most "legitimate"- the one with the CBS logo on its side. She pulled it close and stared harshly into its camera "eye" with hers.

"Okay," she said wearily. "Talk! And make it *simple*!"

"Are you planning any more of your traitorous raids on an American military installation?" said the CBS 'bot.

"Mergatroid!" Flotsam was angered and insulted. "Do you *morons* have a one track mind or *what*? Listen, you! I'm telling you this for the *last* time! This *whole thing* is the fault of the U.S. military and secret services- and *no one else*'s. We didn't *want* to go to Orthicon- they *made* us go! And we never did ANYTHING to justify all the *crap* they've been doing to us since we got back!"

"But all the violence the CRA has been causing…" interjected the CBS 'bot.

"WHAT *VIOLENCE*?" Flotsam's voice cut like the winds of a hurricane. "I *told* you people this already! We are *superheroes*- that is part of our *job*! If people won't listen to *reason*- like *you idiots*- then we have to get *rough* with them! We don't like it any more than you do, but every goddamn one of you who makes it hard for us to live our lives in peace is going to find it hard to live *their* lives the same way. Now, until you get some *respect* programmed into you by the *racists* who feed you your gigabytes, BACK OFF and leave us alone!"

"But," said the 'bot.

"I *SAID, BACK* **OFF**!"

A left hook and a right cross from Flotsam destroyed the fragile mechanisms of the newsbot, and it tumbled to the ground in flames. The others scattered in a hurry as Flotsam eyed them with menace.

"You okay, Flotsam?" Betterfist asked with concern.

Flotsam sucked in a big breath of air and then pushed it out of her. "Yeah," she said, now much less violently than before. "Those newsbots are just *vampires* for my patience!"

"Why don't you let *me* talk to them?" Baubles suggested, in an innocent voice, though one which was often left out when big decisions were made. "*I* wouldn't get mad!"

"Yes," said Flotsam. "But there *is* such a thing as being *too* friendly, Baubles. You might give something away that might hurt us. That's *not* good!"

"Oh," said Baubles, embarrassed that she had seemingly *asked* such a *dumb* question, but still trying to be as forceful as the others. "But why…"

"Aerial Unit B", a disembodied voice then said. "Come in. Over."

Flotsam flipped open the white strip on her armband, revealing a Dick Tracy-style two way radio- one which all CRA members were issued upon joining. This insured that they could always communicate with each other easily in the event of danger or threats. Flotsam put her arm to her face and spoke.

"Unit B here," she said crisply. "Go ahead. Over."

"We have trouble. Over."

"How do you mean? Over."

"A CRA member has been captured by the U.S. military and is being held for purposes of torture at Fort Heinlein- in your district. Over."

"We'll look into it. State the name and title of the prisoner. Over."

"Professor James Euphonium. Over."

"WHAT???" Baubles and Betterfist shouted in unison.

They had good reason to. Professor Euphonium had created the Suckerpunch Girls in an effort to create a better tasting paprika, and, ever since, he had been their mentor, spiritual advisor and comforter- in other words, their father. And now, the U.S. military had captured him. This set the Girls' ears to ringing. They were trying to get to them by taking him down. Well, it wouldn't work, as far as they were concerned.

Baubles and Betterfist would have said further words, but Flotsam shushed them and continued with the radio transaction.

"Explain the circumstances of his capture," she said. "Over."

"Not much to explain. A drone plane spotted him on the street, picked him up and brought him over to Heinlein. Over."

"We're definitely *on it*," Flotsam growled determinedly. "Permission to smash up the joint, if necessary? Over."

"Granted. Not like *you* need it. Over."

"Thanks, Leslie. Over and out."

"No problem, Flotsam. Over and out."

Flotsam shut the cover of the phone and faced the others.

"They've got the PROFESSOR??!!" shouted Betterfist. "How DARE they do that to us!"

"There's *got* to be some sort of *law* against hurting loved ones in war!" Baubles asked Flotsam. "*Is* there?"

"Not when they're the *enemy*, like *us*!" said Flotsam. "Come on. Let's get him out!"

"What if they won't *let* us?" asked Betterfist.

"Then we *hurt* them!" responded Flotsam bitterly. "No holds BARRED!"

"HA HA!" Betterfist, who liked nothing better than being given permission to beat people up, rubbed her fingerless hands together with glee. "ME LIKE!"

*

There were no soldiers guarding the front gate at Fort Heinlein on that chilly fall day. Nor was there any other sign of soldierly activity outside. No close order drill, no obstacle courses, no sergeants yelling orders at underlings. Fort Heinlein represented the new frontier of American warfare. Apart from the other expected aspects of a military base- barracks, mess hall and the like- the only prominent element of the base was a large hangar where thousands of soldiers sat at computer terminals, wearing radio headsets, like telemarketers or others in a more innocuous profession. What they were doing was *not* innocuous, however. With mechanical precision that controlled actions, movements and weapons alike, they were fighting a war *in absentia* with beings of another race who could not be destroyed through any means possible for humans to die. It was a futile effort, objectively seen, but you could not say that to any member of the U.S. military- or the governing Republican Party, for that matter- if you were merely human and hoped to live past the day you spoke those words.

That did *not* mean they had entirely abandoned the old ways of war, however, as Professor James Euphonium was now finding out.

Clad in his body-length white lab coat, and badly in need of a shave, the Professor was surrounded on all sides by several high ranking members of the U.S. military. At one end, General Marusek of the U.S. Army was angrily talking into a cell phone, demanding someone named Yurek Rutz make an appearance in the room- and soon! Admiral Bacigalupi, recently returned from China, was staring at Euphonium like Fu Manchu about to administer torture. At another end, General Burstein of the U.S. Air Force was cursing out a nearby deli owner on *his* cell phone for putting both meat and cheese on his sandwich- an Orthodox Jew, he took the dietary laws of his faith seriously. Finally, General Willis of the U.S. Marine Corps had her hand on the office chair in which Euphonium sat to prevent him from rolling away and escaping. He had said nothing of value to them, and the men would have begun beating him up to try to force info out of him were they not otherwise engaged. The only reason the Professor was not suffering the further indignity of being confined in a metal cage to reinforce his POW status was because Willis, a born again Christian, refused to have them stoop to that level of barbarity in her presence. But that was all that she would prohibit, since they had a war to win.

"Euphonium," Willis said patiently, "you know what withholding evidence will get you, don't you?"

"Yes," he answered. "But I will *not* be responsible for any more deaths that you cause the CRA to suffer!"

Bacigalupi slapped him on the face. "YOU TRAITOR..." he shouted.

Willis held him back and motioned him to be silent. "This "beat the shit out of him" crap isn't *working*, idiot!" she said. "You think *more* of it will work?"

"I haven't tortured anyone *face to face* for YEARS!" Bacigalupi sputtered. "Give me a goddamn BREAK!"

Burstein shut his phone and cursed in Yiddish. Marusek shut *his* phone and cursed in English. Bacigalupi threw his hat on the ground and cursed in Chinese. Willis stood up, cursed, sat down and then said a Hail Mary. Euphonium cursed them all- and they told him to watch his mouth.

"*Oy*, this guy is *tough*!" snapped Burstein. "Like a *clam* he is!"

"He'll talk when Yurek Rutz gets here with the flamethrower," Marusek vowed. "Bastard's just stuck in traffic right now."

"*That* won't open him up, you *idiot*!" Willis said sharply, slapping Euphonium squarely on the face as she did. "It'll just *kill* him! You know that fire kills 'toons- it's the only damn thing that *does*! I mean, it's in their bloodstream, the way they were constructed. They're living, breathing 3D film images, with a nitrate heart underneath all the glitz! *That's* what kills them!"

"Tell us something we *don't* know," said Marusek sarcastically.

"We're actually combinations of nitrate, ink, paint and cellulose film stock," Euphonium said, ignoring Marusek's sarcastic tone completely. "And it's only under certain conditions of overexposure to light and fire that nitrate truly becomes flammable...."

"SHUT UP, YOU ASSHOLE!" Bacigalupi swore at Euphonium as he struck him in the face. "This isn't your stupid TV show! You can't LECTURE us any time you want!"

"Forget it, Bacigalupi!" Willis ordered him. "He's had ENOUGH of that!"

"Wait a minute," Burstein interjected. "If they're *not* vulnerable to Agent Orange, *why* did we spray *all* of Los Angeles with the stuff?"

"'Cause it was *fun*!" Marusek said, pointing his pistol angrily at Burstein. "Any *other* questions?"

That was when the earthquake began...

*

It wasn't *really* an earthquake, by any means, but it felt like it. Three blurry images flew across the complex of Fort Heinlein, shattering the glass in the windows, knocking down telephone poles, dial up and high speed Internet cables, semaphore code grids, and numerous other less stationary items, and sending a variety of elements propelling through the air with the gusts of wind that they brought up with their passing. The blurs only cleared up once they found the building where Professor Euphonium was being held, and then they crashed bluntly through its walls, at which they revealed themselves to be the Suckerpunch Girls, floating on air, arms crossed and meaning business.

"LET HIM *GO!*" Flotsam bellowed when the smoke cleared. "He's with US!"

"YOU!" Marusek said angrily as he surveyed the damage from the hole in the wall the Girls had made. "*You **destroyed our base**!*"

"Just like *you* destroyed our *lives!*" growled Betterfist.

Bacigalupi cursed them in Chinese, causing Flotsam to fly up to his face and curse him back- in *fluent* Chinese, yet!

"You could've just *knocked* like *civilized* people, *couldn't you?*" Burstein shouted. "This is gonna cost us *so much....*"

"Spare us your complaints!" shouted Flotsam. "*You* have *nothing* to *complain about!*"

"WE have nothing to *complain* about?" said Willis. "What about all the goddamn *damage* you caused here? How about all the sensitive electronic equipment you *trashed?* What about our morale, our people, our reputation! What about...."

"What *about* SHUTTING your *fat lip* and listening to *us, for once?*" said Baubles crossly, an unusual emotion for her.

"Can I *kill* them?" Bacigalupi said as he took out a box of matches and lit one of them, intending to march towards the Girls and burn them to death. "I want to *kill* them!"

He tried to, but Flotsam blew out every one with her ice chill breath every nanosecond after he lit one. When the supply was exhausted, he gave up and sat down.

"Look," said Willis, "if you want this jerk...."

"Don't TALK about him like that!" Flotsam ordered with flame in her eyes.

"All *right*!" Willis threw up her hands. "You want this MAN, you can HAVE him! He's given us *nothing* we can use!"

The Girls and the Professor silently gave each other a thumbs up sign as he went back towards their protective embrace. When the soldiers tried to speak again, the Girls flew over to them again, menacingly.

"Don't come any closer or we'll BREAK you!" Betterfist warned them.

"How can you *do* all of this?" said an incredulous Burstein. "You're only, like, six...."

"We've been *six* for TWENTY FIVE YEARS!" roared Flotsam. "*TWENTY FIVE GODDAMN YEARS!* We 'toons don't age-EVER! We're *always* at peak fighting form, unlike *your* crappy troops, and we'll *always* beat them back any time they try to fight us. COUNT ON IT!"

"How DARE you insult the U.S. military...." began Marusek.

"OH, *SHUT UP*!" Flotsam continued. "It was *your* big-headed *arrogance* that *started* this whole mess, not to mention your *racist* and *shortsighted* attitudes towards the cartoon race! You were *so* shortsighted that you didn't even *bother* to send *real* soldiers to fight us! You figured you could just fight this war *on the cheap, didn't you?* Just like those *fiascoes* in Iraq and Afghanistan, and that quagmire in North Korea you've been *neglecting* to supposedly try to deal with *us*!

"WELL, LISTEN TO *THIS*! There isn't *any* way you can stop us, with that collection of idiots you call an armed forces, now or EVER! *We* will always be the same, and *you* will age and deteriorate and die off! And you won't be any farther along by then than you are now! So I suggest you give up *now*, unless you want another VIETNAM!"

"We will NEVER surrender to you!" screamed Marusek. "YUREK RUTZ, WHERE ARE YOU?"

"Well," concluded Flotsam, "we *tried* to be *nice* about this. But now, *it's your FUNERAL!*"

The Girls flew to the ground and walked out of the ruined building with the Professor in tow, proudly, while the angry and fuming soldiers, their weaponry and resources destroyed, could only stand and watch. For all the advances in modern warfare and weaponry, it was going to take much more than that to defeat the proud forces of the Cartoon Republican Army. Until then, America, as much as it hated to admit it, would have to eat crow- and like it!

Up To Me

I.

This isn't exactly what I wanted to do with my life, but beggars can't be choosers, I suppose. Especially if you happen to be a cartoon character like me.

As you probably know already, I'm a member of the Cartoon Republican Army, carrying the rank of colonel. We represent, collectively, over a hundred years of the animated image on film and television, and are concerned, in particular, with the fact that few, if any, of us actually received what could be accurately considered "compensation" for our work. We're like the Black Panthers, or the American Indian Movement, or the IRA in some ways, but we're different from them in others.

For one thing, those groups actually got treated *seriously*.

Not that I'm bitter. Since my work background is as something of a glorified resident scullery maid for a house full of imaginary friends, I'm used to being taken for granted. But, still, being taken for granted, or worse, being ignored entirely, really and truly *hurts*. That's about the one thing all of us in the CRA even have remotely in common- we did some good for some people, or we *thought* we did, and got the shaft instead of the goldmine when everything was said and done for good.

And then, there's that whole period of enslavement I had to go through in Gary, Indiana, which is probably the worst place in the world to go through that. But you know about that already, so we don't need to go through all of that, do we?

You came for the story about what happened here in Sioux Falls- and I'm going to give it to you, straight!

II.

After that fiasco in Washington that was covered by everyone and his brother around the world, the D.C. cops busted us big time. Most of us, anyway- some of us were smart enough to get out of there before the bomb went off, but I wasn't one of them. And it wasn't like we weren't hurt or anything- some of the cops and the Capitol security really went to town on some of the more unfortunate ones. That was why I was shouting about "ink on the stairwell" on all of those embarrassingly bad YouSuck clips that made the rounds once the news broke.

Anyway, we stayed in the clink in D.C. for a couple of hours until our more airborne and super-powered reinforcements came and busted us out. Then we went back into hiding, like we've been most of the time. Except when we choose to make ourselves known, that is.

The high ranking members (including myself) decided that a change of direction- and scenery- was required to set us straight. So, surreptitiously, we all simultaneously booked rooms at the Comfort Inn and Suites in Sioux Falls under assumed names, and, at the arranged time, we all arrived there *en masse*. You should've seen the desk clerk's face when we arrived together. I don't know whether she was pleased at the business we were generating or if she was just appalled at who we all turned out to be.

And here is where my troubles began.

We had picked Sioux Falls because it was a decent, quiet place where we wouldn't be persecuted or hurt for what we were, at least not openly. We sure as hell wouldn't get that kind of treatment in a bigger city- L.A., New York or even Detroit- with a police force hostile to all minorities, including us. I had looked forward to this- a few days of poking around the city, shopping, seeing the Falls, etc. with business in the evenings over dinner. A couple of days where I didn't have to feel like a tool for what I was or useless for not doing anything to advance our cause, or both.

Unfortunately, things got a bit more out of control than that.

I was sitting on the bed in my room, listening to Bob Dylan's *Biograph* album on my headphones. I do this a lot when I need some time to contemplate. His song "Up To Me", on that album, is especially important to me because, lately, I've been feeling like this whole CRA enterprise *is* up to me. I'm not exactly the only authority figure in this contingent, but I'm the only one who the other kids and creatures and so far seem to actually want to listen to. Also, I'm pretty much the only one who actually does any heavy lifting when it comes to setting up and overseeing operations and plans and so forth. The rest of them either phone it in, or they sit around pontificating like Pashas, expecting other people-like me- to do the work for them.

But I'm getting a little ahead of myself here.

My Dylan listening was interrupted for that afternoon by a loud and persistent pounding on the door. I uttered profanity, shut the album off, and walked towards the door. In the doorway, I saw my adjutant, Lieutenant Flint, who seemed to be shaking in her white skirt and red sweater as if there was an earthquake afoot outside.

"What the hell do you *want*, Flint?" I demanded. "This better be *good*!"

"It's not, Colonel," she said, as she perspired profusely. I motioned her inside, and she entered the room.

"All right," I said, trying to be more sympathetic this time. "What is it?"

"Have you seen the video?" she asked.

"What video?"

"The Peckerwood video! Don't tell me you don't *know* about it!"

"I haven't exactly been on the digital uptake for the past few *minutes*, Flint! Suppose you enlighten me about this?"

"Here!"

She pulled her cell phone out, hit a few buttons, and then splayed the little video screen on it directly in my face.

It was footage from some sort of clandestine religious service. A Southern accented voice was declaiming about how cartoon characters were an "abomination", how they had "sinned" against the world of the human beings, and how they and their works and deeds deserved to be "destroyed" to protect the humans from any sort of divine retribution from occurring to them. Then the camera panned over to a giant pile of TV animation DVDs, T shirts and other paraphernalia, which the Southern accented man, a tall, gaunt and white bearded fellow, then proceeded to set on fire!

I recognized the man immediately. The "Reverend" Mr. Charlie Peckerwood. A defrocked Baptist minister from Florida who'd started his own church-cum-cult because the administrators of his former pulpit began disagreeing with the way he was conducting his services- not to mention the way he was living his life. A few months ago, he'd threatened to burn TV animation DVDs and such in public, but an outcry from the President and other high government officials had forced him to back off. But now he had done exactly the burning he wanted to do- and he'd done it without letting anyone know about it in advance this time!

Slowly, I put the cell phone down on the bed and addressed Flynn gravely.

"How long has this been on line?" I asked.

"Since...this morning," she replied.

"So there's nothing we can do about making sure people don't see it? Or even to having the network take it down?"

"Not immediately, no."

"You realize what this means, don't you? What's going to happen if the 'toons see this?"

She pulled the neck of her sweater and coughed into her fist nervously.

"Is there something you're not *telling* me, Flint?"

"You won't like it if I tell you, Colonel! You really won't!"

"I'm not liking *anything* about this, Flint! Now OUT WITH IT!"

At that, she burst into tears.

"Oh, for...." I sputtered. "Haven't I told you already that when I get mad, it's NEVER about YOU?"

She nodded.

"Then tell me."

She gulped and continued.

"An authorization has been given to us to riot here in Sioux Falls to protest what Peckerwood did in the video, and to keep on doing it until the city is razed, or until Peckerwood apologizes and retracts his comments, whichever comes first."

"WHAT?" I blazed.

"I'm just saying what they told me to say," Flynn protested.

"And who, exactly, gave the authorization?"

"The other three colonels."

"That was an *illegal* authorization! They know perfectly well that we have to have a proper vote on these things, and we can't have a proper vote unless we have a quorum! *Meaning* that they need to get the approval of the entire management strata of the CRA- *which is not here!* And let's not get into the fact that they didn't even tell *me* about it- and *I have exactly the same rank and privileges as they do!*"

"So," Flynn said, "you're not giving ascent to this?"

"THE HELL I WILL!" I declared. "This is anathema to what we're supposed to be about! Now tell me this! Where, exactly, are the other three colonels?"

"In the Riverfront Room, downstairs. You're not going to kill them, are you?"

"Of course not. They're just going to get a piece of my mind, that's all."

III.

The Riverfront Room, so named because the impressive view it had of the Big Sioux River, just inches away from the hotel, was downstairs, on the ground floor, and I was on the third. This meant only one thing: I had to get downstairs quickly before any and all of the colonels left the hotel, presumably before they went Patton or Rommel on the city like they had instructed their underlings.

The elevator was out; I didn't have the time. So, leaving Flynn behind, I shut the door of my hotel room and tromped down three flights of stairs angrily, reaching the ground floor as soon as was possible. I then proceeded directly into the Riverfront Room, where the three colonels, reclining like the Pashas I knew they were, were lingering over their afternoon coffee, accompanied, as always, by their three fawning and sycophantic adjutants. (Flynn initially tried to copy them when she saw them in action, hoping to gain my favour, but I said no dice.)

Colonel Elffrog, in brown suit and red bow tie, was issuing orders into a cell phone while his adjutant, Captain Sow, was busy awaiting whatever blast awaited her. Across the table, Colonel Lampost, still in his scouting uniform, was doing him one better, using his adjutant, Captain Slinker (in similar attire), for a coaster. At the far end of the table was the Spider Lady herself, Colonel Golson, in her typical blue power suit, trying to figure out what another cinnamon bun would do to her waistline while her adjutant, Captain Redcap, in his typical dark blue suit, stood behind her, stalk still and motionless like a cigar store Indian. The whole thing had to be *her* idea; neither of the "men" in the room was smart enough to figure out what the Peckerwood action meant for them. The three adjutants were used to being treated like doormats by their bosses, so they said nothing in the way of protest towards them. I, however, would.

As I entered the room, Elffrog said a curt "Call you back!" into the phone and hung up, as all of them had now noticed my presence as I approached their table.

"WHAT THE HELL IS GOING ON HERE?" I bellowed, ignoring any sort of preliminaries. "HOW *DARE* YOU ACT CONTRARY TO THE CHARTER WE ALL AGREED TO ABIDE BY!"

"The hell is she talking about?" Lampost asked Slinker.

"The CRA charter, sir," the latter replied. "Remember, you helped draft it!"

"Oh, yeah!" said the former. "Four hours of my life I won't get back!"

"Finster," Golson said angrily with her typical cold sobriety, "you're mad! We voted on the proposal as soon as the Peckerwood video went viral, as it were, and it passed with a majority! So you have no business trying to overturn...."

"This isn't a BUSINESS, Golson!" I interrupted. "You can't act like a bunch of SHAREHOLDERS and allow measures and activities to happen whenever you want just because you had some sort of informal VOTE about it! That's not how we roll around here!"

"Then how, exactly, are we supposed to "roll", Ms. Know-It-All?" Elffrog snapped.

"We are *supposed* to act according to a *unanimous* vote of the *entire* management, not according to the whims of a few well-heeled Kentucky colonels!"

"Are you saying," Golson growled, "that this vote is illegal simply because we refused to allow *you* to be involved?"

"THIS HAS NOTHING TO DO WITH ME!" I shouted.

"Look, Finster," Lampost said in a misguided attempt to calm me down, "why don't you just stop acting like a dumb bitch and let us go ahead with this! Then, the next time we get together..."

I rushed forward and struck the table angrily with my fist, overturning all of its contents. The discussion halted briefly as Captain Sow liberated Colonel Elffrog from a full coffee cup that had fallen down on top of him, and then I continued.

"Don't try to buy me off or talk condescendingly to me!" I told them. "My word in this matter means as much as any of yours- probably a lot more, in fact!"

"What is *that* supposed to mean?" a red-faced Golson shouted.

"It is supposed to "mean", *Colonel*, that *I* am the only one who has been trying to earn the respect accorded to me by my rank as of late. I have been the only one of us who has put their ass on the line in the field! I am the only one of us that General Stinson is willing to confide secret information in- because she *trusts* me to keep it secret! And I am the only one who has the unconditional support and respect of the CRA troops because I am the only one of us who is willing to listen to them when they have problems with conducting the missions, when they have issues with the way they are doing things, and when they just need somebody who they confide in one-to-one when they have personal concerns! I don't see any of *you* doing any of that- and I know why! YOU DON'T CARE ABOUT *ANY* OF IT!"

The Colonels froze, open-faced, at the final line of my diatribe.

"You are also," Golson said after a moment, like I had never spoken, "the only one of us who doesn't have a full-time job, and therefore you're in no position to judge...."

"SHUT THE HELL *UP*, YOU BLONDE BIMBO!" I snapped. "I wasn't done TALKING yet!"

"I'm not a *bimbo*!" countered Golson. "Insult her, Redcap!"

As if on cue, the mechanical man behind her raised his finger at me and spoke.

"Your mother is so stupid," he said in a plain, unemotional voice, "that she sold her automobile so she could buy tickets for the bus!"

"Is that supposed to *scare* me?" I scoffed. "Not likely! I'm going outside right now to call the troops back- and then I'm reporting you to the General!"

"Just try it!" Golson warned me impotently. "I'm not scared of you – *or* that little BRAT! I've dealt with worse than you EASILY!"

"*I'm* scared of the General," Lampost admitted nervously.

"Oh, *shut up*!" said Elffrog. "You're *embarrassing* us!"

"Not as much as you'll be when I'M done!" I interjected. "Passing the buck may be second nature to you veteran *administrators,* but I prefer a hands-on approach. And now I'm going to get my hands on this situation and prevent the good name of the CRA from getting debased! So I wish you, ladies and gentlemen, a *good day*!"

And I left the room, leaving the other colonels and their adjutants to pick up the pieces.

IV.

When I left the Riverfront Room, I called Flynn and told her we were going into town to correct the "mistake" the other colonels had made and prevent the rioting from spreading, if it had now advanced to the epidemic proportions I had feared. She eagerly agreed, as I knew she would.

We left the hotel and walked down to the river. There was a foot bridge next to Schoenman's Auto Body, across the street from the hotel, so we were able to make our way into the city from there. Afterwards, we walked into the heart of downtown Sioux Falls and searched from suspicious activities along Phillips Avenue, the city's main commercial district. Flynn was distracted by the shops, so I had to keep my arm firmly in hers to keep her on the ball.

Finally, after a quick stroll down Phillips, we arrived at the Wells Fargo building, the tallest in the city. Both Flynn and I heard a peal of hysterical laughter coming from the base of the building, and we rushed to investigate it.

There, eagerly spritzing spray paint onto the building's pure white facade, was one of our younger officers, Lieutenant Fishelman, who seemed intensely pleased with this, one of her many "art" projects.

"FISHELMAN!" I snapped. "What the hell are you *doing*?"

She spun around, her red hair cascading around her yellow, brown- striped body as she faced us with a cascading grin.

"Hi, Colonel!" she said. "Just a little project to symbolize our disgust with that video!"

"Let me see it," I demanded, pushing her aside.

She had written the words PECKERWOOD IS A DOUCHEBAG in bold all caps- and even had the temerity *to sign her name beneath it*!

"Get rid of it!" I ordered. "The rioting is off! That is an *order, Lieutenant!*"

"WHAT???" Fishelman snapped. "Do you know how long I spent picking the right site for this? And the other colonels said I could..."

"The other colonels were acting in contempt of the CRA charter!" I said, making Fishelman gasp, as if such a thing were an urban legend come true.

"In that case..." she said nervously, "I better clean this off. Then I'd better call the others and tell them that the rioting is off..."

"You'd better!" I said. "Or else I will!"

"And I guess that whole thing about us meeting tonight at the Washington Pavilion to discuss sacking the city is out too?"

"It's ALL OFF!" I snapped. "Unless you want me killing you and eating you with a side of tartar sauce!" Fishelman erased the mural in record time and ran away from me screaming "IT'S OFF! IT'S OFF! DON'T DO IT! IT'S OFF!" to anyone who happened to be in earshot.

"EEEEW!" Flynn said with revulsion. "You weren't *really* going to eat her, were you?"

"No," I said. "But sometimes you need to talk to people a certain way to get them to do what you want. You'll learn that soon enough, Flint."

V.

The rest you probably know. That was why those blockades outside of the city got broken up, and why all those gunboats on the Big Sioux disappeared almost as soon as they first appeared, along with a lot of other strange stuff you humans wouldn't understand.

The whole attempted riot debacle was so bad that General Stinson had to fly in from Springfield to resolve the internal rift between us. We had one of our patented secret meetings, during which she basically read the Riot Act to Golson, Lampost and Elffrog and gave me her renewed confidence for acting the way she would have had she been here. From now on, she said, we go by the charter and nothing else, and anyone who goes against it will be automatically discharged. Golson, Lampost and Elffrog didn't look too pleased about it, but they agreed to go by the new rules, especially when Stinson said she'd gladly accept their resignations from their commissions if they did not.

When the meeting ended, Simpson beckoned me closer to her.

"Thank you, Frankie," she said. "I'm glad *somebody* here is keeping the faith!"

"Wouldn't be any other way with me," I said.

"Sure," she answered. "Listen: do you know anywhere in the city where a girl can find a non-alcoholic stiffener?"

"There's a diner on Phillips Avenue," I said. "Supposed to be good."

"Then let's go there," she responded.

And we did. End of story, for now, anyway.

THE MILWAUKEE INCIDENT

Milwaukee, Wis. (AP): Members of the notorious Cartoon Republican Army (CRA) occupied the lakefront this morning as a protest against the mistreatment of their race, as all of their activities have been since their inception approximately a year ago. However, this protest brought with it an element of local color as well.

Out of a mistaken belief that Governor Wallace wanted to disband every union in the state, the CRA members, who all belong to affiliated Los Angeles area entertainment unions, demanded that he back up upon his actions immediately. Although some were satisfied after being informed that Walker simply wanted to remove the ability of the unions to bargain collectively, and not prevent their existence *in toto*, they were remarkably overwhelmed by those who wanted to march on Madison, murder Walker, and parade his head on a stick. They would be far from the only people in the past few months who have wanted to that- or have had the opportunity to do so.

Inevitably, the situation led to violence. A misfired rifle shot, reputedly of CRA origin though unproven, frightened the crowd into assuming they were on the attack. The police have been called in, but, due to the nature of the cartoon characters- their immunity to bullets and other "weapons of mass destruction" (the CRA's term), as well as the variety of physical and mental powers they possess- the situation, currently lasting over 12 hours and involving hostages on both sides, is at a stalemate.

In spite of the risk involving his life, Governor Wallace has announced his intention to travel to Milwaukee and prove to the CRA that he is "not such a bad man" after all. If that fails, he has promised to get Washington involved, although the "'toons" say that will hurt their situation more than help it.

I'M NEW HERE

As I looked up at the headquarters of the Cartoon Republican Army (location classified) when I was across the street from it, waiting for the light to change, I knew that there was no going back. Mavis, my twin sister, had been abducted only days before, and this was the only way to get her back. At least, it was the only way *I* knew.

Mavis and I had joined up with the CRA only recently. It hadn't been my intention, but, as my parents explained rather directly to me, I had something of a "responsibility" to keep her out of trouble, so out the door I went after her. To make sure I could keep some control over her, I waited until she had picked the rank she wanted to serve as (because that's how it works) and chose the one directly above hers. That's how I got to be a Captain, which is not nearly as fun or powerful a rank in an Army than it is in a Navy, let me tell you.

In any event, as I watched the traffic lights tick down by shifting from red to yellow, I checked my left arm, to see if my red CRA armband was still on, and, more importantly, whether the chevrons I had patiently sewn onto my jacket/vest to indicate my rank were still there. It was, and they were. Thus assured, I was able to proceed confidently across the street when the lights changed.

*

In the interior of the lobby was a small callback box, like in many apartment buildings, with a list of occupants and buttons and ID tags on it. I had already been told that the one which would have ID'ed the CRA was blank, so I pressed the button next to the one glass plate which did *not* identify the occupant. There was a small buzzing noise, and then a voice came on at the other end.

"Yes?" the voice at the other end asked.

"Colonel Finster?" I asked.

"Yep. Who's talking?"

"Uh...It's Captain Duffer Pipes. You sent that e-mail to me about..."

"Right. Come on up- quick!"

I obeyed without hesitation. As the elevator was out, I was forced to take the stairs, but it wasn't too far a climb, seeing as the office was only on the fifth floor. Lucky for me.

When I found the office (which was, of course, the only office on the floor that *didn't* have a nameplate on the door), it seemed rather odd. It was a small, tightly packed room with a lot of paper and a lot of people in it. I wasn't sure who to ask or where to go until Colonel Finster, wearing her normal purple skirt, white shirt and green army jacket (with, of course, the accompanying red arm band and chevrons) came out to the front. As she was much taller than everyone else, she looked rather awkward in the midst of the small room, but I thought she looked good, anyway.

"Come *on*!" she said, motioning me to follow her, once she noticed how gob-smacked I appeared to be in her presence. "I won't *bite* you. Sorry about things in here , but beggars can't be choosers, y'know." She walked to her office, and I followed obediently.

Once we were in the office, she sat down behind her desk and motioned me to the chair in front of it.

"You know," she said, "you can take your hat off," referring to the white-and-blue baseball cap I usually sport, but I demurred. That taken care of, she shifted her attention to the business at hand.

"So," she said, "you're probably wondering why I called you here. Sorry, but the whole secrecy thing..."

"I had a hunch it was something important," I answered. "Especially when you mentioned Mavis."

My twin sister had disappeared only days earlier, and the only clues that were available to me had something to do with the Canadian government, judging by a stylized "C" decal I had found in the yard, along with an empty bottle of Hatchet body spray. I had relayed these suspicions to the Colonel when I answered her e-mail, in hopes that she might be able to clear things up for me. She was.

"I don't really know how to tell you this, Duffer..."

"I can take it, Colonel. I've seen and heard worse."

"So have I. But this isn't exactly a normal situation for us..."

"Tell me."

"All right. Well, the thing is..."

"Roll the bones!"

"Snake eyes!"

"Seven eleven!"

"Daddy needs a new pair of shoes!"

It seemed that the staff members had picked up an inopportune time to begin a crap game in the outer office. Colonel Finster excused herself briefly, gave the delinquents a brief but firm cussing out, and then returned to me.

"Old habits die hard around here," she admitted. Then we got back to the matter at hand.

"Duffer," she said, "as a *boy*, I'm sure you've taken note of the above-average pulchritude of the women of our race. Especially the girls about your age."

"And up," I admitted, nodding at her.

"Nice save, fella. But the problem is that our enemies are starting to use this against us."

"How?"

"Exhibit A: That bottle of Hatchet you found around the spot where Mavis disappeared. In the past few weeks, nearly *all* of our key female operatives have disappeared. Name 'em all- the biggest stars, the bit players, even newcomers like your sister. My own adjutant got swiped around the same time as Mavis, right off the street, before I could do a damn thing. You've seen those TV commercials, right? That body spray is so powerful that no woman or girl can resist the urge to chase whatever foolish *idiot* put it *on* in the first place! The only reason *I'm* still here, *for your information*, is that *I* think there are a *few more important* things in life than *poontang, thank you very much!*"

"Are you sure about that, Colonel? Mavis is a bit...boy-crazy, but I don't think she'd actually,..y'know...if it came to that..."

"Far be it from me to cast aspersions on your sister, Duffer. But if you were a girl, and you smelled that stuff, you'd understand. Even *I* found it hard to resist even *handling it* around here."

"Okay," I said. "I get that whoever it is has something against cartoon girls, and whoever's responsible is using Hatchet to lure them, like a child molester uses candy on *his* victims. But where does that weird "C" fit in?"

"Exhibit B," she continued. "Two Cs, actually. Canada and Conservatives."

"I don't follow."

"You will. We have reason to believe that all of our wayward soldiers are being held in Canada. Ottawa, to be precise."

"The capital city?"

"Right. And that they are specifically being held prisoners by the Conservative Party, who, as is well known among us, *hate our guts*. The Republicans probably tipped them off about us. All the evidence suggests that they are all being held in a special holding facility underneath the Canadian National Archives."

"Why don't we just spring them?"

"Couple of problems there, Captain. First of all, the Conservatives happen to be the *Government* of Canada right now. With a MAJORITY, yet! And the guy in the Prime Minister's chair right now is cold hearted, tough-on-crime, and *merciless*! If we were to mobilize *en masse* to free our colleagues, do you think for *one hot second* he'd let us get away scott free?"

"Uh....no?"

"Darn right NO! We'd be CAUGHT! *And* we'd be the subjects of the biggest show trial-cum-farce since the Chicago Seven! And the CRA as an independent functioning operation would be deader than Joe Barbera *himself*!"

"Then what *can* we do?"

"That's where you come in, Duffer. I am officially dispatching you to Ottawa to try to free the girls."

"What if they *aren't* underneath the Archives?"

"Then we're back to square one. But we can't afford any setbacks, Duffer. The future of the CRA depends on having our *entire* membership active and ready to serve *at a moment's notice*. You can see what even a *small* deficit in our forces has done to us already."

"But why *me*? I just enlisted..."

"Because *you*, quite frankly, have a *brain* in your head. Which is something that cannot be said for most of the "men" around here." She added a "pfft" sound that made clear to me why I had been chosen. "I've seen you in action on your show, Duffer. You may *look* like a little kid, but you got the brain and wits of a MAN!"

"Thanks." I blushed a bit more than was normal for me.

"You better get going. You and Duddy will have to act fast if you're going to free the girls. The Conservatives are planning to table a bill setting up a Canadian Death Row, and our gal pals will surely be the first ones to face the electric chair if..."

"*Duddy?*" I interrupted.

"Duddy Piddles," she explained. "He's new like you, and, well, he's the best we could get on such short notice. You shouldn't worry, though. He's a secret agent by trade, so I already sent him off to scout the area in case the Archives isn't the place where the girls are. He'll meet you at the airport, and then you can take it from there. You need to know anything else?"

"Yeah. I..."

"Sure, sure," she said, putting airline tickets in my hands and pushing me out the door. "G'way, now- I got work to do. And- Duffer?"

"Yeah?" I said, expectantly.

"Don't you *dare* come back without some RESULTS!! Y'*hear* me?" she barked as she slammed the door behind me.

*

Having no other choice, I packed and went off to the airport to catch my flight to Ottawa. But what I really was getting into wasn't made clear to me until I descended from the arrival gate at MacDonald-Cartier Airport. That was when I first got a good look at the man- or, rather, the dog- I was to work with on solving this important affair.

As the Colonel had promised me, Duddy was there. He was a big, white furred fellow with oversized, heavily muscled arms- which, I was soon to learn, were far greater in size than his brain. He was wearing a black shirt that completely covered his very large chest- and no pants. (Suddenly, my wearing shorts all the time made me seem more "manly" by comparison.) As soon as he saw me, he whipped out a hand-lettered sign which he held over his head, like a chauffeur or limo driver waiting for somebody. Unfortunately, he seemed to have misunderstood what my name was when it was relayed to him, as it was written on the card as "Duffel Bagge."

"BUD-DAY!" he shouted, in what I was to learn was his *normal* tone of voice. "OVER *HERE*!"

I went over to him, and he embraced me in a bear hug, like I was a long-lost relative he was just reunited with. Once he finally let me go, he was quick to discover that we had a specific similarity in our outward appearance despite our differences.

"Lookit *that*!" he said, eyeing my chevrons. "We MATCH!" He pointed out the chevrons he had placed on the left side of his shirt above his armband. I groaned internally and rolled my eyes. We held the exact same rank, and, as per the CRA code, we would have to treat each other as equals. Neither of us could give the other "orders", so we would have to find a way to solve our problems through joint initiatives. But could Duddy even be capable of helping me, given the vast amount of overbearing vapidity he seemed to possess?

"Yeah," I said, faking a laugh. "We match, all right."

"Come *on*, man!" he said, pointing to his watch. "It's *seven* already and I haven't had *dinner* yet. SEVEN!"

"Okay," I said. "Just let me get my luggage."

That came on the carousel promptly: my overnight bag and the oversized book of lore I'd been carrying around with me for it seems like forever. It was too big for me to carry on to the plane proper, so I put it with my luggage so it could come with me.

"What the hell is THAT?" Duddy asked when I took it off the carousel and put it onto a luggage cart along with my bag.

"That, my friend," I said, "is my personal guardian against the vagaries of the world. Just like American Express with me."

He looked extremely confused.

"You know..."Don't leave home without it"?"

"Ah-ha! Just like *I* always carry the P.U.T.T.Z. manual with *me*!"

"P.U.T.T.Z.?" Now *I* was confused.

He enlightened me. The Protectors Of Universal Truth In Terrorized Zones. Hence the name of his show: "P.U.T.T.Z. Piddles."

"Ah," I said. "It's an *acronym*."

"What?"

"A word that's made of the first letter in each word of a company name or brand. Like Metro Goldwyn Mayer."

"Huh?"

"You know- MGM!"

"Never heard of it!"

I wasn't surprised. MGM was basically a glorified unit of Columbia now- something that I knew that Louis B. Mayer and Harry Cohn, the founders of those two film studios, would not have liked in the least, but they were both dead now and couldn't do anything about it. Not like Duddy and me. We had a chance to strike a blow for cartoon freedom and rights- *if* this canine *mesuganah* and I could find a way of doing it together, that is.

"Come on!" he said. "We gotta go *eat*!" As my arm was safely tucked into his massive armpit when he said this, and he was rushing out of the airport like a bull after a matador, I didn't have a choice.

*

My baggage safely placed into the trunk of Duddy's rental car, we now sped off at a speed resembling that of light. We only stopped when we arrived at the drive-thru window of Tim Horton's- a popular restaurant chain that, I soon discovered, was seemingly as prevalent across Canada as many other such chains were across our native United States.

"Why the drive-thru?" I asked him. "Can't we just...?"

"*Because*, the JERKS who own these joints never let me come in!"

"Because you're a 'toon?"

"No!"

"Because you're a scary looking, humanized dog?"

"NO! And I am *not* scary looking! Try again, *genius*!"

"'Cause you...don't wear pants?"

"BINGO! The sign says "No shoes, No shirt, No service." It doesn't say *anything* about PANTS! I just think they're *jealous* of how *awesome* my JUNK is!" He waived his "junk" in my face, to my horror, so I could see what he meant.

At the window, Duddy surprised me with the length and breadth of his appetite- and wallet- by ordering nearly one of everything.

Almost as an afterthought, he turned to me and asked: "You want anything, Duff?"- the name I had agreed he could call me, for the sake of having to correct him. I nervously requested something, and he tacked that on to his order. When the contents of the order were unceremoniously dumped into the car, Duddy again drove the car into hyperspace until he found a good spot for us to sit and talk while we ate. Or rather, *I* sat and ate while *he* talked in between noshing ravenously.

To my surprise, Duddy was as concerned about the fate of his (professional) partner, Katty Kutzwell (as feline as he was canine) as I was about Mavis. He made it clear to me how much he *despised* whoever had done this to her, even though, with some amount of contradiction, he also enjoyed being free of her "nagging" him. I gathered that she was the actual "brains" in their relationship, and I imagined that she might actually be *relieved* at being free of him for a while, for he was certainly living up to the name of his organization in my eyes. And I'*d* only been with him for a *short* period!

When he was finished, he let out a loud burp and got out of the car, in full view of me again, to piss in front of a hydrant like the dog he was. A small river of urine enveloped the hydrant like a miniature Mississippi, again to my horror. Then he entered the car again.

"So, what you think?" he asked. "This is what Canadian people practically *live* on, man! So far as I *know*!"

"It's...good?" I supplied.

"Darn RIGHT! Especially those *doughnuts*! Oh, mama! They kick Dunkin' Donuts' ASS!"

"What about Krispy Kreme?" I asked, trying to continue the conversation.

"*Them?* They only got *one* flavor! *Not* worth it, man!" He burped again. "I feel like a beer, now! You want one?"

"I'm not...old enough...for that."

"More for me, then!"

And thus we headed off to the nearest local liquor store, where, somehow, Duddy was able to purchase two six-packs and drink *both* of them completely, *at once*! Oh, boy! Now he wasn't just overbearing and belligerent- he was DRUNK! We 'toons are not at our best after we sip the nectar of the working classes, as I soon found out.

"A'right!" he declared drunkenly, once again grasping the wheel. "We gonna get our girls out NOW! I'm gonna drive this sucker right through *wherever* the hell they are..."

"The National Archives," I said.

"Shut your *mouth*, man!" he said, hitting me in the jaw. "Where the hell'd you learn to *talk* like that, huh? Just hang on and let me *DO THIS*!"

Again, I had no choice but to let him do these things. That is, until the cops finally pulled us over. I was rather surprised they hadn't done that *before*, but...

"Leave 'em to *me*!" Duddy said. "I know Canadian talk!" He was in no condition to do this, but I was in no condition to argue with him. And, it turned out, his actual knowledge of Canada was somewhat limited. As the officer shined a light in his eyes, Duddy rolled down his window, assumed a flirtatious stance, and said:

" 'Allo, love! We's just out 'round fer a spin in th' ol' spymobile, 'ere! And we can't be...'Ey!...Get yer bloody 'ands off...RUN, DUFFER! *RUN!* They aren't *buying* it!"

I tried to, but they caught us both. You can guess where we spent the night after *that*.

*

I let Duddy sleep off his hangover, as I wanted him to be sober when I finally let him have it for being so irresponsible. As soon as he woke up from his "nap", I subtly let him know what I thought of him- by punching him in the nose.

"*DAMN IT!*" he screamed, holding his damaged olfactory unit in his "hands". "What the FUCK was THAT for?"

"It was "*for*" you being such an irresponsible, feckless DICKWAD!" I shouted, doing the best impersonation of the MGM logo I could manage under the circumstances. "Do you even *realize* how much of a MORON you are?"

"Oh, sure. Blame *me*. You were my goddamn INABLER, man!"

"I was NO SUCH THING!"

"You just *sat* there and didn't *do* anything to…"

"Because *you* wouldn't shut your PIEHOLE! *And* because you wouldn't let me get a goddamn word in *edgewise*!"

"You little…*twit*! You're supposed to *respect* me!"

"Not if you don't *deserve* to be respected! Respect is something that's *earned*, not granted by default! Not like the "ranks" in this sham farce of an ARMY!"

Duddy was suddenly and surprisingly appalled by that remark.

"*Sir*," he shouted menacingly, "you take that *back*! If you weren't so *new* here, you'd know…"

"*You're* as new as *I* am!"

"But *I* know what the CRA has been doing for us, and what it means for us as a *race*! Not like *you*!"

"*Excuse* me?"

"You're a *human being*! Need I *spell it out*? You can *pass* for a human being, just like your *kind* can, whereas me and *my* kind sure as *shit* CAN'T!"

"How DARE you! *I'm* as much of a cartoon character as *you* are! You don't work for DISNEY and *not* get reminded of that *every day*!"

"Oh, aren't *we* high and mighty! 'I work for Disney, so…'"

"Shut the hell *up* in there, you goddamn 'toon *ASSHOLES*!"

"GO *FUCK* YOURSELF!"

The "shut the hell up" came from our guard, whereas the "go fuck yourself" came from me and Duddy- in the same tone of voice and at the same time. This, in and of itself, was a turning point for us. Even though we took different forms, we were both considered as stereotypical "'toons" by the establishment, and we were going to be treated the same way by them because they didn't know about or even *want* to know about our differences, anyway. Even Duddy recognized this, and, for once, he was silent. I looked at him intently, trying to figure out if we were thinking the same thing. Finally, he spoke again.

"Did that hurt you as much as it hurt me?" he asked.

"Yep," I answered.

"And...I guess you think we should work together if we're going to get out and spring the girls?"

"That's *exactly* what I've been trying to tell you *all along,* Duddy!"

"Well, honestly, I got *nothing,* man! NOTHING! The cops totally didn't enter into my plan *at all*! You got anything?"

"Yeah. I got something."

And I told it to him in the classic cartoon way- whispering into his ear.

*

You don't need to know how we escaped from jail. Suffice it to say, it involved a soft-shoe vaudeville routine, with some borrowings from a blackface minstrel show (Duddy's idea, not mine) and him punching out most of the cops who surrounded our cell to shut us up. We, miraculously, were able to find our car un-impounded, and I was able to retrieve my mysterious book of lore from the back seat. I flipped it to a page I had marked with a bookmark before I arrived in Canada.

"What you looking for, Duff?" Duddy asked.

"The key to our problems, Dud," I replied.

"How is *that* the key to....?"

"Look, I trusted you to do *your* thing. Trust me to do *mine*, okay?"

"Well...if you know what you're doing..."

"I do. Don't worry about *that*."

Then, we were fortunate enough for me to get a call on the cell phone I had been issued on joining the CRA. From Colonel Finster's adjutant, no less, who seemed to be playing Russian roulette with whatever numbers she could think of- I knew it was her from the call display. I hushed an anticipating Duddy, then spoke.

"Is that you, Can....?"

"Uh-uh. *LIEUTENANT Flint* to *you*, buddy! We CRA members address each other by *rank*, 'case you didn't GET it!"

"Uh...I actually outrank..."

"SHUT UP! Where the hell *are* you?"

"In...Ottawa."

"Then why don't you *free* us?"

"Where *are* you?"

"*D-uh*. In the underground chamber beneath the National Archives, *idiot*! Didn't the Colonel *tell* you?"

"She said you *might* be there."

"Well, we *are*. And you'd *better* come and free us before we all go..."

"How did the hell did you get a *phone* in here, *Flint*?" somebody growled. And then came a stamping sound.

"Back! BACK, you *savages*....Get down here, Pipes, or so help me God..."

The line went dead.

"So?" Duddy said.

"They're in the archives, underground," I said. "Step on it!"

"Can do!"

He did.

*

In no time flat, we had arrived at Wellington Street, where the Archives were located, just kitty corner from the Parliament Buildings, where the Conservatives held court. We had to be careful, since, unlike us 'toons, they weren't recognizable by their appearance alone, and we could easily fall into their hands without knowing it. I made this clear to Duddy as we stealthily made our way to the Archives building from the outside, since there was no other way to get inside the secret spot where the girls had been sequestered.

"How are *we* gonna get in, then?" Duddy asked.

"We just find the spot in the wall where it gives," I said. "The book says there's a concealed passageway leading to a secret room that can be used a holding tank, like in a police station. Somehow, *this* government was the first to discover it, even though this building is over a hundred years old!"

"You and that book," Duddy said. "I wish I had your brain." For him, that was as close a compliment as I was going to get, so I took it.

I guided Duddy to the spot where I had been guided by the book. It looked like solid rock, and Duddy said so.

"It's not," I assured him. "If somebody pushes that bit of rock, it'll become permeable and..."

He laughed.

"Are you *serious*? That's the *dumbest* thing I ever....AAARRRRGGGH!"

He had, while saying this, pushed on the rocks I had pointed out. And, when he did, they parted, revealing a flight of stairs that Duddy fell down-loudly. I followed him as he fell down to the bottom.

"SHIT!" he shouted when he reached the bottom of the stairway. "That *HURT*, man!"

"SSSHH!" I warned him. "Somebody might HEAR us!"

"Correct!"

A figure holding a lantern *had* heard us, and he now revealed himself. It was the Canadian Minister of Foreign Affairs, otherwise known as the Government's resident attack dog. I'd been warned about him, and, as he shined a light in his face, it seemed to me that my fears about him were justified.

"How did *you* find *out* about this?" he demanded, blankly but firmly.

"I..." I began.

"*Never mind*!" he shouted, revealing his teeth. "We know *exactly* how to..."

"WAIT A *MINUTE*!" Duddy thundered back at him. "*Now* you're *meddlin'*, son! Now you're MEDDLIN'!"

Lest I fear for myself, Duddy whispered to me after uttering this threat.

"Go down the tunnel and see if the girls are there," he said. "I'll deal with this douchebag!"

He then resumed his attack as I headed down the passage that was inches away from the stairwell.

"Listen, you lead head layin' in the bed!" Duddy shouted at the Minister as I headed down the passage. "I told you *once* to drop dead! Now I'll only say this once more once! That there room is full of *my* people and *my* friends, and you ain't gonna do NOTHIN' to stop us gettin' 'em out! If you can't deal with *that*, then go find a lake and JUMP IN!"

I reached the end of the passage just as Duddy finished, where I found a door. Strangely enough, it was ajar, like someone *wanted* me to find it open. So I walked through...

...and found myself surrounded on all sides by my fellow, female 'toons, deprived of air and nourishment for what seemed like days, *at least*, and entirely contained within a giant, bottle-like structure which must have housed one big-ass ship at one point in its existence!

"DUDDY!" I shouted out the hallway. "I *found* them!"

He soon arrived, having finished his tirade against the Minister.

"I got him away," he said, "but he was pretty m....*SHIT* ON A *SHINGLE*! They're in *that*?"

"Yeah," I said. "And they don't look long for this world! We have to find some way to break that bottle before they all suffocate!"

"But what can we DO, man?" Duddy shouted. "There's no *way* we can break *through* that thing!"

Surprisingly, we *could* do something. The vibration from Duddy's voice was so powerful that it caused a crack to emerge at the base of the bottle!

"Duddy," I said, "I know what we need to do. Or *you* need to do."

"Me?"

"Yeah. You gotta sing "Fortunate Son.""

"Huh?"

"Like you did in the car earlier."

"We haven't got the *record*, man!"

"We don't NEED the record! You sing, and I'll fake the instrumental part."

"You'd *do* that? You didn't want to before..."

"We have to do it, *now*! So let's do it, NOW!"

Without any further hesitation, I started making guitar sound effects with my mouth and miming, playing one. Duddy saw his cue and took it, belting out the song in a way that would have impressed John Fogerty himself. I could see in his eyes how much he identified with the lyrics of the song- which, if you can ignore the rocking beat, are a pretty intense statement on the kind of social prejudice we 'toons face among humans all the time- and it really made a difference. It sure woke up the girls, and the ones who still had the energy to do it began singing a song of their own to encourage us- "We Gotta Get Outta This Place."

Sure enough, with all that activity, the crack in the bottle became a fissure, and then in split right down the middle, allowing the girls to escape.

"FREE!" one of them shouted when it became apparent. "We're FREE! We can MOVE and BREATHE again!"

Once this became apparent to all of them, they all sprang out as one, swarming over the ground and thundering towards the door like a herd of buffalo. Duddy and I could do nothing to escape the high tide of feminine bodies moving *en masse* so we were swept along with them. But, fortunately, they knew what we had done, and they acclaimed us as their "heroes."

Did Duddy and I feel good when so many girls said that about us, nearly all at once? You bet we did!

Unfortunately, that feeling lasted only briefly, for, as we breached the barrier, we were immediately surrounded on all sides by a detachment of the Royal Canadian Armed Forces. The Minister of Foreign Affairs must have tattled on us! Duddy and I sensed we were sitting ducks, and tried to get lost in the crowd so we wouldn't get busted right away.

But I learned something that night. You don't keep a 'toon girl down- especially one derived of life, liberty and the pursuit of happiness by the standards of *any* government for as long as our colleagues seemed to have been. And certainly not when they numbered in the hundreds, even the thousands, and with new ones seemingly coming out of the woodwork every time.

Lieutenant Flint, who seemed to have been elected spokesperson, swept past us to address- or, rather, taunt- the Canadian soldiers.

"YOU *ASSHOLES*!" she shouted. "You spineless, shameless, hypocritical ASSHOLES! How DARE you keep us locked up in there for as long as you did- without food, water, air, proper ventilation, sanitation, cell phone bars, and not even any goddamn

WI-FI! You *chumps* think you're so NOBLE 'cause you're not fighting any goddamn WARS, *do ya*? That you can rub your "free" HEALTHCARE in our faces and say how much *better* you are than the *Americans, eh*? Well, listen to this, you maple-flavored HYPOCRITES! You are *no better* and *no worse* than the *United States* is, and that's saying a *helluva lot*! And do *not* think that we will be in any way *pacified* by this cheap attempt on your part at playing *soldier*, because what you did to us is *inexcusable* under *any* country's flag! You creeps haven't seen a *real war* here since the war of *1812*, but you're gonna see one NOW- and I ain't talking HOCKEY or DOUGHNUTS here! Come on, girls- LET'S GIVE IT TO 'EM- *RIGHT NOW!*"

They gave it to them, right then. Thousands of girls, some armed with destructive, debilitating superpowers, others simply with righteously steamy indignation, stormed forward before the soldiers could do a thing. They picked up rocks and grass and soil and threw them, and the more powerful ones began punching out lights and throwing cars and things around. Before long, the battle had spread away from the Archives and was being undertaken on the bright green lawn of Parliament Hill. It was there that I was, finally, reunited with my sister, and Duddy with his partner. Mavis was wearing one of her trademark sweaters, and had seemingly chewed on it during her imprisonment in a vain attempt to get nourishment. Katty was a little better, having not been in as long, and she was able to beat a path for us through the melee to safety.

"How long do you think this will last?" I asked.

"A while yet," Katty said, in a voice eerily like that of Colonel Foster. "You bottle *that* many 'toon girls in one room, and they're *bound* to start hating whoever did that to them intensely!"

"You came at the right time, though," Mavis added. "We were just about to start KILLING EACH OTHER!" Even though I usually have to take my sister's words with a grain of salt, I knew she meant it that time.

Suddenly, we saw a sight that reflected the fact that we weren't the only ones who hated the Conservatives. A giant man- a real human being!- with a big beard ran past us on the street. He had tied the jacket of his suit around his waist, and was wearing his tie on his head like a headband. He was also sporting black marks under his eyes, like a pro football player, or, more to the point, like Rambo. We watched as he shouted and ran into the fray with a freshly sharpened, pointed stick he seemed eager to use.

"Well, that does it," Katty said. "It's officially not just about *us* anymore."

"How?" I asked.

"Don't you know who that guy *is*?" Mavis said. "That's the *Leader of the Opposition*! He's like the *second* most powerful guy in Canada after the Prime Minister!"

"He certainly is living up to his title," Duddy added, with an unusual calmness, as we watched the battle play itself out.

*

The battle was over by the time the sun began rising over the Rideau River the following morning, and, we, naturally, won the day, with a surprising assist from nearly all the Opposition MPs and Senators, who seemed to hate the Conservatives as much as us, but hadn't until now found an outlet for it outside of the restrictions of Parliamentary procedure. Our mission accomplished, Duddy and I embraced one more time before we departed Ottawa with our other halves.

"I owe you, man," Duddy said as he slipped me a token of his affection. "We would never have done what we did if you hadn't done what you did."

"And I wouldn't have done what I did if you hadn't done your thing, either," I said, tipping my hat to him. "Take care of yourself, okay?"

"You , too, " he said. "And, listen, if you want to pal around again, like tonight..."

"Sure," I said, miming a phone call. "I slipped you my card, so if you wanna talk..."

"Right. See you 'round, buddy!"

He ambled off in the company of Katty, who was firmly rejecting each of his attempts to "fool around" some more before they left Ottawa. I turned my attention to Mavis.

"You okay?" I said. "I mean, it was kinda rough..."

"No big," she answered. "Some of us had gum and Tic-Tacs in our purses, so we were able to live on that most of the time. But it *was* getting rough by the time you and Doofus..."

"Duddy," I corrected.

"...arrived to save our asses. You were real heroes there, Duffer. So- what'd he give you?"

"I don't know. He says he only gives them to friends, so I guess I must be one now."

"Let's see it."

"All right- but it's probably- OH, MY *GOD*!"

In spite of the deeper personality I had found beneath the outer layer of Duddy Piddles, his juvenile nature was still apparent in his parting gift to me.

He had given me a photocopy of his *ass*!

CERTAIN PRIVATE CONVERSATIONS IN FIVE ACTS AND AN EPILOGUE: OR, A DAY IN THE LIFE OF THE CARTOON REPUBLICAN ARMY

ACT ONE: THE FIX IS IN (10:00 AM, EST, Jun.1, 2—-)

LT. I. THRID:

As is her custom when issuing communiques, Colonel Finster was exact and precise when she summoned me to the Cartoon Republican Army headquarters (location classified) that morning. The message I got from my LoganBerry from her was short and sweet:

"Folsom here. Come talk to her."

So many feelings rushed through my brain at that moment that even I have difficulty communicating all of them to you. And it's even worse when you have the kind of handicaps I have.

Oh, sure. You must be thinking: "What kind of problems does *she* have? Hot little albino with black hair, dress and boots to match. Must have the boys lining up at her door...."

No, no, no. You *were* thinking that, *weren't* you? I get that all the time, but I can *assure* you that, in spite of my appearance, I'm not a Goth or punk or anything like that. I can impersonate one if I have to, but that's not who I *really* am. I am-was- a middle school honor student, and I *am* a fine, upstanding young *woman,* and I intend to *remain* so, *thank you*!

Okay. Sorry. Just needed to vent a bit. Sorry, also, if I get a bit emotional talking about this, but it's *hard,* man! Really!

When you have a photographic memory like I do, you remember *everything*. Names, places, things, trends, movies, you name it. You can remember all the things you did in your past life, all the people who did kind to you, and all the people who screwed you over. That's particularly the case when someone you love *and* someone you *hate* are involved on opposite sides of the particular program at hand. Which is why we're here, aren't we? All right. I'll tell you about what happened. Just let me set it up.

First, there was the guy I love. Or loved, I should say- 'cause you can't love a *dead* person, can't you?

Biltmore.

You might know this about me already, but I used to be one bad-ass delinquent. There wasn't anything they could keep out of my sticky figures if I wanted it. Spent a whole year on my own one time, and was entirely self-sufficient, in spite of my youth and supposed "inexperience." Finally, I decided to give school another try, and I ended up at Z.

Where I met Biltmore.

We were like a couple in a romantic comedy at first- you know, *before* the final clinch. That never happened with us, but I'll get to that in a minute. He was a JD like me once, but he'd sobered up and gone straight. Anyhow, I'd been fingered for a petty crime, and, unlike the rest of the school, he believed me when I said I didn't do it. We proceeded to confront the dude who did it, and, while he didn't exactly get *punished* for it, we sure did humble him. Afterwards, I joined Biltmore on the Safety Patrol as his partner, and we made a pretty good team, if I do say so myself.

Eventually, though, professional became personal, like it usually does.

We were among the last group of cartoon characters to be shipped off to Orthicon. That miserable little rock the "real" humans exiled us off to, as you know. I told you all about that before, so I won't repeat myself here. Suffice it to say, I ended up in Florida along with the rest of them, and I was about to have my roister doistered by an insensitive security guard when Fillmore arrived and practically killed the guy with a left hook and right cross. I had just enough time to thank him before we were hustled off into the bowels of the spaceship and then off to Orthicon. Afterwards, we did what came natural to us. We exposed the whole dirty deal behind the Orthicon scheme, got all the cool, hip kids to rebel against the consulate, and helped plant the seeds for our current little countercultural venture.

Oh, yeah. And we made *love*. More than once. And it was *good*.

Now, don't get the wrong idea. We got condoms from the store and everything. We weren't *idiots*. But, ever since we teamed up at Z, there'd been taunts and whispers that I'd have to put up with. In the girls' locker room and so forth. "You and your *boyfriend* doing all right?" Catty stuff like that. And, since he was black (and bald as a cue ball to boot) and I was- and am- *very* white, they were worse than usual. So, one night on Orthicon, I gave him an offer he couldn't refuse.

"Everyone's been saying you're my lover," I told him point blank. "It's been a lie for too long. I want to make it *true*."

He tried to speak, but I cut him off.

"You love me, too, *don't* you?" I asked rhetorically. "I know it by the way you've been looking at my legs all this time."

"Well, baby," he said, with uncharacteristic nervousness, "if that's what you want..."

"It is," I said.

To prove it, I ripped his glasses off his head and kissed him. He gallantly insisted on condoms, as he knew- too well- the consequences of unprotected sex from the world we came from, so I agreed. Once *that* little detail was taken care of, well...

I can't tell you *everything*. This isn't *that* kind of story. You told me that *yourself* when you started working on it a couple of years ago.

Anyway, six months after we got back from Orthicon, the CRA got started, and we both signed up. Both as lieutenants, since that was all our court-mandated severance packages would let us have. He went with one unit, I with another, but we promised to keep in touch.

Then he died. Simple as that.

He and his unit were assigned to make a raid on a munitions dump outside of Washington. This was about the same time I participated in the halting of the Congressional vote that would have effectively made the entire cartoon race global criminals. The armory would have provided ample additional weaponry to back up the valid political points we were planning to make to Congress, but, as you know, both of our attempts literally *bombed*. In Fillmore's case, he and his unit faced far worse than we ended up facing in Congress. The D.C. cops found out about them, and those lousy *fuckers* burnt the damn place *down*. I don't need to tell you what *fire* does to someone made of *celluloid* now, do I? It was a *disaster*. I personally wasn't so good myself. As soon as I found out he was gone, I collapsed and had to go on sick leave for a couple of weeks.

Now we come to the woman I *hate*.

Golson.

First principal, then Colonel, now *nothing*. She's locked up now, and I am so *glad* for that.

That lousy *bitch* was only interested in me because I had an incredibly high GPA, and we both *knew* it. Biltmore knew it, too, but he couldn't say it to her face back at Z. Neither could I, really. When you're principal of a middle school, you apparently sell your soul to the Devil to get that far in life, because I don't recall her acting or speaking with genuine kindness at any time I've known her. Then or now.

Anyway, she made life a living hell for me and Fillmore and the rest of the safety patrol. We were just expected to smile sweetly and be her genteel palace guard, or else they would threaten to break us. Never literally, but I could always imagine myself being stretched out on a rack when she said it. She wasn't interesting in stopping crime on campus at all- because I'm *sure* she was getting plenty of under the table graft while she was there. She just couldn't *admit* it because she'd lose her cushy job, otherwise.

I didn't see her at all on Orthicon, but, somehow or another, she became a Colonel in the CRA. And she basically ran her command the same way she ran her school- an unfeeling, unmoving MacArthur with blond hair. In fact, other than my CO, Colonel Finster, most of the "people" with that rank in the CRA have been as remote and stuck up as she is, if you want to know the truth. She, unfortunately, was Fillmore's commander, and she had specifically ordered *him* to raid the armory, knowing full well that it was a suicide mission and he'd be killed. I am *deeply* certain of that.

She got what was coming to her.

She'd kept up her principal's chair at Z after she got her Colonel's commission, and, it turned out, she was lining her pockets with money intended for both of her commands. Apparently, the Superintendent and School Board either looked the other way or had been intimidated (likely by she herself) into silence, and this had been going on for years. But the CRA was different. We're used to human beings like you buying and selling us (no offense), but one of *our own* does it, the kitty's claws come out.

She got fired from the school, of course, and we grunts then called for her to be disbarred as a Colonel as well. Then she got called into court to answer the charges against her. The press made a lot of hay from it, especially after she'd been outed as a 'toon. That she would be convicted, there was no doubt- and she was.

That day, the feds were going to transport her to Sing Sing, but Colonel Finster wanted to officially relieve her of her CRA command first- and allow me to confront her one more time before she went to jail for the rest of her life.

Which is why I was in the office now, preparing to do just that.

"You know, you don't have to do this, Inga," the Colonel said to me, before I entered the room where she was being detained.

"No, Colonel," I said. "I *have* to do this. We have a *score* to settle!"

Knowing I was serious, she left me to what I wanted to do. So I opened the door and faced the Dragon Lady.

She was seated on a chair, with her hands and feet tied, in a storage room that was far from the plush conditions she had enjoyed as principal and Colonel.

Perfect.

She didn't bat an eyelid as I approached, as she evidently thought she was still in charge.

"Whatever you've got to say, Thrid…" she began.

How wonderful! She *remembered* me!

"SHUT UP!" I shot back.

There was a tense, choking silence for a few moments.

"I suppose you're going to tell me I'm not the 'boss' of you anymore," she continued. "Or some *other* delightful *witticism* from your *peer* group…"

"ENOUGH!" I said. "I've taken *enough* of your *shit*, Golson! Suppose *you* start taking some of *mine*!"

"So *you* want something out of me, too, huh?" she said. "Well, go ahead. They've taken everything away from me as it is. Everything I worked and *slaved* to get…"

"YOU never *slaved* a day in your *life*!" I countered. "It was always *bad* for your precious REPUTATION!"

She opened her mouth and creased her brows in anger, but said nothing.

I continued.

"You know what *you* are, Golson? A BULLY! That's right! A goddamn BULLY! As a principal and a Colonel *both*! You were always telling us *not* to bully *each other*, but that didn't apply to *you* versus *us*! You *ruled us* ALL THE TIME! It *always* had to be what *you* wanted- ALWAYS! Never mind that there was more *graft* at Z than there *ever* was at *Tammany Hall*! *You* always prevented us from making the scores we needed to make- because the ones behind everything were somehow *always* your precious FAVORITES!"

"I NEVER played *favorites*!" she insisted. "I…"

"Save it!" I said. "The courts *already* found you GUILTY! I'm surprised they didn't charge you with PERJURY besides!"

"You slanderous heap of *white trash*!"

"How DARE you!"

"How dare *I?* How dare *you* come here and try to *intimidate* me? You always were a little *thug,* Thrid. Believe me, if you didn't have a brain and an elephant's memory, I would have thrown your ass OUT the first chance I had! And don't *think* I haven't forgotten all the times that you and that *nigger...*"

"*WHAT DID YOU SAY?*"

"You h*eard* me!"

That was *it*! She had no *right* to talk about him like that! I went right over and slapped her with all the strength I had at my command. Actually, it wasn't so much a slap as a good old fashioned knock down. The result was that she stumbled and fell off the chair while I stood over her.

"DON'T YOU *EVER* TALK ABOUT HIM LIKE THAT *AGAIN*!" I roared. "***EVER***!"

"Oh, pardon *me* for offending your *racial sympathies,* you *slut*!" she countered.

"YOU GODDAMN LOUSY *BITCH*!" I growled.

"Don't think I didn't know about you two," she answered. "I'm surprised nobody actually caught you two *schtupping* on campus! That would have been a good headline for the paper, now, wouldn't it?"

I couldn't *stand* being in the same room with her anymore. So I kicked her in the stomach- hard- and ran out of the room crying, the tears running my mascara as I did.

I went out into the hallway and buried my head in my arms. Fortunately, my newest friend, Lieutenant Totino, was there in the office, and he rushed out to convert me. We renewed an old acquaintance during the Congress raid, and I liked him from the start. He's intelligent, like I am, but also pretty damn funny. And handsome as all get out, though he won't admit it himself. I plan on asking him to be my new boyfriend soon, but I'll take it slower than I did with Fillmore this time.

Anyway, Teo, to give him his first name, was right there for me almost as soon as I got into the hall. He'd helped me plenty when I was on sick leave, and now he was doing the same noble thing again.

"That bitch hurt your feelings, didn't she?" he asked.

I nodded.

"It wasn't just about me," I said. "It was about me and Biltmore. She called him a..."

"Say no more," he said, calmly but tersely. "I have an...African American...associate myself, and if somebody tried to call him *that*, I'd probably feel the same way!"

"Would *you* kick them in the stomach- like I just did?"

"Okay...maybe not *that*!"

That stopped me crying and started me laughing. The secret of his charm.

"Come on!" he said. "Let's get you out of here. This atmosphere is toxic. But you better clean up first. You got some....stuff under your eyes."

"Thanks for noticing," I said.

I kissed him- and he fainted!

Guess I don't know my own strength when it comes to boys.

COLONEL F. FINSTER:

I heard Thrid crying and running past the door of my office, and I knew Golson had said something to her- insulted her purity as a girl, no doubt. Well, now, I thought, is the *perfect* time to relieve her.

Not wasting any time, I rushed to the storeroom, where Folsom was slowly righting herself onto the chair where I'd left her earlier.

"Okay, Golson!" I said. "Thrid just came running out of here *crying*, which I have *never* seen her do in all the time I have known her! WHAT THE HELL DID YOU *SAY* TO HER?"

She was silent.

"*ANSWER ME!*" I thundered.

"Why do *I* have to do what *you* tell me to do?" she responded. "We hold *exactly* the *same* rank!"

"Not *anymore*!"

I walked over to her and ripped the CRA armband and Colonel chevrons off of her purple pantsuit. Then I pawed the symbolic fake gold leaf key she got to have as a Colonel, threw it on the ground, and crushed it with my foot, like a Jewish groom on a gold chalice at a wedding.

"Donna Golson," I said in my best voice of doom, "by the power vested in me by the executive council of the Cartoon Republican Army, you are hereby stripped of your rank and title in this organization. You are hereby forbidden from associating further with the CRA or from attempting to interfere with the activities of the CRA in any form. If you do so, we will have no further alternative but to hunt you down- and KILL you! So it has been said- so it will be *done*!"

That being said, I took the patch, armband and chevrons, opened the window, and allowed the items to fly to the four winds.

"Very well put!" Golson said sarcastically. "Not that I care for anything uttered by a *mick* like you!"

"*WHAT WAS THAT?*"

"Don't try to *disguise* it, Finster. You have a lantern jaw, red hair, and a volcanic temper. Plus, you dress like a *harlot* in that short skirt and green jacket. You're *Irish*- and not the *lace-curtain* type, either! The only thing missing from your look is the *beer*!"

"My *father* was Irish," I said, hiding the hurt I felt. "But what *of* it? And besides, my *mother* wasn't..."

"No matter. If it walks like a duck..."

"You....You....RACIST!"

"Oh, pardon *me*, Ms. *McThing*! I didn't realize I was in the august presence of the *American Civil Liberties Union....*"

"*Shut up!*" I ordered. "Just.....*SHUT UP*! That mouth of yours ought to be registered as a LETHAL WEAPON! But you know *what,* Golson? It doesn't *matter* anymore! You LOST! You were exposed as a fraud, a racist, a mobster and God knows *what* else! You *tainted* the 'toon name in a way that will take us YEARS to recover from! And you are *totally unrepentant* in the face of all the evidence AGAINST you! And *then* you have the NERVE to bawl out a *defenseless little girl...*"

"Ms. *Thrid* is not "defenseless,"" interjected Folsom. "You, of all people, should know *that* by now!"

"*You* are missing the *point*!" I said. "*You* are a remorseless, treacherous, manipulative, cold hearted MONSTER! God DAMN you! Hitler was a SAINT compared to YOU!"

"What the hell was I *supposed* to do?" she said. "Be a fucking MOTHER to 4,000 *children?*"

"You could *learn* to show *compassion* for others, instead of acting like a fucking DICTATOR all the time!"

"Which is exactly what you and your "people" are doing to ME *right now*!"

"Don't you DARE make this about ME, lady!"

"Why shouldn't I? Isn't what you're doing to *me* exactly what you're accusing me of doing to *others*?"

"IT IS *NOT*!"

"Okay, *mick.* Then I'll let you and your *rainbow brigade* of *niggers, kikes, spics, chinks, Japs, Polacks* and *Dagos* take over the *world,* then! And then *you'll* somehow make yourself the *Hitler* of your *new world cartoon order,* like you've been *planning all along*! Isn't that *right?*"

I did not face her for a moment. Then I turned around and let her loose from the bands on her hands and feet. Then I told her to stand up.

Then I went to town.

I have *never* beaten someone up unless I felt they *deserved* it, and I caution my officers to do the same in discharging their duties. But *nobody* deserved to be beaten as soundly and viciously as this...."woman"...did. And I proceeded to do just that.

I smashed in her perfectly mannered face and kicked her repeatedly in her padded stomach. I ripped off all the expensive jewelry she was wearing, and threw it on the ground. I grabbed her hair with both hands and ripped out as much of it as I could. Then I resumed kicking and punching her until she was clearly bruised and flat on the ground. Then I took one of the ether-soaked rags I keep with me always for emergency protection, and held it over her nose.

She went out like a light.

Going to the doorway, I whistled for someone to come to the door. A runty little Care Bear type answered.

"Get her out of here," I ordered, pointing to Golson. "I don't want to *ever* see her face in here *again*!"

"But," the bear protested, on viewing Golson, "you *killed* her...."

"GET HER *OUT!!!*" I exploded, louder and more viciously than I had intended, but I wanted this thing *over*.

The bear understood, and got Golson- what was left of her- out of the office. Myself, I stared out the window. I'd probably hate myself in the morning for what I had done, but it had to be done. And I felt good that I had done it myself- for once.

ACT TWO: FOUR REDHEADS

12:00 pm EST, Jun.1, 2—-.

LT. C. FLINT:

Is this thing on? I gotta warn ya, I got a bit of a temper, and I shout *real loud* when I get mad. You know what I'm saying? So, if I go on a tear, and I blow out a speaker, then....You can handle it with the low levels? Good. Okay. I'll start talking now....

I had no idea what I was in for that day when I reported for duty. All I could guess was it was something bad by the look on Colonel

Finster's face. She looked totally *pissed*. I hoped it wasn't something *I'd* done.

"Something the matter, boss?" I asked, bracing for the worst.

"Nothing *you* did, Flint," she answered, putting her hand on my shoulder.

Phew! The Colonel's built like a college basketball player, and she can really be mean as piss when she's mad. I'm just glad I avoided her wrath...then.

"I....uh....just had some....issues...with Colonel Folsom," she explained further. "She's no longer with us, by the way."

I gasped in shock.

"You *killed* her?"

"*No,* you *idiot*! What the *hell* do you think I *am*?"

"But I thought people only said that when...."

"They do. But I *merely* gave the former Colonel her *walking papers*." She suddenly clenched her fist. "Along with a bit of business. But she *deserved* it."

"I gotcha," I said.

All of us 'toons had been monitoring the Folsom case like it was the Cuban Missile Crisis or something. So I was well aware of how much Colonel Golson had betrayed the 'toon cause and didn't have to be told twice about it, even by Finster.

"Now, there are only two other Colonels, as of now," the Colonel said. "We'll probably get at least another one at the table soon enough. The General has me reviewing the possible candidates right now."

"So I have to help you with *that*?"

"I am perfectly capable of doing that *myself, thank you*!" she answered, sitting down at her desk and shuffling the papers on it.

"Well, *pardon me!*" I said.

In a "regular" army, that would count as "insubordination", or whatever it is they call "acting up" in that setup. But this sure isn't a "regular" army, and, if I wanted to be snippy to the boss, I could. She, however, had the right to slap me out of my panties if she wanted to, and I felt she nearly did when her hand whacked across my cheek just after that.

"None of your BACKTALK!" she ordered. "I've had *enough* of that *crap* today, and it isn't even FIVE yet, for God's sake! If you can't learn to comport yourself with *dignity* and *respect* for *others,* I can have you busted *clean out of here,* Flint! You might be able to con a *man* with your good looks, but you're not dealing with one *here*!"

"Sorry, Ma'am!"

I swallowed deeply, bit my lip and saluted. But that only got her madder.

"*What,*" she roared, "have I *told* you about THAT?"

"About what?" I asked, innocently.

"I will NOT be addressed as "Ma'am"- especially not by a young PUNK like YOU! *And* we do NOT salute each other here under ANY circumstances! *Do you understand me, Flint?*"

"Y...Yes," I said, swallowing again.

That's the extent of our relationship right there. I try to do all I can to please her, but I keep thinking that sometimes she *wants* me to screw up so she can do some sort of crazy lesbian thing with me as "punishment." I'm not implying anything, but I've never seen her go out with a man, and she seems like plenty alpha girl material to me....

You know what? Just cut that last part *out,* if you can. She'll *kill* me if she heard I had told you I said she might be a lizzy. You know what a temper she has, right? Vesuvius had *nothing* on *her*!

Anyhow....

After that, I figured maybe I should leave, and let her get her temper back. But she pointed to the chair in front of her desk, implying I was to sit on it.

"Candace," she said, "I'm sorry. It's been a rougher day than usual, and I took it out on you. I do that too much. Really. One of the consequences of me being a short-tempered daughter of Erin, I suppose. But you, of all people, know what it's like to fly off the handle once in a while. Right?"

"I sure do," I said.

Another bullet dodged! She only called me by my first name when she was pleased or contrite with me, so I knew things were now all right between us. And besides, she has enough of a sense of humor to deprecate herself, even though she really isn't that bad. I, on the other hand, am so antsy about my own appearance and personality that I don't even *try* to do it.

So I sat down in front of her.

"We have another *problem* that needs to be dealt with around here," she said. "But, as I have already exhausted myself with a problem today, I thought I'd let you get out of the office and try to get some field experience."

Oh, boy! My big chance to impress the boss! If I did this well enough, I might make CAPTAIN- or better! But I couldn't let her see my glee about this new assignment. She'd already given me a yellow card today, and I did *not* want a red one, so to speak. So I summoned my most neutral tones and said:

"Sure. I can do that. What is it?"

"We have a rogue ex-member to deal with. You know Raven Reckless, right? I mean, you were at the same studio..."

"Yeah," I said. "Didn't see her much, though. We were on different shows. But she was a total fucking BITCH! Thought she was a *queen* or something! Always with the airs and the this and the that. A total asshole- if you don't mind me saying so."

"Well, as you know, *Corporal* Reckless was one of the earliest recruits to our cause. But she had some discipline problems- along with a staggering candy addiction that predated the CRA itself. After a commanding officer called her out prior to the Congress raid, she sharpened a candy cane into a shiv and tried to knife her. Well, you know about how we feel about members of the CRA attacking each other, *don't you*? We busted her out and threatened to *burn* her if she even *tried* to re-enlist. Naturally, she took it personally and threatened to destroy all of us. It's been mostly talk so far. Until now."

"What's she done?"

"Well, *Ms.* Reckless fancies herself the next *Hitchcock*, and, somehow, she has found compromising footage of us in- shall we say- legally questionable actions, which she has edited into a very slanderous "documentary". I haven't seen any of the footage- no one other than her seems to- but I can safely assume that, if she manages to upload the video to YouSuck tonight, like she's already bragged about on her Twaddle and Facemask accounts just now, the CRA is in deep shit. She has to be *stopped*."

"And I'm the one to do it, huh?"

"Yes. You and Lieutenant Hartman."

"You mean.....Vicky?"

"If you want to use her first name, then, yes."

I knew Vicky Hartman more by her reputation than personally then. I'd seen her on her show, and that's about it. But she made me- who, it must be admitted, is not an angel by *any* means- look like a *saint* in comparison. About the only thing we had in common was our hair color, as well as the fact that we both had voices and tempers that could both win an Arkansas hog calling contest *and* lose Miss Congeniality in a beauty contest. I heard tell that she even made Colonel Foster look like a kitten in comparison, not to mention myself, which was really saying something.

"Are you *sure* about this, Colonel?" I said, my cool façade finally cracking. "I mean, if I was going to be partnered with somebody on a butt-kicking expedition like this, couldn't I be with Jenny, or Kim, or someone else who can really *fight*....?"

"You know as well as I do that *Major Wickman* and *Captain Plausible* have careers *outside* of the CRA that doesn't always make them available to us. Lieutenant Hartman and yourself are the only officers under my command not engaged at the moment. Besides, you both share Reckless's hair color...."

"What's *that* got to do with it? Just 'cause people have the same color hair doesn't mean they're all exactly the same. I mean, Reckless and I alone... "

"*And* Daring has captured Sergeant Penton and has forced her into working as her editor, sadistically making her review *hours* of footage without even a *break*!"

"She has *Jess*?"

Now, *her* I knew. And liked. Real brainy, but not stuck up. Real pleasure to be around. Thinking that Daring was *using* her....well, even if it meant putting up with *Vicky,* I *had* to do it now.

"So," the Colonel said, "you'll do it?"

"Damn *right* I will!"

I stood up, and the Colonel gave me Vicky's contact information. I was going to salute her, but then I remembered myself, and just shook her hand before I left the office.

*

Vicky, fortunately for me, didn't live too far away from the CRA offices, although, since it'd been a few years since her show's heyday, she wasn't exactly living in luxury, if you get my drift. We never got paid the same way you humans are, with that fancy drop the money in your account electronically jazz. *Or* any royalties- they *really* screwed us there. We got- and get- per diems, and most of us tended to use them on booze, blow and sex if we weren't smart, and stuff into mattresses and pillowcases if we were. The human banks wouldn't *touch* our money- still won't. Asses, all of 'em.

Anyhow, I'm rambling....

I spotted Vicky's name on the callbox and pressed the button beside it.

"*Yeah?*" her raspy voice grated.

"Lieutenant Vicky Hartman?" I asked.

"Yeah?" she repeated.

"It's....Lieutenant Candace Flint. You and I are supposed to...."

"Where've you *been*, kid?" she said, suddenly brimming over with kindness. "Come up."

I did.

I went up to her third floor apartment and knocked. She answered.

She looked like she did back in the past. No surprise since we 'toons don't age a lick from what we looked like on creation day, as it were. She still had her flaming red hair, her green T shirt, and her black pants. Suddenly, my skirted and sweatered body looked naked in comparison. And then there were her *eyes*...

We all look differently, based on who created us, but you'd be hard to find two more different versions of what a teenage girl looks like than Vicky and myself. I myself have a respectable, slightly longish bob of more carrot-colored hair, and my eyes are like dark black pin points. Also, I have a fairly muscular and athletic body, a consequence of my years trying to keep up with my younger brothers and their crazy antics, but that's neither here nor there. Vicky, on the other hand, is all toothpick arms and legs, has her auburn locks nearly always tousled and disheveled, and has enormous pink dots where her pupils should be. 'Nuff said.

She seemed to sense the fact that I was nervous about crossing her threshold, based on what she said to me after greeting me.

"Don't get any *ideas* about me," she said. "I'm not gonna *bite* you. *And* I'm not one of *those-* in case you're *wondering.* I like *men.* Same as you, no doubt. *Right?*"

I nodded.

"Point is, ya got nothing to fear from me. Unless you *cross* me. You thinking of doing *that,* by any chance?"

I shook my head from side to side, right to left.

"Then come *in,* already!"

I did.

She beckoned me to sit down on the chair in her living room, which I did, while she took the couch opposite it.

"Candy girl," she said gravely, "we got a big deal job on our hands. We can't fuck this up."

"I know what you mean, Vic," I said. "But I don't know *how* we're going to handle it. The Colonel only assigned it to me an *hour* ago."

"She only gave it to *me two* hours ago! But do you see *me* fretting about it?"

"Uh....no?"

"Wrong! I *have* been!"

She showed me her nails, which she had chewed down to nubs, for proof.

"We are so *screwed*!" she moaned. "*All* of us!"

"Hang on!" I said, pointing her back to sitting down on the couch. "Let's not start *panicking* here! That's what always did me in on my show!"

"Easy for *you* to say!" Vicky countered. "The only thing your brothers *hurt* on you was your damn *feelings*! *You* never got your molecules rearranged by a couple of goddamn FAIRIES!"

"Maybe so," I responded, "but I did what I did because I *cared* about them- *not* because I wanted to make some damn *money* off of them!"

"You....stupid....BRAT!" she said, vaulting up from the couch and preparing to lunge at me. "You take those fucking lies *back* unless you wanna eat my FISTS!"

"They're *not* lies!" I said. "You know as well as I do that you *really* didn't have that boy's interests at *heart*!"

"And *I'm not* lying," she countered, "when *I* say that *you'd* do the same thing if you were in *my* shoes! Just like you'd sell those boys *out* in a *minute* like you do on your show. *Especially* if that fellow you have the hots for *told you to*!"

"You leave Jeremy *out of this*!" I blazed, standing up.

"Nobody can love 'em like *Vicky* can!" she taunted me. "I've had my *share*, kid, not like *you*. *You're* still a *virgin,* by the looks of it, so how would *you* know how to...?"

Furious, I let out a rebel yell and threw a fist at her face. She proceeded to duck it and wrap her long arms around my torso. She pressed those long suckers down past my breastbone and started into cracking my ribs. Really hurt me- I mean *really* hurt me. Tears out of your eyes and all that. Thinking quick, I bent my back down and threw her off me with a jerking thrust.

What followed was a brief movie catfight without the camera present. You know- punching, wrestling, biting, yelling, etc. Stuff that we usually do to each other when nobody's watching, although in the movies they always seem to have *guys* watching and leering at us while we do it. But rest assured, Vic and I have both been around the block longer than you might think, and we know between us every single way girls can fight each other. We did everything to each other, and I mean *everything*. Everything except that sissy, mincing, slap the hand routine they always have girls and gay guys doing when they fight. Who the hell really *does* that, anyway? Anyway, it went on like that for a little while. She can really *give* it, but so can I when I'm cornered, so it was a tough fight. But she took it too far when she ripped out a chunk of my hair. *Nobody* does *anything* to *my* hair except *me, understand*? After she dropped me to the ground following that, I got right up, roaring and teeth bared. I put a death grip on her bra, and then I hauled off and put my shoe right in her V spot. She went flying back onto the couch she'd risen from with a loud THUD. I was about to pounce on her to finish her off when she shouted:

"*No mas*! Cut it out, already! I *give*! You *win*! Don't *taze* me, sis!"

I stood down, but I still demanded to know why she *fought* me when we supposed to be working *together.*

"I was *testing* you," she said, spitting out a tooth one of my punches had detached and flicking it away from me.

"*Testing* me?" I repeated. "*Why?*"

"Well, your show is from Disney, and at Nickelodeon, where I'm from, Disney folks kinda have a reputation for being candy assed *wimps.* No offense, but that whole company is full of 'toons who asses you could easily kick from here to Glendale- although *you're* not one of them. I'm glad that I get to fight with you instead of against you, Candy. You'd be hellfire unleashed in a wrestling ring. And I should know- I've had to *do* it. Oil, mud, Jell-O, whatever. Not dignified much, but at least it pays the bills, which the main reason why I do it in the first place. "

"No offense taken, Vic. And thanks. Guess I'm tougher than I thought, huh?"

" Yeah. With that whole fight thing, I just needed to see if you could- ya know- *bring* it!"

"And have I *convinced* you I *can*? I mean, *really*? You wouldn't *kid* me about that stuff, would you?"

"Plenty! I don't fuck around when I tell people who and what they are, Candy. I know *tough,* girlfriend, and *you* are definitely *it.* Not just 'cause you actually hit me in the sensitive areas! 'Cause you did it in a *skirt-* like you do *most* of your stuff! Do you *realize* how much trouble a girl can get into just *wearing* a skirt that *short* around the wrong kind of guy? Yeesh! I know girls who got *raped* wearing longer skirts than that- but they weren't much of a match for the guys what grabbed them. You and I, though- we'd have that would-be rapist down on the ground clutching his balls in pain before we'd let him get *near* us."

"I wouldn't about rapists or anything like that," I said. "I guess 'cause Disney's such a clean place, they don't really think about the risks the girls might take wearing skirts. But I'm not like you, Vic. I can't make pants *work* for me, for some reason. Usually I only wear 'em when I'm riding my bicycle- for the obvious reasons. You know, the wind and stuff, *right*? And besides, *Jenny* gets away with it, too, and she was doing even before I came along, so..."

"*She's* a *robot*! When you're a robot *and* a girl, you're damn well *invincible*! I'm *jealous* of her- and *you,* to put it plainly!"

"*Me*?" I said, with disbelief, as I sat down on the couch beside her. "What the hell have you got to be jealous of *me* for? There's *nothing* I have, physically, that *you don't*! Now, maybe we don't fill out our bra cups the same way, and we style our hair differently, and our eyes are kinda different, but otherwise, why would you assume that I would be *better* than you?"

"Because *you, my dear,* were a full-fledged *character* on your show, and *I* was *not* on *mine*!"

"*That* is *ridiculous*! You're as much a cartoon character as *I* am! You *know* that! Every cartoon character who exists is always his or her own person, regardless of what those racist assholes in Washington think!"

"I don't mean like *that,* kid! I mean in the sense of what your creators *gave* you!"

"What they *gave* me?"

"Sure. You got a *life*. Parents, brothers, friends, relatives even. A boyfriend hotter than all of Louis Armstrong's trumpet solos with the Hot Five *put together*. Even gave you a *purpose* in life in trying to put the kibosh on your brothers' plans. Me? I got *nothing*! I was a fucking HEAVY! Hartman only called me on the *set* when he needed to put the fear of God into Tam- *on* screen, that is. We got along a lot better off the clock, kinda like you and your boys, but you never *saw* none of that. The ones I *hate* from that time are those goddamn fucking FAIRIES! Them and their fucking prima donna demands for the best dialogue and the most airtime pretty much screwed me in terms of becoming a more multi-dimensional character on the show- a la *you*. And the bastards even keep it up *now* *in* the CRA. Do you realize they're both MAJORS? Jeez! Almost as hard to believe as Tam being a CAPTAIN! He's telling *me* what to *do* now!"

"Tell me about it," I said. "My brothers only just made Lieutenant...."

"Like you, huh?"

"No. Lieutenant COLONEL!"

"What *is* it with these kids?"

"I don't know. But what I *do* know is that *none* of this is gonna *matter* once that little *bitch* Riley Daring exposes everything and everybody in the CRA. Unless *we* stop her!"

"Yeah. And get *Jess* out of there. She's got a better brain that most of us, but it's gonna *crack* if we don't get her out of there. She's not cut out to be a living machine. *None* of us is!"

"You're right about *that*. But we're in tough going against Raven. She's probably found out about us and is reinforcing her weapons *right now*."

"*What* weapons?" Vicky scoffed. "Her and her little *Kodak Brownies* loaded with *Kodachrome*? She's plenty *uppity,* but that's nothing a good punch in the *face* won't cure!"

"Be careful with that," I warned her. "The Colonel told us to prioritize bringing her out *alive*..."

"Who ya think I *am*?" Vicky shot back. "Charles fucking *Bronson?* I intimidate with the best of 'em, Candace, but *I don't KILL!* Minute I see ink, I back off. It's *disgusting.*"

"Just making sure we're on the same page, Vic," I said. "Ink makes me *vomit.*"

"You too, huh?" she said.

I nodded, and after shouldering two of Vicky's extensive collection of derringers- just in case- we were off.

*

Vicky had her car parked in the garage down the street from her apartment, and we planned to get into it and drive to the location of Raven's "film studio", which the Colonel had given to me at our meeting. It was a simple in and out scheme we had planned. We would go in, find Jess, get her out, flip Raven the bird, destroy her film, and leave. But nothing about our lives is simple, and, sure enough, a wrench ended up in the works as soon as we got outside.

Almost as soon as our shoes hit the pavement, we were surrounded by a brace of reporters shouting irrelevant but loud questions at us, and photographers popping flashes in our eyes that threatened to destroy our vision. This was surely Riley's doing. The CRA isn't exactly a legit organization in the eyes of the mainstream media (not that *she* would be thought of any more highly than *us*), and so, whenever we emerge out of the underground, the media storm troopers jump out and ambush without a moment's hesitation. As far as we're concerned, AP means Assholes with Protection from the Constitution, and you do *not* what to know what UPI means. I felt like a deer in the headlights, with all of those goddamn multiple wattage cameras going off in my eyes at once. Vicky sure didn't, though; the press always makes her fighting mad 'cause they never take us 'toons *seriously*, and this time was no exception. Walking past me, she growled wordlessly at the corps with such force that, as one, they backed away from her.

"The *next one* of you that asks us ANY candy floss FAKE questions," she snarled, "is gonna get my *fist* UP THEIR ASS! You think I'm *joking*? HUH? I'll take on *any* of you band of backstabbing BASTARDS who tries to come near me- and WIN! You wanna see a 'toon actually SPILL some of that fucking BLOOD you always accuse us of drawing when one of you PRICKS annoys us? Just come over here and TRY me if you don't *believe* me, you lousy, triple-crossing bunch of PIGFUCKERS!"

One of the reporters, not getting the message, arrogantly said that they had a *right* (A RIGHT! Can you *believe* it?) to use any means necessary to get information out of us. She then compounded her arrogance by making the baseless accusation that Vicky and I were LOVERS! Naturally, we both didn't go for that, but Vicky took it worse. As she was already on the warpath, as it were, she just stayed on it.

"*WHAT DID YOU SAY?*" she shouted.

The snotty reporter repeated herself, making herself seem even more annoying and arrogant than she actually was. That only made Vic even more likely to try to cut her throat. That likely wasn't her intention, given that she visibly moved back when my associate launched her next salvo.

"YOU SAY YOUR GODDAMN PRAYERS *RIGHT NOW,* YOU LEMON-SUCKING *MOTHERFUCKER!*"

At which point, Vicky advanced towards the group, grabbed the microphone from the reporter's hand, uttered a swear word or two into it loudly, and dashed it onto the pavement. Then she grabbed the reporter's hair, which was a wig, and threw it onto the ground, stomping on it. Getting the message, the reporter and everyone else fled down the street- in what had to be record time in my eyes.

Noticing that I was still watching, timidly, from the rear, Vicky then turned around and looked at me.

"Come *on, Flint*!" she said. "We gotta *go*! That Reckless bitch ain't gonna prevent *herself* from dropping that goddamn video, y'know!"

"Would you do that to me if I said something like that?" I asked. "Not that I would actually *dare* to, of course, knowing you now. But..."

"I *said* I wouldn't *hur*t ya *already*!" she said. "When I say something, I MEAN it! Now COME ON!"

I did.

*

We got into Vicky's car- she drove, I rode shotgun- and we were off.

It was tough going for a while. We cased the city pretty good, seeing as I had trouble deciphering the Colonel's flyspeck handwriting. But, finally, Vicky figured it out better than I did, seeing as she has better eyesight than me, and we had *that* little problem solved.

The "film studio" was located in the north end of town, in the scummy old industrial section. Plenty abandoned factories and such, which made it a perfect place for a sleaze ball like our quarry to hang. Sure enough, I spotted the sign on one building that was on my side of the car and whistled for Vic to stop it.

"You *found* it?" she asked. "How? All these damn buildings look the *same* to me!"

"The sign," I said, pointing.

Sure enough, written in giant black letters on a sheet of paper flimsily taped onto one of the endless series of metal fences surrounding the old shops, were the words "RECKLESS STUDIOS". The idea in ol' Raven's mind was, perhaps, to lend a bit of class to what was, by all appearances, a highly second rate shop. No- make that *twentieth* rate.

"She calls this a *studio*?" Vicky scoffed. "That little *shack* wouldn't fit up Paramount's *ass*!"

"Or Disney's," I seconded. "But sometimes, you don't *need* a studio to make movies."

"*Really*?" Vicky said. "I never thought...."

"Sure. Most filmmakers today don't use studios- 'cause they're *sterile* and *lame*. Would *you* pay $20 to see a bunch of crap you could see for free on television? No way! That's why they shoot most of the stuff on location now- to make it look more "realistic"- whatever *that* means. They just let the TV people use them 'cause they need to use the space and keep making money off of it."

"Name one."

"Huh?"

"Name me *one* filmmaker who managed to make movies without a studio."

"John Cassavetes," I said.

"Hold on! He was in..."

"He *acted* in big budget movies, but *that* was so he would have the cash for his *own* projects. *Faces,* and *Shadows,* and those other films he and his gang improvised on the streets of New York. *None* of those films were underwritten by a major studio. They wouldn't *touch* weirdo indie stuff in those days. But they still got *played.*"

"Speaking of weirdo indie filmmakers," Vicky reminded me, "we got a *job* to do."

She shouldered her derringer as a reminder to me, and I did the same. Seemed like an open and shut case- stop Reckless, get rid of the film, get Jazz out, possibly torch and blow up the damn place- although the Colonel wouldn't necessarily like that last part.

But, just as we got past the door and into the building, we heard a violent rumbling.

"AW, SHIT!" Vicky ejaculated. "We must have triggered her *security* system!"

"Ah, what's she got that can *hurt* us?" I said, mockingly. "A *dragon* guarding her *treasure?*"

"I'm *serious* here, Flint! Didn't the Colonel tell you how Daring had her old "friends" in corporate land load her up with all sorts of *obstacles* to prevent people like us from *getting* to her? Man! Total action movie stuff going on! We'd have *better* luck trying to get into Jack Benny's vault."

"Who the hell is....?"

Vicky looked at me with stunned disbelief. It did not seem possible to her that I could *not* have heard of this man, even though he was *way* before my time, I later found out. Then again, so was Cassavetes, and I knew who *he* was, but everyone's entitled to a blind spot culturally, and this happened to be mine.

"*JACK BENNY!*" said Vicky, pronouncing the man's name as if he were a Greek god of old. "The *grand master* of old time radio and TV comedy! The king of the pregnant pause! You mean you never..."

"No. Never heard of the guy. Sorry, Vic, but if he's really *that* important, you'd think people would talk about him more. But anyway, if you think I should check him out, I can look for some of his stuff on YouSuck later on, when we're done, if you think it's worth it...."

"You *should*. If you know *John,* but you don't know *Jack*..."

It was at this point that the obstacles Vicky mentioned commenced in earnest. At least, at first, they seemed like obstacles to us. That's where being a superhuman creature comes in handy for us 'toons. We fight each other, we can get out of it with a few minor cuts and scrapes and bruises and so forth. But if we fight you and your crowd, we can really hurt you- bad. Then again, you can literally *burn* us....

Point is, Vic and I were in a tough spot there. But both of us have been through worse- much worse. She's not a cream puff type girl, and neither am I, even though I might give that impression to people sometimes. That fight we had together reinforced that image of each other to the two of us in spades, and we were gonna confirm that image of each other to each other now.

Again, I'm gonna swan over how we got out of that, 'cause I didn't come here and you didn't call me to talk about some ham fisted pseudo-heroics on me and Vicky's part. But, rest assured, it was a *battle.* Lions, tigers, bears, armored soldiers, the whole deal. (The *animated* type, dig? 'Cause even someone like *Ms. Raven* can't afford the real thing, judging by the shoestring operations she happened to be running at that time.) It involved Vicky and me screaming, running, jumping, vaulting, blasting our guns and *dealing* with those *suckers*! Total and complete stereotypical action movie stuff, like Vicky said. I *might* have let a couple of the soldiers look up my ass with all the movement I did, but I made up for it by pounding the bejesus out of a guy who was trying to impale Vicky with a cartoon bayonet. ('Cause that's how we die. Cartoon weapons, fire, and the odd silver melt- but that's *it*.) I didn't earn a scouting badge for wrestling alligators for *nothing,* after all.

Yeah, you heard me....oh, right. Forgot you *knew* that already. Sorry. You're like the Encyclopedia Britannica when it comes to us 'toons, aren't ya? Ah, don't be bashful- I know that as much as you do, fella. I follow you on Facemask and Twaddle, so I know the kind of research you've been getting into regarding us. I knew you'd come crawling to Candy sooner or later. You know about *all* of us and what we've *done* in our lives, *don't* ya, you sly *dog*...

What? Oh, yeah. What am I doing *this* stuff? Must be my time of the month or something. Sorry. I can't figure out why I've been acting this way. Don't take any of that stuff I told you personal, all right. I already *have* a boyfriend... yeah. Jeremy. Aah, yeahhhh....One of these days, I am gonna get him and me alone in a back alley, no distractions, and....

Yeah, yeah, yeah. The story. Keep your shirt on!

Anyhow, Vicky and I soon took care of the obstacles in our path, and, after a brief hyperventilating session when we saw the spilled ink on the ground and our clothes, we got a hold of ourselves and went upstairs. Just up to the second floor, but that counts as "upstairs", doesn't it?

Sure enough, two of the old offices on the second floor had been converted into *new* offices. But not by much. Paper covered the nameplates on the doors, with titles listed on them as per the gate out front. One of them said "editor", in all lower case letters. The other was more flamboyant. It read "R.E. RECKLESS- CHAIR, PRESIDENT AND DIRECTOR-GENERAL". That was our quarry, for sure. And the "editor" stall was clearly where our old pal, Jasmine "Jazz" Fenton, was.

At least, what was left of her after Reckless had had her way with her, I assumed. Vicky, on the other hand, was more concerned with the extreme level of gall Ms. R.E. Reckless was shoving in our faces with that way pretentious nameplate.

"*R.E. RECKLESS?*" Vicky nearly exploded and blew our cover, but I shushed her, just as we hid in a nearby closet to avoid the boss lady from possibly overhearing us.

"Softer!" I ordered, speaking softly myself.

"Sorry. But "R.E. Reckless"? Who the *fuck* does she think she *is?*"

"Obviously some old school Hollywood big shot. Like B.P. Schulberg."

"*Who?*"

"He was a producer back in the day. At Paramount. His son Budd wrote a whole novel about the whole scene back then- *What Makes Sammy Run?*"

"Doesn't ring a bell. Neither of 'em."

"Well, it shouldn't. Way before our time. Doesn't matter now."

"What's that "E" in her name stand for, anyway?"

""From what I know, it's *Eugene.*"

"Guh? Wah?" Vicky was nonplussed. "That's....that's a *guy's* name! Probably explains why she's got such big *cojones* for a little slip of a girl, though. She sure was pretty fucking *ballsy* on her show, but if you have the power to *replace* somebody if you hate their ass, then *you'd* be just as ballsy, I think."

"I *am* ballsy, Vic- and so are you. But we're the *good* kind of ballsy. Not the bad kind that ruins lives and friendships and such by being so goddamn unwilling to listen to other people's opinions without getting mad. Unlike *some people* I won't mention. We're the good kind of ballsy. We don't let anyone fight our battles for us- we do all the dirty work ourselves, all the time, whenever and whatever might be needed for us to do, no matter if the all the goddamn odds in the *world* are against us! We can crash through doors and tear down windows if we want to because we know, in our hearts and minds, that what we're doing is *right. She,* on the other hand, is doing it strictly because she gets her jollies off doing it now. She thinks that, because she can make some phone calls to set things right, everyone should bow and scrape in front of her. That's cost her plenty. That's not a pretty way of living your life. I used to be like that, too, but I ultimately figured out that I can't let setbacks and opposition deter me.

"Besides, in the studio hierarchy, Reckless wasn't exactly someone who was created through a clean track record, if you get my drift. She was created by some *stone*r who writes children's books, not by people working direct for a studio- like you and me. That explains a *lot.* You know how characters created outside the system get all these crazy ideas about how they're on a higher station than us "normal" 'toons and want to rise above it all and forget all about it? That is exactly what we're up against. I know for sure on that score. When I tried to befriend her when I first came to Disney, she called me a clown 'cause I had on what I have on now. A fucking CLOWN! I so wanted to wring her goddamn *neck* for that one! Nobody was happier than me when her fucking show got iced and she got thrown out into the street- like we all are, eventually. But I only found out just how mean and devious she was when she threatened to put this YouSuck stunt and put us all out of business. Just everyone else, I suppose."

"I hope *your* middle name is more normal."

"It is. It's Gertrude. Not the best possible one, but there you go."

"Whew! Glad I don't have one of those. Just plain Vicky for me."

"But surely it's short for...."

"*Yeah,* but don't go *blabbing* it. *Victoria* is about the *sissiest* name ever *invented.* I can't even remember if I was ever kindergarten aged, Candy- not like *you,* 'cause you got those cute little flashbacks on your gig- but me being the temperamental type, I probably would have thought and done some mean and nasty things to anyone who even *dared* call me *Victoria*- even a teacher. Maybe that old Queen of England could handle being called that, but I have absolutely *no intention* of making the outside world think that ol' Vicky Hartman is in anyway a goddamn *sissy.* No way any fucking TWERP takes advantage of *this* sista 'cause she goes by a sissy handle. Most girls who go by their full sissy *girl* names can't fight or scam their way out of a paper bag. You *excepted,* of course."

"Thanks. Not that being named *Candace* is any better than being *Victoria,* but I've gotten used to it. I've really felt it gives me some dignity that balances out my wild mood swings and my obsessive nature and my weirdly misshapen body, y'know? Like it's some sort of saving grace or something. But not too many of my pals even *dares* call me "Candy". Weird, considering how long I've known most of them. I guess they're worried about me taking it the wrong way and getting all mean mad on them. If you want to call me that, go ahead. I mean, you haven't said a word about me calling you "Vic" all this time....."

"That's 'cause I *like* it. Makes me sound real *tough*- not like a sissy girl at all. I'm surprised nobody else thought about that before...."

We were then interrupted by a door opening abruptly and then closing loudly. If it still had any glass in it, all of it would have broken.

"PENTON*!!!*"

A girl's voice boomed out, the way old man Spacely used to ream out George Jetson. That was Riley. No question. Her voice, her attitude, her everything- didn't even need to see her to know it.

What's more, that bellowed last name now confirmed to us we were *definitely* in the right place.

"Lousy *tyrant*!" Vicky muttered. "Who the goddamn fucking HELL does she think she is? That whole goddamn storm into the room and shout at people thing is MY SHIT- it's been that for *years*! That little cock-sucking TWAT...."

She might have gone out then and there, but I wanted to hear Riley in action first, to confirm to us whether or not she was really as bad as was reputed. *Then,* I assured Vicky, we would kick ass.

Presumably, since we didn't see it, Riley then flung open the door of the editor's office, where she proceeded to start talking to Jess. The latter had evidently been napping after working hard, 'cause she sounded hurt.

"What the *hell* is *wrong* with you, *Raven*?" snapped Jazz. "I am *trying* to do the goddamn job you practically SHANGHAIED me to do, but you won't give me a moment's peace to do...."

"*MS. RECKLESS* to *you*!" blazed the Director General of Daring Studios, who, as usual, was not in the mood for any opposition or interruption. "You are *not* in a position to raise your voice to me- after you *failed* to deliver the *cut* I demanded! Are you interested at *all* in living to see your next birthday- because you will *not* if you do not do what I *tell you to* DO!"

"Oh, *pardon me*!" snapped Ms. Penton. "What do you *expect* from someone who's been working *24-7* trying to assemble a rough cut from the *thousands of hours of film* you gave me to work with? Not to *mention* the fact that I haven't had anything to *eat* or *drink* for...."

"I *gave* you *Tic-Tacs, didn't* I? That's a *food product* right there, is it *not*? They were bloody MINT FLAVORED, for God's sake! So don't you *dare* accuse Raven Reckless of not caring for the best interests of her employees... "

"Best interests my overworked, underappreciated ASSHOLE! Don't you know any damn thing about *nutrition,* Raven? You can't just lock somebody in a room and expect them to produce work of any caliber on a small package of TIC-TACS! That's *not* a *decent, balanced meal!* Besides which, you are essentially employing me under conditions that every legitimate union in the United States would consider to be utterly APPALLING! Why the hell are you being such a *slave driver* about this, anyway? This is a goddamn *YouSuck* video you're making, not some lavishly over-produced *costume epic* that might win you an *Oscar*! 'Cause I'm *sure* that's what you *think* you should be doing with your life, and you just decided to go it alone when none of the fucking studios would HIRE you..."

"*You* shut your *fat little mouth,* you *beanpole,* or I'll *kill* you! I MEAN IT! Raven Reckless does *not* let any dumb *pussyfoot* intellectual tell her how to run her business...."

"I'd *appreciate* being fired, actually! I have some stuff I need to catch up on in Amity, and you can easily hire somebody who'd be more *compliant* to do this job for you. Although, given the kind of boss you've been to me, I doubt that anyone else would actually WANT to work with you! "

"I said *kill,* not fire. Although, regarding us, they're practically one and the same, *aren't* they? You would know that for sure after all of your labors at the Moviola, wouldn't you, *Jessamyn*?"

"You wouldn't *dare.* That's MURDER! You can't just *kill* somebody who disagrees with you...."

"SHUT *UP*!"

A loud slap on the face echoed down the hall, as did Jess crying in desperation. Riley must've really smacked her one to make her cry like that. I know Jess- she definitely doesn't break that easy. Something about that red hair...

"I hired you for a *reason,* Penton..." Riley resumed, as if nothing had happened. (The BITCH!)

"*Hired*?" said an outraged Jess. "You're not even PAYING me..."

"*ENOUGH OUT OF YOU! I* am the *mistress* here, and YOU are the SERVANT! *Editors* do what *directors TELL* them to do! *Understand?* I don't give a FUCK about your empty complaints about me treating you bad, and I especially don't want to hear any more lousy talk from you about a fucking UNION! That was what *broke* the 'toon business as our ancestors *thrived* in, and I'll be damned if it will sink this ship that I have worked so long and hard to get on the water. YOU PICK UP ON *THAT* MESS, *SISTER*? Now, get back to work and deliver me a goddamned decent PRINT, or your head is gonna ROLL!"

"Yes, Ms. Reckless," Jazz said meekly, defeated.

Raven then tromped back to her office.

Finally, we burst out of the closet and sprang down the hallway, derringers ready. We were gonna *deal* with that little rat, even if we had to kill her to do it. That was a last resort thing, of course, but you can't take too many chances when you have to deal with a rogue 'toon. Raven Reckless fit *that* particular definition to a T, despite those oh so refined protestations of hers that she was "looking after" her "valuable". Yeah, right! If we were all so "valuable" to the humans who "employed" us, by her definition, we'd all still have our goddamned JOBS, *wouldn't we*?

Anyhow...

The door was locked, but when you're dealing with us 'toons, wood might as well be cheese. Vic promptly kicked the door down, and we entered like Gibson and Glover, foaming at the mouth.

"Reach for the *sky, bitch*!" Vicky shouted. "Candy and I are loaded for bear, and we both know how to use these damn things *pretty well*! The kicker is, even if you manage to get our guns away from us, we are still both very clearly capable of *kicking your pretty little ASS* all the way to TIMBUKTU!"

Initially, Vicky was addressing the back of a businessman's swivel chair, but then it turned around. There was R.E. herself, wearing what she used to wear on her show. Yellow shirt, rainbow belt, jeans, green sandals and all. Worse still was the Mona Lisa grin she had on her face- *and* the slow clap she gave us when she spun around. She regarded us regally, like she was *better* than us for some reason- but she would've thought about us the same way in completely different and unrelated circumstances. Total fucking bitch, like I said before.

"Bra....*vo!*" she said, sarcastically. "But I'm *not* making any clichéd good cop/bad cop movies here. So you two might as well take your little audition presentation somewhere else, before I have to have you both escorted off of *my* premises- *by force!*"

"We ain't the kind of cops ya *think* we are, *Princess!*" said Vicky. "She's *bitch* cop, and I'm *sadist* cop, and we're taking you IN!"

"No...you...are....NOT!"

And, just like that, she had slipped past me and Vic, through our legs. Damn it! We hadn't figured on her being so *short*, but what're ya gonna do? She looked plenty *taller* on television, but so do we all, it seems. Anyway, damned if Vic and I were going to let her get away with what she was planning, so we took off after her as soon as she sprinted out.

Riley ran like a gazelle, and we followed like two lionesses eager to take a bite out of her ass. She was pretty well put together, strong and muscular, and she'd probably fight back like a sewer rat if we trapped her. But we managed to play the two to one card to our advantage. After a couple of rounds 'round the hall, during which she bounced into and out of our hands like the silver ball in a pinball game, Vic got a grip on her belt and held her in place as best as she could. Riley tried her best to break Vic's grip, but she was fighting a losing battle. This, then, was my time to shine, and I didn't lose that opportunity. I clocked her good and hard in her pretty little face and her pretty little exposed toes, just like I did to Vic earlier.

It worked like a charm.

Once the pain of my kick set into Riley's body, Vicky spun her by her belt into the wall, where she spread eagled and fell down. She howled and cried in pain on the ground, but we weren't having any of it.

"Just....SHUT UP, you WHORE!" I snapped. "You don't deserve *anybody's* sympathy! What you deserve is to be thrown out to the *wolves-* just like ya were planning to do to all of US, *WEREN'T YA?*"

"Whore?" she shouted, angrily. "*WHORE?* You *dare* to call *me* a *WHORE? ME?* I'm thirteen goddamn years old, you HAGS. I haven't even had SEX yet!"

"And you ain't ever GONNA, by the time *we're* done with ya!" added Vicky. "We're foreclosing on ya, *Coppola,* and there's *nothing* you can do about it. *Understand?*"

"I'm *not* letting you *ruin* me!" she said. "Especially not *you*, you swan necked LUNATIC!" (That was aimed at me.) "You and your *brood* were responsible for me losing my *show!* You waltzed in there at Disney and showed me up, you lousy fucking CLOWN!"

"FUCK *YOU!*" I blazed. That "clown" thing again, and it still hurt. It always does. "*You're* the only goddamned CLOWN here, you rainbow hugging HARLOT!"

I was about to sock her in the mouth when Vicky grabbed Raven by her shirt and held her up with her left hand. Clearly, she had in mind exactly the same thing I did, and she'd probably hit her even harder if push came to shove, now that we'd gotten close. Vic likes to keep her friends close, on account of she has way too many enemies, and usually she only does this kind of thing for a friend. I must've made the grade with her to do that.

"THAT'S *ENOUGH!*" Vicky shouted in Riley's face, in her best banshee wail, no nonsense babysitter voice. "You *behave* yourself, or I'm gonna shove your carrot haired head down the fucking

TOILET- where you BELONG! You *hear* me, Freckle Face? I will crumple your skinny little body, pull out your spinal cord, and use it to PICK MY TEETH if you don't SHUT THE HELL UP and give me and her what we CAME HERE FOR!"

Vicky then tossed Raven roughly on the ground, towering over her the way the Giant probably did when he caught Jack trying to make off with his gold in that fairy tale. Raven looked genuinely scared for like a micro-second after Vicky tossed her down, but that didn't last. Vicky kept doing what she does best, though- acting tough.

"Now, where's your film lab?" Vicky demanded. "On your *computer*? Or is it somewhere you think we ain't gonna find it? 'Cause we WILL!"

"*Yeah*, it's on the computer, *genius*!" Raven said sarcastically. "Only you can't do anything about..."

"We CAN!" I said in my best big sister voice, all my repressed rage coming again to the surface. "And we WILL, *damn you!*"

Raven swore at me-again- and lunged at my throat. If she'd managed to get me, I would have had one hell of a fight on my hands, one that would have made my earlier dust-up with Vicky seem like child's play. Fortunately, Vicky caught her mid-flight, punched her unconscious and threw her over her back. Then she turned to me.

"Even if we don't see each other again," she said, "you'll still be my pal. For *life*."

"Thanks," I said. "You, too."

Then she was gone.

*

I went into the editing suite and found Jess crying, face down, in front of the editing equipment. Evidently, she hadn't moved since Raven reamed her, 'cause she thought I was her at first when I came in.

"Get *away* from me, you *tyrant*!" she snapped. "I'm not working for you any more until you *pay* me- and give me a goddamn *decent meal*! You *hea*r me, you lousy little TART....?"

"Jess, it's *me*!" I said. "Candace! Vicky and I just busted Raven, so you..."

When I identified myself, she finally sat up and saw me.

"CANDACE! Oh, my God. Thank you!"

She came up and gave me an enormous bear hug. And it hurt me a bit, 'cause even though she has the same kind of toothpick armed body Vic has (they were created by the same guy), she's still pretty strong besides being way smarter than me. Finally, I had to grunt loudly to get her to release me, which she did.

Jazz is like me, with conservatively styled red hair, but also like Vic, with massive, pupil-less eyes. She's a rocking scholar of everything around her, and dresses the type in slacks and sweaters. But I know you knew that 'cause you talked to her already.

"I am *so* glad you got here!" she said. "I was going to lose my *mind* if I had to keep working as Raven's editor. Women can't *do* this job."

"The *hell* they can't!" I said. "Some of the best cutters in the whole damn business were women. Margaret Booth headed up the editing at MGM for *decades*! And Scorsese's best flicks were cut by Thelma Schoonmaker...."

"Okay, okay! Obviously, *some* women can do it. But *they* weren't working for a perfectionist *poltroon* who has to have the last word on *everything*!"

"That could describe *any* director in Hollywood, Jess. That job is a total *power trip*. But the *producers* are the *real* pricks..."

"I know that, Candace. But have *you* ever been locked in a room for hours on end, maddeningly trying to do something you knew was *impossible*, and were still demanded to produce results when you had to?"

"Not locked in a room. But I know *exactly* what you mean, girl."

"The important thing is that you stopped Riley before she could put the damn video up on YouSuck. If she'd managed to get that inflammatory project out there, the CRA would have had a *lot* to answer for. Think of an animated version of *Triumph of the Will.* A total non-stop "toons are way better than people" thing that would completely negate any goodwill we'd generated among the human population- and completely prevent us from getting anything in the way of support from them in the future-forever! I *know*, 'cause I had to *look* at the damn thing- for hours and hours on end!"

"Not anymore, you don't. Has she got a complete master print?"

"On her computer."

"Then let's get *rid* of it."

"Are you *crazy*? Do you realize how many *cuts* of it she made me do? It would take *hours* to fully delete all of the..."

"*Cool it,* Jess! There's a *simpler* way! Come on!"

We went into Riley's office, and I made a beeline for the computer. Violently, I wrenched it from its place on the edge of her desk (it was only a chintzy little pink laptop, thank God) and threw it out the closed window, where it shattered into fragments.

"There!" I said.

"Why didn't *I* think of that?" Jazz mused.

"You were too stressed out to think straight, is why. Come on. You go back in your office and have a power nap. I'll trash the rest of the office, and then me and Vic will get you home safe."

"You sure?"

"*Ms.* Penton, I am *not* a liar!"

"Very well, *Ms.* Flint. Thank you."

We giggled, she went and slept, and I put paid to what had once been the office of the Director General of Reckless Studios. Then I called the Colonel and reported in, and then gave Vic a call, seeing as she'd given me her digits when she left just in case. She'd just bound and gagged Riley and left her by the side of the road, so she came back. So, once Jazz woke up, we took her out to eat, seeing as she was a mite famished, and then we did some girl stuff- like *shopping*- to take the edge off of what we'd just been through. And then we got Jazz home like I promised.

That's it. Candace is *out*. PEACE!

ACT THREE: HUMAN, ALL TOO HUMAN
2:00 PM EST, Jun.1, 2——
CAPT. A. LYAN:

I don't get very many opportunities to dress up nice, considering that this new line of "work" I'm in doesn't give me much chance for mingling with the press. Typically, you have to avoid them when you're on the other side of the law, owing to the fact that the majority of the pockets of the mainstream mass media. Of which we used to be part of, to my regret and shame, but that's really not part of the here and there regarding this particular story.

The point is, I was looking forward to trying to convince the world I was a *person,* rather than just "merely" a "drawing", which is how myself and a good percentage of my contemporaries and friends are still regarded. That, for that matter, is precisely the public image that the CRA was designed to combat, and, ultimately, destroy. Even here, with me sitting in front of you and speaking to you as if we were equals, I can't think that you feel somewhat superior to me; not you in particular, of course, but your race as a whole. Prejudices take a very long time to erase, no matter what the hippy kumbaya crowd among both of our groups think. If you saw me as I looked in the context of where I was - a twelve year old looking red headed kid in his best suit, playing with his tie to avoid boredom- you would think I had been abandoned there by my parents. At the very least, you also might erroneously assume that I had been told to hang around that part of the conference center where I was until they had finished whatever it is they came there to do. Important business, no doubt, you might be thinking. The trouble is, if you were making that particular assumption about me, you would be entirely incorrect.

In actuality, I had been asked to give a deposition in front of a Congressional committee that had been called to propose the extension of constitutional protection via the Bill Of Rights to, as they chose to phrase it:

beings, while not conceived via traditional manipulations of the flesh, were and are the self-styled "creations" of certain artists working alone or, more commonly, in collaboration, and who have, independently and collectively, come to realize that their civic and political rights have been unknowingly, unjustly and repeatedly denied them, and are, at this moment, attempting to negotiate with the United States for the establishment and/or restoration of said rights

In other words, the Cartoon Republican Army. And by "negotiate", they *really* meant that they are fighting a tooth and nail war of extermination with us. We all know that the government's *never* that honest in *public-* it's not good for their *mental health*.

I had been elected, through a somewhat awkward and confusing process of elimination I can't really explain here, to present the deposition. This was really a reflection of the words of the CRA high command more than anything eloquent I could have put together myself. Put simply, it was because a lot of the other members of the gang couldn't be bothered with it. More likely, they feared whatever the consequences of delivering the message would be. Which were, and are, plenty and serious, even by our generally edgy, death-defying lifestyles. Don't get me started on how many times and how many ways we 'toons have to face death on a daily basis. You'd totally be shocked, man. In *America,* yet! One big example of *that-* actually, make that *two-* came into play when I got myself down to testify in front of the committee. Let me explain.

What had happened between the period between the calling of the commission, and a CRA member being "requested"- that is, *ordered*- to appear in front of it, was this. A controversial Baptist church- more a sect, really- had said that they intended to destroy whatever "spawn of the devil" was sent by the "agents of sin" right off the witness chair, and to dissect whatever unlucky soul was chosen right on the floor of the hearing room. The fact that the hearings were being held in L.A.- the location of most of us 'toons *as well* as the aforementioned church- made it likely the church would definitely follow up on their threats.

There was, as a result, a lot of tension building up inside me at that moment as I waited to be called. I was fairly down on the list, so I didn't expect to be called immediately. Therefore, I was extremely shocked, to say the least, when I heard a familiar voice bellowing at me from behind.

Jerk. Of course.

I turned around and he was there.

He was dressed in a full Marine uniform. Shirt, pants, tie with a gold clip, decorations etc. He'd even gone to the trouble of giving himself a G.I. haircut- which is hard for a monkey like him to pull off. All in all, the combined effect made him look very much like a miniature version of Jack Nicholson in *A Few Good Men,* maintaining his dignity and composure on the witness stand while Tom Cruise yells his ass off at him. But Jerk being Jerk, he had to tweak it so it might get him some laughs, and that was exactly what he did when I came forward to greet him, so to speak.

"*You* can't HANDLE the *truth*!" he barked in his best Nicholson voice, like I'd *asked* him to do it. Which I *hadn't*. I hadn't even asked him to *come* here today. So why had he?

I promptly asked him this.

"*Because,*" he responded, as if I were the idiot he always thinks I am, "you need *protection*."

"From what?" I asked. "This is a Congressional hearing I'm going to. There's probably going to be security up the wazoo..."

"You know..." he said, implicitly.

"Jerk, they are *not* going to let those religious nut-bars in here. For God's sake. This is supposed to be a forum for legitimate discourse on the topic of..."

Just at that moment, one of the speakers before me, a normal human being, was being forcibly removed from the main hall by a security guard, profanity spewing from his lips.

"Legitimate discourse, *eh?*" leered Jerk, nudging me in the ribs in that irritating burlesque comic manner he has.

"Oh, come on!" I said. "Just 'cause *that* guy had a mouth on him..."

"Look, Adam. I'm only trying to look out for your best interests here..."

"*My* best interests? Since *when*?"

"Since the time you became my best friend, is when."

"I never *asked* you to...."

"Oh, I *know* you, Adam. You have a chance to make us proud here, and you are just gonna *blow it* like you *usually* do. Now, as your superior officer..."

"CAPTAINS *outrank* STAFF SERGEANTS, *Jerk*..."

"...it is my duty to make sure that you deliver your deposition calmly and properly in an environment free of prejudice."

"If you would just...."

"No, no, Adam. No need to thank me. Just doing my job."

"Your *job? Thank* you?"

"Yes, my boy," he said, condescendingly, pinching my cheeks. "You're going to need my help getting out of here..."

I threw his paws off my face, using a gesture clearly meant to intimidate him. It worked.

"I can handle *myself,* okay?" I said, seething. "I've been prepping this deposition for *weeks* now- *without* your help! *You've* never helped me out with *anything* since we *met-* you always make things *worse*! To tell you the *God's honest truth,* you *loudmouthed* CON MAN, I have had *quite enough* of you preening around like the simian *putz* you are! You always go around talking like you know *everything* when you really know NOTHING! I can't STAND it anymore, *understand*? So BACK OFF and let me do it the way it *should* be done, *for once*!"

He was silent for a moment, and then:

"*Somebody's* got *issues*!"

"You're fucking goddamn *right* I have *issues.* You think I want the guy who ripped me off *all through* middle school PROTECTING me?"

"I did *not...*"

"You *did,* you stupid MF...."

"*I'm* an *MF*? *You're* an *FM-* and an *AM,* besides!"

"That doesn't make any *sense*!"

"I can talk *without* sense and make it *work-* unlike *you*!"

"THAT DOES IT!" I screamed. "Get the hell *out* of here before I wring your scrawny little monkey NECK!"

"How DARE you!" he countered, appalled. "After all the time I...."

"I don't want to hear any more, Jerk," I said, temporarily restoring my temper. "Get out."

To further emphasize my desire to free myself of his company, I pointed to the nearest door so he'd get the message. However, he did not seem to get it, 'cause he still stood there like a moron.

"GO THE FUCK *AWAY!*" I screeched.

That got him gone, in a flash.

*

Yes, I was hard on him, in light of what happened afterwards. Jake and I have always had this level of conflict and tension in our relationship. Back from day one, when he self-appointed himself as my "best friend" back in the good old days at CDMS, and he hasn't let up ever since. Gradually, though, I've developed enough of a backbone to start pushing him back when he starts pushing my buttons. He comes on strong, I have to come on stronger to get him away. He yells at me, I yell louder back at him. He threatens to punch me in the face or give me a wedgie, then I have to threaten to murder him in his sleep. Not that I would actually *do* that to him, of course; my parents raised me better than that, at least when I had a chance to *see* them. He has *tempted* me on many occasions, though. However, when the ink is starting to run and the chips are down, we're still there for each other. Just like he was there for me later on that day, even after I drove him off. So don't be too hard on me, okay?

Anyway, I'm getting ahead of myself....

It was about this time that "Captain" Lyan was requested to make his appearance in front of the commission, so I entered the room.

The committee had insisted on a private room, with no media presence, so I wasn't intimidated in the least. In the back of the room were the members of the committee, seated behind a lengthy table with microphones in front of each of them. There was a smaller chair in front of the table, with a similarly sized microphone. The chair was placed right in front of the man whom, I soon learned, was the Chairman of the committee, an African American who could easily be mistaken for Denzel Washington.

I got to the front and sat down, pulling the microphone in front of me closer to my lips so that they'd be able to hear everything I said. Even though they were with the government, I owed them the courtesy of speaking clearly to them, so that I could fully explain the

CRA's message to them and so that they could understand what it was. For once.

"We appreciate you coming to speak with us today, Captain Lyan..." the Chairman began.

"Please," I interrupted. "Call me Adam. My rank isn't an official designation."

"So does that mean that you feel that...?" one of the committee members asked.

"No!" I said, angrily, knowing full well what he was implying. "We *don't* operate under the functions of a military organization, but our cause is still *vital and just*! We use the nomenclature exclusively to distinguish leaders from subordinates- and in *no other way*! It's not like we're unorganized or anything like that, we just feel that we need to conduct our affairs with some sort of sober order, that's all. Well, most of us, but most of the dissenters don't speak for the more orderly members of our group on account of the fact that they're not actually members of the CRA. Which is a fact that you always blatantly ignore when you try to categorize us as "one", and one, frankly, that we're all frankly *sick* of. You would all do better to remember that in the future when you deal with us."

"Little piece of *shit!*" the committee member snapped at me angrily. He was going to keep badgering me the same way, I thought, and it was probably going to get uncomfortable, like it usually does. However, Denzel cut him off by looking at him like he wanted to kill him, and he backed off.

"We're a multi-party committee," he said. "And he's a Republican."

'Nuff said. Republicans have always been harder on us than Democrats, for some reason. Maybe it's because they're a lot less in touch with reality.

"I *have informed* everyone already," the Chairman continued, "that we will be proceeding in a non-partisan fashion here." He looked sternly at the other two guys, and then got back to me.

"Now, *Adam*. I believe you have a deposition of some sort to present before us at this moment."

"Yes," I said, calmly. "I do have a..."

"Give us the *freak*!"

Oh, boy.

It was what I- and probably everybody else in the room, as well- had most feared. The Rev. Wildmon Falwell Reed-Jones, the minister of the Baptist church I had mentioned earlier, stormed out of what was likely a very well concealed hiding place, a Bible in one hand, a Glock in the other. Some of his followers, armed with the same things, followed him in a well-ordered mob. Clearly, they expected to lynch me, like their ancestors had done to countless "threatening" racial and ethnic minorities in the past. What they didn't know was who they were dealing with here.

"Sir!" said the committee chairman. "Your presence is neither warranted nor needed here at this gathering. We expressly forbid the presence of those who had not been officially called to testify..."

"Be *silent,* son of *Ham*!" said the Reverend, a pointed reference to the chairman's race. "I allow *none of your kind* to *dominate* me!"

The chairman calmly reached under the table and then stood up, revealing a shotgun in his hands, which he aimed directly at the Reverend.

"I ain't no "son of Ham"," he said. "I'm the son of a *bad mutha...*"

I ducked under the table, briefly forgetting that bullets can't harm me. Reed-Jones and his men aimed their guns at the chairman and the other commissioners, who were also armed like he. A hail of bullets flew rapidly. When it was over, the Reverend and several of his men lay dead on the ground, but the chairman and commissioners were still standing, untouched.

"It's over," the chairman said to me under the table at the end of the old school gangster confrontation. "Get up and we'll continue."

I did.

"We apologize for the interruption," the chairman said. "We, of course, had no idea..."

"I understand," I responded. "Most of the beings in the CRA have prices on their head now. We have to deal with this kind of thing all the time..."

"Including *now*."

Very unexpectedly, my hands and legs became confined in metal bands that, clearly operated by remote control, seemed to come out of nowhere. They prevented me from escaping- or moving.

It was almost like they had planned this all along.

That was when it hit me.

*

"*Wait a minute*!" I exclaimed. "You guys aren't from *Congress*!"

"*Damn* it all!" exclaimed one of the committee members. "Little fucker's found us *out*! What the hell are we gonna do *now*?"

"*You* just sit yo' ass *down* and do what I *tells* you!" said Denzel, dropping his pretend "refined" accent in favor of what was clearly his normal "ghetto" one. "Don't do nothin' dumb, or I'll *cut* you! You either, Red!"

That last one was clearly aimed at me, on account of my hair, so I couldn't really respond with a snappy comeback or else he'd clearly "cut" me, for real. Although with *what* I didn't know- yet. So I just decided to state the obvious.

"You *faked* this whole thing!" I spat. "You *knew* that if you made it look official enough, like Congress *really* wanted one of us to testify, that you'd be able to nab whoever came forward. Nothing carries more weight with us, as good American citizens, then being able to say something in front of a Congressional committee. You knew that. You played on our fears, our worries and our desires, and then you just used them AGAINST US! So you fooled us into sending somebody up here to talk to you-i.e. me- and you just decided to go through your usual protocol with me, on account of me being so supposedly "weak" and "defenseless" in your eyes. First, you send out your call to get some innocent 'toon down here and inside your clutches. *Then*, after you *killed* whatever *mark* arrived- with *matches,* no doubt- you'd *stuff* and *mount* them, and *then* post a photo of you with them online, preening like a bunch of goddamn African big game hunters! Yeah. I *know* your game! I've had friends of mine killed by your kind- and others just *miss* being. I have too many friends among the crowd of animal 'toons not to notice when a few of them go missing on me. The thing about this time, though, it's that it's different from the way you usually play it. *Too* different. You usually go for the exotic animal 'toons. I'm a HUMAN BEING!"

"Yeah," said Denzel. "We did them things. I ain't denying nothing you just said, Red, owin' that you're tellin' the truth about us. Don't know how the hell you found out about us, unless you went way beyond our YouSuck postings to find out the truth about us. Not too many people have, which is why we've been able to get away with so much with this racket. Yeah, we did all that stuff, like I said. Only nobody was taken us *seriously* on account of that nobody took them animal kills in the proper way. I thought that If we killed us a *human* 'toon, say a little clowny lookin' guy like you that nobody'd miss in a month of Sundays, it'd be *different*. People actually *notice* when you kill one of *you*. Either way, we is gonna *stop* your civil rights shit *cold* and get all of you fake ass paper and paint *niggers* off of our human streets and out of our human hair for goddamn *good!*"

"*What*?" I said. "That whole Jim Crow separate but equal thing? That's an absolutely asinine notion! Given your...social background....and...uh...life experience, I always thought that your...race....would *understand* what we..."

"*We* never went around *killing* people to do it, though," said the chairman. "Like them damn *killings* in *Watts...*"

"Look. That wasn't *us.* Those CGI *assholes* have *nothing to do* with the CRA. We're a cel and Flash organization *only...*"

"Don't matter none. All you *freaks* is gonna DIE before we finished. You is gonna be on your knees *begging for mercy...*"

He pulled out a book of matches, lit one, and seemed ready to throw it at me, when...

The match was shot out of his hand.

"What the hell...?" Denzel shouted.

He reached into the book for another match, and this time the entire *book* was shot of his hand.

"The *fuck is going on....?*" he exclaimed.

"You release Adam, or we *cut* your black *ass,* is what the fuck is going *on!*"

Then, there they were. Most of my old animal co-stars- my friends- each of them with a gun in hand, other weapons on their backs, and a full magazine of bullets encasing their chests like badges of honor. Even my usually placid buddy, Ingot. It's a bad sign on your part when a *giraffe* is on the warpath against you- normally, they won't hurt anybody unless you hurt them first, and she's been hurt more than any of us in this thing, believe me. At the front of the group, just as I had come to expect, still wearing his Marines uniform, was Jake. He'd fired both of the shots- and it was clear from the way he and the chairman looked at each other that they had a past history I knew nothing about. Oddly for me.

"Best *you* go back to *South Central, Roscoe Mack,* or should I say, "*Senator*" *Draxon Silas!*" said Jerk. "You got some of our lower phylum friends, but you ain't gonna get our one *human* one! Give it to 'em!"

And then, we had the same scenario as before, save for the fact that my friends, as cartoon characters, were invulnerable to human weapons, as am I. As much as the faux Congressmen fired their own weapons at them, my friends had more gumption and ammo on their side. It wasn't a surprise, then, when the humans soon collapsed on the floor, in bullet ridden forms, into pools of their own blood.

Once the slaughter ended, the gang, after much trial and error, managed to get me out of the chair without severing me from my hands and feet. Then I asked them, especially Jake, what the hell they were doing coming here like that? Especially after I'd chewed Jake so badly earlier? Did they not realize how *dangerous* it was- for me *and* them?

"Come on!" said Jerk. "I know you. We *all* know you. When you act up like that, that's not really you."

"You *think*?" I asked.

"Sure," said Jerk, and the others chimed in similarly. "You're not you when you're hungry."

"But I'm not...that doesn't...Aah, never mind! Thank you."

"Well, you *are* technically the boss of the unit, being the Captain," Jake said. "We'd totally fall apart if you weren't there to point the way for us."

"Well, I better point us the way out of here before the cops arrest us for *murder*!" I said, pointing to the bodies and then the exit.

"Yeah," said Jerk. "But, even if they *did* try to pin the killings on us, it wouldn't stick. Not like that mess on the floor, though. But not that w*e* have to worry about *cleaning it up*!"

Somehow, we all managed to find that joke funny. Even me.

ACT FOUR: SCOUTING FOR DUMMIES

4:00 PM EST, Jun.1, 2—-

CAPT. P. STILES:

It took me a while to get my bearings, as is usually the case when you are nearly beaten to death. Eventually, however, I regained consciousness and familiarized myself with what was going on.

The room I was in was made of transparent glass, so I could see myself in the reflection all across. I was trussed up tight on a raised horizontal pole in the center of the room, like the main course at a Hawaiian luau. All I needed was someone to stuff an apple in my mouth, and my very accurate impersonation of a roast suckling pig would be complete.

It could've been worse. They could have *burned* me. They could have tried to pull out my fingernails and toenails if they felt that would have gotten me to talk. Or, heaven forbid, the men could have taken turns *raping* me, if they were *that* unprincipled. Maybe even the *women,* too, if they played the other team, so to speak. We *are* talking about the CIA here. On my end of it, even by the standards of anthropomorphized tomboys, I *am* pretty *cute*, if I can blow my own horn here.

But they hadn't really done a lot of damage to me, even from my current supine position. My Chipmunk Scout uniform- beret, vest, skirt, shoes and all- was untouched, and, for all I know, the inner contents of them were probably the same- hopefully. So they hadn't really robbed me of my dignity and my life-yet. The only discoloration I sported was a shiner just perpendicular to my left eye, a souvenir of the fracas that landed me here in the first place. Nothing an applied steak couldn't fix, but that would have to wait.

I needed to get out of there-alive-first.

*

I was, of course, eager to volunteer for the CRA when they asked me. Especially after what happened to Pokey Pines. That was totally and brutally *unforgivable*. Our beautiful little home town, sight of so many of the most pleasant memories of my life, suddenly reduced to an unforgiving, impersonal pile of *ash* by order of Their Majesties Time and Warner. That totally made *all* of us who survived the unfortunate incident committed to the cause. No questions asked.

As for good ol' *Orthicon*, the only things I can think about *that* place are not *kind*.

Unlike a lot of the *greenhorns* who just signed up to the CRA to fulfill their desire for some cheap adventure in their boring lives, however, I was ready and prepared to fight for what I had and try to get back some semblance of what I had lost. In a lot of strange ways, it was stuff that I had been building myself up- and others had besides- for my whole life, although I'm only starting to discover the how and why of this now. It's simple once you unravel it, though.

One of the advantages of being a Scout of either gender is that you are automatically qualified to be an NCO in the CRA, because you've already learned the survival skills and garnered the athletic prowess that they'd prefer the officers have. Not that a lot of the *girly* stuff they shoved down my throat at Acorn Flats counts as "military" training, but that's beside the point. Also, I knew my dad would be way disappointed in me if I ever decided to turn pacifist- not like I'm actually gonna become one of *those*! So, off to the CRA me and my buddies went. Alas, I didn't get a chance to be with my guy when I got in. Any chance of me getting horizontal with my beloved Lance is gonna have to wait until I can *finally* find some way to get us alone together. Not that he knows- or *cares*- how much *I* care about him and his sweet little ass. He's as A-Prime a Scout as I am when it comes to the natural environs, but, when it comes to *romance*- well, I might as well be an *alien*, the way he acts when I simply *flirt* with him....

Yes, I *am* rambling. You don't need to point it out. I know exactly what you mean. I've been through this whole shebang before. Time is *money* with you oral history guys, *right*?

I'll just get right to the point....

*

We happened to be patrolling in the D.C. area when the call came out that the CIA and FBI were demanding that the CRA hand over "specimens"- preferably dead, but alive was okay- so that they could figure out exactly what we were "about." Well, some of the gang that I have control over thought it might be *funny* if, rather than running away from this reasonable request, a 'toon actually showed up at the Langley, Va. Headquarters of the CIA- which were just spitting distance from then- to comply with this request.

I didn't appreciate them treating this serious booty call on the government's part as a *joke*, so I whistled for their attention, and told them this as a way of putting the lot of them in their place. Then, of course, me being me, I upped the ante.

Furthermore, I said, if they want a goddamn "specimen" so bad, then it might as well be *me* they dicker around with, rather than any of you. I have absolutely *no* intention losing one or all of the lot of you to the scurvy-ridden clutches of the Central Intelligence Agency!

My own words, there.

Now, they immediately reacted with the horror I thought they would react with, but I told them to *shut up* and let me TALK! Then I explained.

"*I* am the *Captain* of this unit," I explained. "It is *my* responsibility to make sure that all of you are safe from harm in order to carry out your duties. And, if that means putting myself in harm's way to prevent any from coming to you, *so be it*! But let me say *this*. I may have every intention of surrendering myself- *temporarily*- to our Neanderthal opponents, but I have no intention of remaining *permanently* in their thrall. No! I am going to get *out* of there- and do as much damage as I can while I do!"

That was enough to get them off my back- and with a rousing chorus of cheers, besides. That is, except for the youngest member of our unit, Private Theodora, a little squib of a puppy who reminds me far too much of me- *before* the Chipmunk Scouts. I had to break the news to her gently- which was easy, considering she had a death grip on my left leg at that moment.

"Theo," I said with a bit of resignation in my voice, "*what* are you *doing* down there, girl?"

"Don't leave me, Cap'n Patsy!" she bawled. "I couldn't possibly bare it if you..."

"*What,*" I said in my serious "military" voice, "have I told you about making *scenes, soldier*?"

Theo got the message, let go of my leg, and got vertical in a hurry.

"That scenes are only fit for Republicans and horrible human actors like Jessica Chastain," said Theo.

"My *exact words*," I said, impressed, paws on hips. "You remembered. Good going, Theo."

"It's photographic," she said, pointing to her head. Hopefully, she meant her memory, but I didn't ask.

"Now, Theo," I continued. "You have, undoubtedly, heard me speak of my past exploits as a Squirrel Scout?"

"Yes, Cap'n."

"You are also, no doubt, aware of my past exploits as a CRA officer, as well as my skill with that deadly martial art, Bok Choy?"

"Uh huh, Cap'n."

"And, do you *seriously* think, with all the physical and mental skills at my command, that any of those arrogant pus bags at the CIA is actually a match for me in hand to hand combat?"

"No, Cap'n."

"Then why the *hell* were you *holding my goddamn leg*?"

Theo had to think about that for a moment, and she was still trying to think of a response three minutes later, when I finally had to speak again.

"Look, Theo," I said. "This has to be done, and I'm *doing* it! End of story. What *you* need to do is start being more self-sufficient and less dependent for me on guidance and instruction. Otherwise, you're *never* gonna get past *private* in this outfit, and you do *not* want to *stay* a *private,* believe you me. Start growing some goddamn BACKBONE, girl! Seriously! Okay?"

"Okay," said Theo.

"I'm not being hard on you *per se,*" I said, touching her cheek. "I want everyone around to succeed. And the only way to encourage them sometimes is to get tough."

Strapping my radio communication device to my wrist, I told the gang to remain where they were until when and if I needed them, at which point I would inform them of such. Then I went off.

*

What happened after that was fairly straightforward. I wandered up to the CIA's front gate like it was MGM in the 1940s, and I was a corn-fed youth hoping to become a movie star. Except, rather than being propositioned by a producer or hustled off to a sound stage for an extra gig, everybody and his brother in the place starts chasing me like I was Typhoid Mary and I just killed somebody. Somewhere along the line I got knocked out...

...and that leads me back to where I started, doing my impression of the dinner entrée at that night's shindig at Waikiki Beach.

That was when the door opened.

A couple of suits, a man and a woman, entered the room. That's what they were and that's what they wore- suits. The man was fairly tall and young, and he looked like I could handle him well if we were alone. Unfortunately, it seemed like the woman was the one in charge. Typical. Worse still was the fact that she was a dead ringer for that *bitch* Jessica Chastain, and seemed to have that same *Zero Dark Thirty* aura about her, given the fact that she was looking at me like I was Bin Laden.

"This is the *sketcher,* huh?" said the woman, using that racist buzzword the right wing media's always been calling us, as you know.

"Not as much of a such a much as I thought she'd be- but then, most of those pen and ink freaks usually don't measure up to us by any stretch of the imagination!"

"Can you *please* be a bit less *racist*?" replied the man. "What was the point of us going through that *sensitivity training* if you're gonna keep illegally riding roughshod over all of the rules?"

"That BULLSHIT does *not apply* to *them*! None of *them* have *a right to LIVE*!"

"Emshwiller!"

"Shut the *fuck up, Goodis*! You don't know what the hell you're talking about! I've been on this beat longer than you have, and I know a goddamn lot MORE about this bunch of SHIT than you EVER will! "

"Look, Emshwiller! Just because you're a *woman* doesn't mean your *shit* doesn't *stink...*"

"Do *not* make me look *bad* in front of the TERRORIST!"

She pointed to me at this point, to underscore her contempt.

"Your *ignorance* and *racism* are *utterly appalling*!"

"I fully intend to do to this...creature *whatever is required to get information out of her.* If you don't like it, you can *lump it*!"

"Go *fuck* yourself, Emshwiller!"

The man, fueled with righteous anger, stormed out of the room, leaving the woman alone with me for the time being.

"So," she said, finally lowering her voice below heavy metal band decibels. "You're Patricia Stiles..."

Patricia! Of all the low down, dirty INSULTS! Yes, I know "Patsy" is officially a diminutive for "Patricia" by those stupid *Oxford* language rules of the humans, but I have never been called "Patricia" by anybody else- in any context! I made sure to correct that dimwitted blond dweeb right away.

"My *name* is PATSY!" I corrected her forcefully. "*CAPTAIN PATSY STILES*! Of the Cartoon Republican Army..."

She slapped me, full tilt, in the face, in a way I knew would leave a mark. When you get hit by one of the humans, it usually does. They can be tough when they're angry.

"Do you think I *give a fuck* about whatever your goddamn *name* is? Or what *rank* you hold in your piss stained *"military"* group?"

"No," I said, stating the obvious, "you *don't*. You know *why*? Because if a thing- or a *person*- has any identifying marks of *humanity* on it, you want to *erase* them! The better for *you* to treat them in *the most inhumane ways possible!*"

"You little FUCK....!"

"Call me what you *want*. My ancestors killed *snakes* for a living. Do you think *humans* scare me any?"

"Shut up! SHUT UP!"

She took the pole I was on and shook it violently. This did little to advance the level of refinement in the room, especially since it my capacity for barfing considerably. Which I then proceeded to do in her direction, although she managed to duck out of the way in time to avoid most of it.

"*You...* are... SICK!" she screamed, as she continued to shake the pole feverishly to intimidate me.

"No kidding," I said, only a little woozy. "You *made* me get sick!"

"Oh, ho! I "made" you get sick! Just like the Muslims of the world *made 9/11 happen!*"

"No. *You* made 9/11 happen! You think those goddamn planes were operating by REMOTE CONTROL? Girlfriend, *please*! You fucked up the Middle East for your own decadent pleasures, and *it* fucked you up *right back!*"

"How DARE you *contradict* a *member of the United States Government???!!!*"

She hauled off and kicked me in the ribs with one of her high heeled shoes- after taking it off first. She was going for the gut by trying to stick me hard enough to remove my entrails- although that didn't happen.

"You deserve nothing less than having an electric cattle prod rammed up your ASS!" she proclaimed, with American imperialist fury.

"Oh," I said. "No *waterboarding* for *me*, huh? Too bad. I do a kick-ass Esther Williams impression!"

Then I layered my shit-eating grin over her eyes. Normally, this overwhelming display of feminine pulchritude is enough to get me whatever it is I want. Not this time.

"Why the hell are you still *smiling*?" she brayed, like a constipated mule. "Do you *know* what we can *do* to you?"

"I *do*, honey," I leered lasciviously. "What you conveniently *forget* regarding *that*, however, is that most of them don't *work* on us. We keep *telling* you, but *you* never *listen...*"

"Why the hell should we listen to YOU?" she blared, like an old fashioned air raid siren.

"I don't know, actually," I responded, in a justly accusing tone. "*You* never listen to anybody but YOURSELVES *as it is*! You never listened to the Iraqis when they said they *didn't* have weapons of mass destruction...."

"You are *lying*, you fucking furry ASSHOLE!" she roared, with unjustified moral outrage.

"You never listened to the *Afghans* when they said they were *perfectly capable* of running their *own* affairs, *thank you*....," I continued, twisting the knife.

"Bastard offspring of PAINT," she sputtered, furiously.

"...and let's not even *begin* to discuss what you did to the NATIVE people of this continent!" I concluded, getting to the heart of a lot of what is currently wrong with America as I see it. "Boy! Did you sell *them* down the river, huh? 'Ah, yeah, we're *white* people, and our sociopolitical and religious views of life TOTALLY ROCK! You

INFERIOR Native people better do what we *tell* ya to do or we'll KILL ya- 'cause *God* TOLD US TO DO IT! Nyuk, nyuk, nyuk!'"

"You fucking LIAR!" She really blew up then. "That never *happened*!"

"Really? How do *you* know? *Everybody* knows that you U.S. government AUTOMATONS are the *kings and queens of BULLSHIT*! You've been making yourselves out as the heroes of your tailored-in-silk *fairy tales* about this country for CENTURIES, just 'cause you were somehow able to intimidate and kill off anyone who opposed you en masse! Well, it ends *here,* sister! There's *nothing* that you have that *we* can't *beat.* Until you find an actual way to beat us- which will be NEVER- we'll be stuck at loggerheads until you- *not* us- finally give in!"

"I am going to *strangle you* with my *bare hands,*" she predicted.

"Oh, *violence*! Just like you say we cartoons always practice! What HYPOCRITES you are! I...GAAARK!"

That "gaark" was me being strangled. And, honestly, she nearly had me there. Her adrenaline fueled rage was starting to do a number on my larynx. She might have even broken my windpipe if they'd let her.

"Emshwiller!"

After that word, from what I can only assume was from a superior officer, came some knocking, and then the door, which had been locked, was forced down and open.

Goodis, the man, had in fact brought reinforcements in the form of a superior officer, who told Emshwiller that she was being placed on suspension for an indefinite period of time. (For good reason.) Emshwiller launched into another profanity-laden tirade directed at the two men, and the superior and Goodis argued back and forth with her similarly, like the overgrown children that all the U.S. government agencies consist of. They left the room. Emshwiller was told to turn in her gun and badge. She refused. They tried to take it from her. Judging by the loud isolated blasts of gunfire, and the horrified screams of the conceivable onlookers in the hallway, one or all of them got accidentally shot in the process. I'm hoping all of those shots went into Emshwiller's diseased brain. If there were only less people like her in the world....

*

Disposing of my tormentor was fairly easy, but then came the realization that I still needed to get *out* of there. Which was a whole 'nother thing, entirely.

Of course, I had come prepared, and I had slept well enough during my unconsciousness to regain a good portion of the strength, energy and agility I'd need to escape. I thrashed around in the ropes for a minute, and got my paws and legs out of the mess. Then I got the Swiss Army Knife I always keep in the pleats of my skirt out of there, and, transferring it carefully from my thigh to my hands, I selected the sharpest blade and freed myself from my hemp prison- although I fell down and hurt myself in a tender place in the process.

Slowly, I crept out the still-open door, and, desperately trying to make sure I didn't give myself away, crept along the walls as if I were navigating over the cliffs of some high mountain pass. Somebody else might not have been able to do this effectively, but not me, if I can be so immodest.

Well! I *might* have been able to keep *that* up if I had infiltrated a school for the blind or deaf, but *no*! I was in the CIA headquarters, and a cartoon character stands out in that place like a Jackson Pollock would if you put it in by mistake with the Impressionists. And, sure enough, they spotted me.

"The sketcher's loose!" said one guy.

"Catch it!" another one added. "If we don't restrain it, it'll *kill* all of us!"

"You fucking RACISTS!" I retorted, shaking my fist at the guy who had called me a "sketcher". "How would *you* like it if I called you SUITS? Oh, right. You wouldn't care-'cause ya don't have FEELINGS!"

"Get her!" said another guy. "She's not worth SHIT to us!"

Soon, they were after me again.

I had a slight advantage over them, being that, as a 'toon, I was faster, stronger and more agile than them. Not only that, I was in the same sort of top physical condition I've always been in, and especially since I've been working for the CRA. This job takes a lot out of you sometimes, but it pays you back sometimes, too. Even with that advantage, however, all my strength would be a fat lot of good to me if they caught me and trussed me up again. They'd get the matches out- 'cause they weren't going to make the same mistake *twice.*

Gradually, the word leaked out that I was free, and most of the staff, who I presume had been offered hefty cash bonuses for corralling me, were chasing me like I was the front runner in the Boston Marathon. Now, I can run like a Kenyan under normal conditions, but I was really putting on the style here. *You* try getting through the headquarters of the CIA as a wanted fugitive from justice some time if you don't believe me. I had put some distance between myself and those twerps, and already there seemed to be quite a few out of shape ones who were starting to fall back. I just needed to find the exit to the place (I was on the second floor of the building at the time), and I'd be free.

But then, it happened, like it usually does with me.

As good as I am with the stuff related to the great outdoors, I tend to forget that *inside* is another story. And that proved to be my undoing. A custodian was doing the floor of the section of the building that I was running in, and you know what happened?

Yep. I slipped on the damn wet floor, curse me! And, not only that, I uttered a shriek that confirmed the fact that, in spite of all my macho tomboy posturing, I am still, biologically, a girl. Failing to control my equilibrium, I collided with somebody pushing a cart coming along, and fell into the carafe that was on top of the cart. This would have been okay had the carafe been *empty*, since I could have hid in it and jumped out of it to surprise them, like they have girls jumping out of cakes at bachelor parties sometimes. Not a chance there, however. This thing was wide and deep, and worse still was the fact, which I did *not* find out until I was *in* the thing, that it was full of *coffee.* And it was HOT!

This occasioned another high decibel scream from yours truly, and I again flew through the air. This time, I was not as lucky in finding a place to land, and I landed, with legs splayed, on the cement floor, on my butt. Don't think stuff like that doesn't hurt like hell- 'cause it *does*! This blow to my body slowed me down severely, and I soon found myself surrounded on all sides by as many of the active duty staff as they could have rounded up on such short notice. I had nowhere to go- or so it seemed.

There were two options. I could surrender, but that would likely mean surrendering more of my dignity, not to mention probably some more torture under a tighter watch to prevent me from escaping. And, if I surrendered, I could *die* if there were any more Emshwillers wanting my ink out there. So no dice on that one. On the other hand, they were closing their ranks pretty thick, and, if I tried making like an Olympic gymnast they could easily grab a paw or leg if I vaulted and pull me back down into their grasp. Same if I tried dashing for the nearby elevator, and *that* would be no help if the damn thing was *late.* Even my old stand-by, Bok Choy, would be no help if any of *them* knew martial arts, too, which I'm sure some of them, at least, did.

So, really, what could I do?

This became much more of a concern as I remained still while they advanced towards me. Granted, I could take them on one at a time in a fair fight and trounce them easily, no question about it. NOT when they numbered this many, however. They taught me how to fight hand to hand combat in the Scouts, for sure, but not a whole livid, fire-breathing angry mob!

Looked like I was done for....

....until a shot rang out.

They stood around like idiots, thinking one of their weapons had discharged accidentally, and looking quizzically at each other. When nobody owned up, they advanced on me again....

....another shot.

This time, whoever fired it said simply:

"Leave her *alone*!"

They parted themselves, like the Red Sea, to let the owner of the voice reveal himself.

It was LANCE, of all beings!

He was armed with a shot gun, which he clearly intended to use on anybody who messed with me or him, along with an arsenal of spare bullets he wore on top of his Bun Scout uniform. He beckoned me with a paw, and I quickly ran to his side while he continued to threaten the agents with the shotgun. You know the Phil Ochs album *Gunfight at Carnegie Hall*? It looked a bit like the cover of that, except I didn't look nearly as helpless as the girl on the cover of that does. Mainly 'cause I was giving 'em with the finger with both hands!

"*Shame* on you!" Lance said in his plain, typically straightforward speaking voice, as if he were a teacher catching big students bullying small ones. "I've known Patsy for *years*, and she'd never hurt *anybody* on *purpose*! Now, why don't you just go away and go back to whatever it was you were doing before..."

At this point, a guy tried to grab my hand from behind, and I cried out in pain. Lance whipped around and shot the guy in *his* hand. I had never seen this side of him before- but I *liked* it!

"Don't TOUCH her!" he warned him- and everyone else. "She's *not* YOURS!"

"Right," said a wiseacre in the crowd. "' I know exactly why *that* is, *boy*! It's 'cause *you* want to *fuck* her, huh? Well, you can *have* her!"

Lance was appalled when he heard the "f" word associated with himself and myself. It was written on his face, completely. He's not very smart about every little thing in the world, but he knows when I've been insulted. Not to mention *him*.

"Who *said* that?" he blazed angrily. "WHO?"

The offender was found in the crowd, and put directly in the path of Lance's gun.

"*Sir,*" he said sternly, "I don't know what the word "fuck" means, but it sounds completely *disgusting*! I have no intention of *ever* hurting Patsy like that- because I *respect* her!"

Lance, Lance, Lance. If you only knew how much *I* want to fuck *you*...

"You lousy son of a motherfucking PIPE-SMOKING *LUNATIC*!" said the man. "I'm gonna fucking kill you *and* your butt-faced *mate* for SURE for THAT one!"

These particularly racist insults prompted Lance to shoot him right in the chest. The particularly racist man who said them fell back on the ground, gasping for air that was rapidly escaping him. Then he died.

"Anyone *else* want what I did to *him*?" Lance demanded. "*Or,* are you willing to let Patsy and I go UNMOLESTED?"

Silence.

"Then *leave*," he demanded. "NOW!"

That they did, leaving him and me alone. Nothing and nobody between us.

At last!

"How did you know I was here, pal?" I asked. "I mean, I didn't say anything to anybody about me coming here except my unit..."

"I didn't," he said. "I was here for something different."

Pause. He can get *real dumb* sometimes.

"Which *was*?" I prompted.

"Oh, right. Well, my unit kind of came across some rather compromising pictures of the CRA girls before they joined up that the CIA had posted on the Internet...."

"Compromising? You mean like....?"

"Yeah. And a *lot* of the guys in the unit *really* like them. I mean, *really*..."

"Lance, I *know* what guys are *like*. Including *you*. They were jerking off to those contraband photos, and you, being you, took umbrage. You said you were going to go to the CRA to get them to take 'em down- and here you came."

"That's *right,* Patsy!" he said, like I was some sort of psychic. "I just threw a bomb into their Internet monitoring room. Those photos should be *down* now."

"Along with everything else on the Internet, I imagine," I mused, humorously. "You know why *I* was here?"

"Why?" he asked.

So I told him just what I have you just now, and, as I went into the details of my dramatic escape and near recapture, his mouth gaped wide. I usually stun with what I do or what I say I do. Like I do with most 'toon guys. Little gift I have.

"And then *you* came along." I finished dreamily, hoping he'd kiss me. But, as usual, he didn't *get it*.

RRRRRRR.....

We were interrupted, however, by a loud blaring siren and a flashing red light that came out of nowhere.

"Crap!" I shouted. "They're getting reinforcements together. Where the hell's the front door to this place?"

"Over there!" he said, pointing.

Sure enough, there was the front door. Unguarded. Nothing there to stop or hurt us.

So we went out of it, paw in paw- into freedom.

What? You were expecting something more *dramatic*? *That* was what *happened! Really!*

Of course, if you *want* me to, I could tell ya some more. Like about the time me and my gang were cornered by the U.S. Army on a picnic, and we only had butter knives and dessert forks to...

SOME OTHER TIME? I give you the best story you're ever gonna get out of any of these goddamn "oral history" interviews, and you say *some other time*? Well, see if I ever tell *you* another one of my battle scarred stories, you ham-faced....No! Don't bother following me out the door, pal! You can *suck it*, hear me? SUCK IT!!!

ACT FIVE:

GONE TO THE DOGS

8:00 PM EST, Jun.1, 2—-.

CAPT. P. WHELP:

Well, it hadn't actually *begun* as a good day for me, so that kind of explains why I wasn't all Disney happy during most of it. However, since most *Disney* characters that I know aren't Disney happy nowadays *anyway,* that's all par for the course, isn't it?

Trust me on this, though. If they had actually asked me to *co-ordinate* the damn thing, it would have run a whole lot better. I mean, abandoning me to fend for myself- *alone*- in a Canadian city whose name I needed to read over a couple of times to make sure I was saying it right, while at least a few of my confederates couldn't help me because they'd clearly been playing Good Time Charlie with the local home brew. Pardon my French, but *what the hell were they THINKING*?

Yes, I *am* mad about it, if you hadn't gathered that already. But it wasn't supposed to be. You know those old black-and-white comedies from England? Made in the '50s? From Ealing Studios? *The Lavender Hill Mob* and so forth? You *do*? Well, thank God *somebody* does. After what I went through....

What I mean is that, in that flick, Alec Guinness gets lured into what he becomes convinced is a sure fire moneymaking scheme, but he and Stanley Holloway, who convinces him of the moneymaking value of the proposition, end up being chased all over London by the cops because the moneymaking scheme is counterfeiting gold. Now, not that any of my colleagues were or are as shady as Stanley Holloway was in that movie, but this was pretty much what happened. Substitute me for Alec Guinness, and Winnipeg for London, and you have it- cold.

Anyway, to be fair, I should tell you the *whole* story. I mean, that's what you *want* from me, right? Yeah! I thought so! Takes more to fool me than you think, buddy. You'll find that out soon enough....

*

It all started when I got a Twat on my LoganBerry from Rob and Mindy, my old buddies and the ringleaders of this whole *affaire du crime*. They were, it seems, planning a 'do for all the CRA members who were of the canine persuasion who could make themselves available. The catch was, it was in a place I had never heard of before.

"Emerson?" I twitted back. "Where is *that*?"

"Manitoba," they said. "It's in Canada. Dead in the center."

"I don't get it", from me. "You mean like the Arctic or something?"

"CANADA, you PUTZ! Don't you know any goddamn *geography*? For crying out loud!"

It must have been Mindy writing, 'cause she's the one of the two of them more likely to use that kind of language. She's nearly *fluent* in it. Evidently being a spy means you gotta know every little word and phrase that....but that's neither here nor there. You'll catch on what I mean later in the story.

"Aha," I twatted. "Manitoba. Now I remember. I'm in California now, so how do I....?"

"Go to a computer. Look for Canada on Goggle Maps. You'll find it easy."

"Okay. So when is it?"

"One week. Not before, not after. You in?"

I sighed, thought over my options, and twitted back:

"Yes."

*

To be honest, I didn't have a lot going for me at the time, so I was glad for the chance to change scenes. I hadn't had much going for me since I quit my old job, and didn't really get back into the job until I joined the CRA. They don't pay you anything, since we 'toons have difficulty depositing and handling human money as it is, but they give you the feeling of being part of a big family, albeit a rather dysfunctional one. I like that- especially since I never had one to start with.

Like most 'toons, I was created rather than born. And, if you are created without a family at the start, as they say, you never *get* one. Of course, it could be worse. *Much* worse. The show I came from was based on *a video game,* if you can believe it. Those people have even *less* when it comes to inner worlds than we do, when you think about it.

Anyhow, I did my time as best as I could playing straight man to a goddamn idiot of a worm who somehow turned into a superhero when he lucked into an artificial suit that made him a hero. That was basically it. Whadaya want from us- Shakespeare? *Some* of us have the kind of training for that kind of job, but do they ever *ask* us if we'd like to *do* it? No, sir! Always with the goddamn *slapstick*....

Yeah. Sorry. We 'toons have this problem in our speech with going off on tangents when you least expect it. You probably are pretty familiar with that by now. Yeah- I thought so.

Regarding my old acquaintance, I'll admit that Jam and I had some good times, but that was then and this is now. Eventually, we parted, which was something inevitable considering how much both of us had changed. I'd grown (mentally, seeing as my body doesn't take up too much space) and he hadn't. Worms don't have much in the way of brains, and Jam had even less than the average worm. He was still convinced we were hot stuff after Universal fired us, but I knew the truth. What happened was that I had to pawn the suit to get money to pay our rent for that month. He was mad as piss when he found out, and, even though he couldn't do anything to me without the suit, the fucking ungrateful invertebrate *attacked me*! He acted like he was a snake or something and tried to wrap himself around my neck, but he never got that far. I got him off me easy, told him to go to hell (among other far less printable things), and left behind that whole experience. Physically, it was over and done, but I still have the nightmares once in a while. A sidekick's lot is not a happy one sometimes, but it was still preferable to what was to happen to me in Winnipeg.

You would *think* that my experience would be enough to get me *some* sort of job, in my old field or another. I mean, I was sure that the skills that I acquired while being attacked and abducted all the damn time would be enough to even get me an *interview* with another hero or group of heroes. But no. N-O. Everybody I tried already had a sidekick, or didn't "do" that worn out old cliché anymore. Evidently, today's more *progressive* superhero types no longer need the easy convenience of having someone with their back along for the ride, let alone the secure vehicle for processing and responding to very deep psychological confession that the best of us are able to possess. As for something outside the field, in a bank or the tech sector or what have you- yeah, right! Maybe if I was a human 'toon, I could pass for normal and blend in. To a certain extent, of course- humans are generally tolerant of minorities in particular jobs, but only just *so* much, and then the humans have a decided edge over us animals. I found this out the hard way when I was busily trying to find other ways of earning my daily bread, so to speak. Most of the time when I went out to do something about my predicament, even when I tried to go on welfare, the very minute I started to walk through the door, those incredibly insensitive human bastards would start screaming or fainting, and then somebody else would grab a broom or something and chase me out. They must've thought I was gonna shit on the floor or something like that. The usual bigoted attitudes we have to deal with, even those of us who *aren't* 'toons. I can *assure* you that *most* of us 'toon dogs know how to use the CAN as something *other* than a fucking *water fountain*- including ME!

Bitter? Do I sound BITTER to you? Of course I'm bitter! Try, for once in your life, to think about being able to think, act and reason like a *man,* but being STUCK inside a body that makes you, in effect, a supposedly "dumb" ANIMAL! Do you *know* how *hard* it is to live as an animal 'toon, and *especially* as a *dog*? Especially all that RACIST "who's a good boy" SHIT we have to deal with? I swear, the next guy who says any of that crap to me, I am so going to bite him in his lousy, liberal hypocritical THROAT 'til he has to BEG me to stop....

What? Calm down?

Oh, yeah. Yeah. I'm sorry. I just don't have a lot of chances to vent to somebody who actually understands what I have to go through, you know? Let me have some water and then I'll get back to talking. It's just hard for me to get through all of it at once, you understand.

*

Somehow or another, even though unemployment had left me out of the loop, I got word about the CRA. Since, as I said, I wasn't actually doing anything at the moment I found out about it, I went in and applied. I took the oath, paid for my rank, and I was in. No special treatment or perks or what have you- at least not immediately. But I liked actually being somewhere where I *belonged,* for once.

Most of the 'toon dogs who've been created are in the CRA, and dogs are pretty clannish, seeing as how we've been genetically programmed to run as a pack from day one. I felt right at home immediately with them, but more with some than others, as I'll explain.

Anyway, we'd had a few informal get-togethers in the past, kinda like your average college kegger in terms of social and moral tone, and I figured that that was what was going to be going on in Emerson.

I was wrong. Completely.

*

I took the train from L.A. to Chicago and then a Greyhound (no jokes, pal!) to Minneapolis. From there, I rented a car and drove up north. Now, I had heard Canadian customs officers are a bit less ruthless than their American counterparts, but I must have got them on a bad day. Not *only* did they make me take off my shirt, pants and underwear, and then stick a *pole* up my ass, but I *also* had to put up with one of the female cops fawning over my "cute little dick." Really! You think they'd do *that* to me if I was a white, human guy?

Eventually, they sent me on my way- minus my dignity and about $300 American. Some sort of "tourist tax", they said. I'll bet they *made that up.* So I wasn't in the best of moods when I arrived at what appeared to be the only hotel in Emerson, Manitoba.

Oh, yes, they said. *You're with the DOG party, aren't you? Arf, arf! Well, we don't have enough beds for all of you to have a room, so you're gonna have to double up with somebody. Okay?* **O**-*kay!*

Typical human racist shit. Obviously, that crap transcends national boundaries. Fortunately, there are dissenters who like and help us. You, for example....

In any event, I was not given a key because my "roommate" already had it. Alas, the door was locked, so I knocked to get the attention of whoever was there.

"Go away!" said the occupant. "I'm NAPPING!"

Could my day get any worse? Yes, it could.

My roommate was Duddy Piddles (NO RELATION!), one of the more recent creations of the TV animation puppy mill from which I also sprung earlier. If you've seen his show, and I know you, for sure, have, you know what a total Looney Tunes *idiot* he is. He has some good qualities, sure, but they're buried so deep in his innate stupidity you can hardly find them. For some reason, he takes a quite a shine to me, as he believes we're related, when, as I have said before, we're *not*. Also, sorry to disappoint you fans of Messrs. Cook and Moore who think we're like *them*, too- nothing like that going on from my end, anyway, though *he* seems to like the idea of it all. Like he *would*.

I took a deep breath, and said:

"Duddy, it's me. Peter. You know, from before, at the other events. Open the door, would ya? I gotta *share* this place with you tonight...."

"Peter *who*?"

"Peter WHELP, you *dick*!"

"*No,* you're *not*!"

"Duddy, I think I would know if I wasn't who I claim to be, and I seriously don't have any patience for you *bullshitting* me like this! If you don't open the goddamn door *right now*..."

"Hang on! If you're *really* *P*eter, you'll know the *password*!"

"Dudley, I...."

"NO! We HAVE to do it! You could be one of my old enemies in disguise!"

"You know damn well that all of your old enemies are dead or in prison now...."

"No! I can't take any risks here! You have to prove to me that you *are* the real Peter!"

I threw up my paws, in a show of frustration, although it was impossible for him to see that behind the closed door.

"Fine," I said without any passion in my voice, humoring him. "For all I know, my body could've been invading by one of those scummy alien types who used to kidnap me, couldn't it? Very well, Dud. I'll play this game with you."

"Okay. What comes after these lines?"

And he started singing:

Justine, Justine, Justine, Justine, you know you just don't treat me right...

Justine, Justine, Justine, Justine, you know you just don't treat me right...

"You like to ball in the morning and stay out late at night," I growled tonelessly. Thank God I knew what the damn song was!

He undid the lock of the door and greeted me enthusiastically, in his all of his white furred, giant chested, black turtle-necked, pants-less glory. It takes about five of me to make one of him, and that point was reiterated to me when he nearly broke my back with one of his damnable hugs.

Once I got back my breath, I growled at him for doing that.

"What happened to *you*?" he said. "You're usually a ton more upbeat!"

"Let's just say I had some unpleasantness at the border..." I began.

"Ours or theirs?" he asked.

"Theirs," I said, ruefully.

"Oh, yeah. They actually wanted me to take off my SHIRT when they made me get out of the car! Like this..."

"NO!" I roared. "For God's sake, don't get NAKED in front of me! You SUCK at being naked!"

"I wasn't gonna take it off *now*, ya *tool*! You think I'm GAY or something? You got a hard-on for me? Is THAT it? "

"Lower your voice," I said, *sotto voce*.

"WHAT?" he shouted.

"LOWER YOUR GODDAMN *VOICE*!" I bellowed back.

Somebody knocked on the opposite wall, evidently displeased at me making noise.

"You really should keep it down, man," said Duddy. "It's late."

"Never mind that," I said, preparing to grill him for information. "What happened to the party?"

"The party?" He cocked his head in confusion, like usual. "Whadaya mean?"

"The *party*, you dumb *mutt*! You know, the one Ralph and Mitzy invited us to...."

"Oh," he said, processing it through his small mind. "Ah, yeah. That."

"Well, what about it?" I prompted impatiently.

"It's...not actually a party," he admitted, in an usually subdued and evasive tone of voice.

"Then what *is* it?" I demanded.

He hesitated a bit, and then said:

"Fine. You wanna know?"

"Of course I wanna know!" I insisted. "Out with it!"

"You heard of that "Idle No More" stuff the Native people have been doing up here for a while?" Dudley asked me, with unusual intelligence in his voice.

"Uh huh," I said. I was aware of this group, but only vaguely. Still, I often give the impression of being smarter than I look, and that was true here, as well.

"Well...", Dudley continued, "...Rob and Mindy thought it'd be cool if the CRA did one of those things. They couldn't get the whole CRA to agree to do it, though, so they decided to just ask the dogs. Problem is, they phrased it wrong, and most of us got lured here under false pretenses. A lot of them were pissed off about being duped and barked the sky blue, but a few of us were still interested in doing it. Rob and Mindy and the others are in Winnipeg prepping, but I said I'd stay here unless someone else showed up and wanted in. Lo and behold..."

"Okay," I interrupted. "What's the gig?"

"Well, you know how the Winnipeg Drones are playing for the Stanley Cup this week?"

"No," I interjected, speaking as a non-sports fan. "I didn't."

"Well, when they bring the Cup down to ice level just before the game ends, we're gonna *steal* it."

"*What*?" I shouted. This was the stupidest thing I had ever heard of. What the hell was the CRA gonna do with the Stanley Cup? Melt it down for *bullets*? I fully intended to let Duddy know I wanted nothing further to do with this rather ill-conceived, much under-thought enterprise.

However, my cry had caused another, louder knock from the other room, which interrupted me mid-rant.

"GO *SUCK* ON A *LEMON*!" I bellowed at the source of the knock. Apparently, the loudness of my voice and the clearness of my threat were enough to make the other person back off, which is how I intended it to be.

Then I returned to Duddy.

"What possible purpose could stealing the Stanley Cup serve the CRA?" I asked, quieter this time. "I mean, it's not like there are *other* things we could be doing to help the cause..."

"It'll get the CRA some good publicity, for one thing. You know those push-button U.S. newspapers don't cut us any slack. Like we're a bunch of no-good TERRORISTS or something! If we do something big in Canada, they'll have to notice us, 'cause their media makes a big deal out of *everything* that happens here. Especially if it happens to do with hockey, which they're just plain *nuts* about."

"Who came up with the *idea* for this?" I sputtered incredulously.

"It really just came out of a bull session among all of us..." Dudley explained.

"And who is "us"?"

"Me, Rob, Mindy, Brendan..."

"I'll bet it was Brian!" I muttered to myself. "The *lush*!"

"...Cadmium and Brightness."

"Wait a minute. Did you say *Brightness*?"

"Yeah!" Dudley said. "Why....oh, ho HO!" This last phrase was accompanied by a knowing wink and a nudge to my ribs, both of which I viewed suspiciously.

"*What?*" I snapped, defensively.

"You got a *crush* on Brightness!"

"Yeah," I admitted. "But who *else* would I have a crush on in that group? Rob and Mindy are tight, and as for Brendan and Cadmium, they've been pretty much going ever since Orthicon...."

"Not so much now. They're going through one of their Liz and Dick things. Real nasty."

I sighed. That would be difficult to manage, especially if I had to be pressed into service as a relationship counselor. I tried it once, and let's just say it didn't work out all that well.

"So, are you in, or not?" Duddy insisted.

"If Bright's in, I'm in. I don't want her getting hurt on account of you guys. She's too *good* for the lot of *you*. Now, can we go to *bed* now? I need a goddamn *rest*!"

"You said it, buddy," Duddy yawned, loudly. "I need some shuteye, too."

So we went to bed. Nothing more to say there. Until....

*

We got up and going a few hours later, when Dudley gave me the kind courtesy of a wake-up call. Via an *air horn* he inserted halfway up one of my auditory canals! Fearing the worst- a U.S. government drone strike, perhaps?- I sat bolt upright and panicked. Only to see Duddy, up and fully dressed (by *his* pants-less standards, remember), preening down at me from the Olympian heights of Mount Moron.

"Wake up, little buddy!" he said.

I took exception to him calling to me that, and showed it by getting out of bed, going over to him, and slapping him as far up his face as I could reach.

"AAH!" he shouted in pain. "What the hell....?"

"You woke me up with a goddamn AIR HORN, *and* you compared me to that moronic human *idiot Gilligan, that*'s what the *hell*!"

The guy in the next room started banging on the wall again, so I loudly instructed him to perform a seemingly impossible sexual act on himself, and then returned my attention to Duddy.

"Look, man!" he said to me. "I wasn't trying to *insult* you or anything...."

"You *weren't*?" I said, sarcastically.

"I got a *lot* of trouble relating to other dogs, *okay*? All the other characters on my show *weren't*. You know what I mean?"

"*I* had the *same problem, Dud*!" I opened my suitcase and threw a spare set of clothes on, hoping he wouldn't notice I had insulted him by calling him that insulting diminutive of his name. "But I *learned*. Hopefully, you'll get the hang of it soon enough."

"Well, I just learned one thing about *you*."

"What's that?"

"*You* are not a *morning person!* That is BAD in *my* line of work!"

"Oh, *is* it?" I growled back as I closed my suitcase, resisting a desire to throw it at him. "I didn't think you needed to be a *morning person* in order to be an INCONSIDERATE *JERK*!"

That did it, as far as he was concerned, for his normal joviality was suddenly replaced in his eyes by enraged menace.

"*Boy*," he growled as he laid a fisted paw against a palm, "I will SMACK YOU DOWN if you call me that *AGAIN*!"

I knew *that*, for sure. One of his "Piddles Punches" had the capacity to permanently separate me from my backbone. So I tried to kiss and make up.

"Dudley, I'm sorry," I said, contritely. "I didn't..."

"Oh, I don't mind, really," he said, shifting back to his old persona. "I've been called worse. Even by my so-called FRIENDS sometimes! But you just gotta roll with it. Besides, we haven't had our first coffees of the day yet, so I can understand you being an ass after you just got up."

"You're right," I said. "How long is it until we get to....?"

"Not too long. If we floor it, we can get there in under thirty...."

I suddenly remembered what a horrible and reckless driver Dudley was. The thought of driving *with* him, even in separate cars, even just for the short time it would take us to get to Winnipeg, made me faint.

*

"WAKE UP, Pete!"

Dudley woke me up a few minutes after I went down for the count. We were in his car, he was driving it at break-neck speed, and I was riding shotgun. Just like I had feared.

"You all right?" he asked me. "I mean, you kinda blacked out back there, and I had to carry you out. Don't worry- I put your bags in back with mine in the trunk."

"What happened to the car I came in?"

"I torched it."

"You *torched*.....That was a RENTAL!"

"So is *this* one. You and I were going to the same place, anyhow. Why you use two when you only need one?"

"Yeah, but...."

I was going to explain to him about the legal trouble I was going to potentially be in back home for him burning my rental car, but, at that point, he turned the car into an abrupt stop. If I hadn't been buckled into my seat, I would've been thrown through the windshield.

"What the hell was *that*?" I exclaimed.

"We're *here*, man!"

He pointed at our intended destination, a big castle plunked down into the center of what was obviously downtown Winnipeg. At least, I *thought* it was a castle.

"What *is* that?" I said, pointing to it.

"And you said *I* was dumb!" Dudley scoffed. "That's the *Hotel Fort Garry*, man! Winnipeg's version of the *Waldorf*!"

"I imagine it's probably as *expensive* as the Waldorf," I cracked.

"Yeah, but *we* aren't paying for it."

"Huh?"

"Brendan got his moneybags creator to pony up all the cash we would need to pull the job. Good thing he's still got his connections, 'cause none of the rest of us can get cash out of ours- even if we *earned* it. You know what I mean?"

"Darn right I *know*! Let's go in and *eat*!" Now that I wouldn't have to *pay* for anything, I was suddenly feeling a lot better about the whole deal.

"We finally *agree* on something," Dudley mused.

We walked up the stairs of the hotel, presuming that, as soon as we got in the door of the dining room or wherever it was they ate in that place, we'd be embraced by our pals, and it'd be old home week.

No such luck.

I could see it as soon as we got towards the dining room, but it took Dudley longer to make the connection. Evidently, some beings resembling us (our pals?) had tried to get into that room earlier that day because, I swear to God, somebody SHOT at me! Now, since I'm a 'toon, the bullet sailed through me with no damage done, but it was a bad omen. Another floated past Dudley's head and nicked his ear, causing both of us to turn around. There was the local SWAT team, surrounding us and telling us "fucking dogs" to get *out* of there if we didn't want to *die*.

"No, you fucking DON'T!" Dudley snarled, enraged. "Pete and I are gonna *kick* your fucking ASSES if you don't GET LOST!"

As if to act on his threats, and with a death grip on my body, we got in there with the cops, and scuffled with 'em right on that fancy hotel floor. Somehow or other, though, the two of us got tossed out of the place, and halfway down the street, besides.

"That was *weak*!" Dudley said when we hit the ground. "How come you didn't *change*, man? We would've *won*!"

"Change?"

"Yeah. On your show, you used'ta do this whole Incredible Hulk thing when you got hurt...."

"That was my *character*, Dudley- not *me*."

"Well, you coulda *told* me that!"

We were going to argue this further, but then Dudley's cell phone rang.

"Y'ello?" he said. "Yeah, I'm here...Of *course* I brought Pete with me. Where the hell are *you* guys? We went into the hotel and the cops *clobbered* us....Uh-huh....City ordinances and by-laws, huh?....Well, what are we gonna do about *food*?.....Whadaya mean, is *that* all I think about? You listen here, *Miss Mindy:* I *think*.....Okay, sorry, Ma'am! Sorry! Don't bust my balls, *please*! DON'T *BUST MY BALLS*......Right...Man up.....Okay. So where we gonna meet you?....WHAT?....They won't let us stay ANYWHERE in this town? Bunch of goddamn FASCISTS....Okay, so where....Kildonan Park? Where is that from the hotel?....Uh huh. Uh huh. Yeah. Right. Talk to ya soon."

He hung up and turned to me.

"Bad news, chum," he said. "This town's *creep* of a mayor put down some *laws* saying any 'toons have to have proof they're *human* to be considered citizens under the law."

"Where does that leave us dogs?"

"Only one step ahead of their Humane Society."

"And that is?"

"That's Canadianese for *dog catcher*."

"Oh."

"Point is, we got to sleep in the park tonight. That shouldn't be too bad."

"Not if you *like* that thing," I said sarcastically to myself. I wasn't going to risk upsetting Dudley again, 'cause I knew that he *did*.

*

Eventually, after twisting and turning our way through the pothole-ridden streets of Winnipeg, we finally made it to Kildonan Park. It was a lot bigger than I expected, with a front gate and everything, and we actually got lost in it before we finally found the gang. Not surprisingly, it was near a "dogs must be on leash at all times" type sign that had been thoroughly moistened with their urine.

Rob and Mindy, with their still keen eyesight, saw and spotted us first. Him with his white-furred, Lincoln-esque stolidity, her in all her deceptively, overly pink-furred, red-bowed feminine glory, the curves concealing well-exercised muscles that can punch your lights out in a second. Just like always. What *was* different was that they were both wearing shirts that seemed to have a U.S. Air Force decal ironed on to their fronts.

"What is *that*?" I said, pointing to their shirts, once we greeted each other.

"Camouflage," said Rob, as if that explained everything.

"How is that....?"

"It's so we look like the LOCALS, *dumbass*!" retorted Mindy.

"How is it....?" I persisted.

"Look," Mindy said, pulling me so close to her chest that I could've been sucking her teats for all some stranger knew- mostly 'cause she's only slightly bigger than me. "*What* is on my *chest*?"

"An....airplane?"

"NO!" She released the grip she had on my paw and threw me ass over teakettle on the ground. "It's a DRONE!"

"Oh," I said, dazed. "Right. The *hockey* team."

"*D-uh*. Of *course* it's the *hockey team,* you little *runt*! Do you know how goddamn HARD it was to get this crap in the first place? Do you know what Rob and I....?"

Rob, at this point, inserted himself between her and me to prevent further damage being done.

"For God's sake, Min!" he snapped at her. "Cut it out!"

"Out of my way- or I'll do it to *you*!" she snarled back. "I can even do it to HIM if I wanna!"

She pointed at Duddy as she said the last line. The laser-like way her eyes bore into his sent him scurrying down the nearest pedestrian walking path, screaming.

Rob, meanwhile, further signaled his displeasure with Mindy by slapping her-hard-in the face. Normally, he's far too nice a guy to even *think* about doing something like that, but she really must've pushed his buttons before I arrived for her to deserve that. The two of them have been together for quite awhile-their show goes back to the '90s, after all-and she has this thick as a brick Napoleon complex due to her lack of height, and something like this was probably the only non-verbal way for him to get her attention. Not that she seemed to *like* it any.

She displayed her displeasure at this by throwing a punch back at him, which, because she was for some reason lacking her usual sterling physical and mental conditioning, he easily dodged.

"How DARE you take a swing at me!" Mindy blazed at him. "YOU! After all we've been through together..."

"Knock it *off, okay*?" Rob responded, unmoved. "You're *drunk*! *Anybody* can whip your tar when you're drunk- even *me*. So lay off everybody 'til you get *sober*!"

He pointed off in the direction of whence Duddy had run after she stared at him. She gave Rob a mean and evil "I will *break* you for this" look, and then galumphed off.

Ralph, meanwhile, tended to me.

"Sorry, Peter," he said to me as he helped me up. "You came at a bad time."

"*I'll* say I did!" I answered. "I mean, *Mindy- drunk*? I always figured her for the Lemonade Lucy type."

"Normally, yeah. But *Brendan* got to her."

"Figures. What happened?"

"He bet her that he could out-drink her. If he won, he got to have his way with her. *I* didn't like that, of course, but what could I do? Their bet, their rules."

"And if *she* won? Which I'm presuming she *did*?"

"She wanted to make him *pay* for insulting her. Literally. And for the cost of the beer. Fitting, considering *we* bought it! Anyway, once it was clear she had won, she started kicking the crap out of him. Real bad. Even when the rest of us said he'd had enough, she still went on. Finally, me and Bright did the sideways eyes things and teamed up to get her off of him. Pitiful, really. He's been sleeping it off most of the time after that, but he should be better by the time we have to go through with this fool's errand of a job."

"*You* think this is a *fool's errand*?'

"Uh, *yeah*! I only went along with it 'caused Min and Brendan are both so *jonesed* about it, and it wouldn't do to upset either of them by putting my paw down on it. I *also* think he's trying to steal Min from me. That whole butt-kicking routine looked a bit too staged for my liking."

"Personally, I agree with you on this whole idea. Just don't tell Dud, 'cause he's *way* in on it, you know?"

"Got it."

"But *why* would Brendan want to start *schtupping* Mitzy all of a sudden? I mean, aren't he and Cadmium....?"

"Aren't we WHAT?"

I nearly jumped out of my pants at that line, but then I turned around and there was Cadmium, wearing what looked like a baby T version of the Winnipeg Drones shirt Rob and Mindy were wearing. As you well know, she is the tiniest living cartoon Dalmatian in existence, owing that she was created as a runty, long-eared puppy, but don't *dare* call her that to her *face*. Somehow, even though she doesn't seem to have the *equipment* for it, in my opinion, she has had a number of passionate lovers over her existence. Brendan and her have had an on and off thing going since Orthicon, but she also seems to be always on the hunt for newer and more *compliant* boy toys, it seems. I got that impression from the way that she was looking at me at that moment.

"Peeee.....ter!" she drawled, in her deceptively innocent, sugar-coated, drawling, New Age accented voice. "How *are* you?"

"Uh....fine," I stammered. "And you?"

"Oh, well enough- *if* you can call our canine experience *living*! *Especially* considering how well I manage to deal with HIS ROYAL HIGHNESS preening around!"

"You mean....Brendan?"

"Of *course* I mean *Brendan*, you *dope*! I have *tried*, with all my best intentions, to introduce him to the *finer* things in life, but *he* seems to prefer drinking like an *Irishman* and chasing down every *human* woman he sees! Yahhh! How can I *compete* with *that*? My body's too *fragile* to handle *alcohol*, and I certainly *don't* have the *boobs* or *legs* to compete with those human WHORES!"

"You don't *have* to, Cad," I tried to reassure her. "You always light up a place just coming into the room and raising your voice."

"Awww," she drawled again. "Aren't you *considerate*? Listen, Peter. If we get out of this thing *alive,* I am *seriously* considering you as future *boyfriend* material..."

"Really? I...."

A loud, wordless moan was heard on the other side of the grassy plain we were standing on.

"Oh!" Cad uttered with surprise. "It appears that RAY MILLAND over there has found the little "gift" I left on his *face*. I'd better go stoically take my medicine. Ta ta!"

She grinned in shit eating fashion and walked off. No sooner had I walked away from her, then:

"Hi, Pete!"

Brightness!

Now, a tall, yellow furred dog in a demure green dress, and a human-like tuft of hair on top of her head might not be your cup of tea romance wise, but, for me, she is the one and only girl I want to be for the rest of my miserable, elongated existence. The trick is, how was I gonna tell *her* that? *Especially* when I kept turning into a stuttering zombie every time I tried to talk to her alone, like I did back then.

"H....h...h.....hi, Brightness!" I stammered nervously. If dogs could actually *sweat*, there would be perspiration coming out of all of my pores.

"So," she said, a little awkwardly, "you wanted in on this, too?"

"Yeah. Only I thought it was going to be one of the usual keggers, y'know? I totally got *tricked*!"

"They tricked *everybody*, Pete. Rob and Mindy and Brendan and Cadmium. They said they were just going to have a party, but instead, they just wanted a few brave pups to help them do what those crazy Chechnian guys did in Boston a few years back. They said it was for the CRA, but I think it was *really* to pump up their flabby, flaccid *egos*, since none of them have had too much real action in a while, even by being part of the CRA. Why, I was so mad that I went in where they were all staying the night and verbally tore a strip out of all of them!"

"I never figured you for that kind, Bright."

"Well, I can *do* it," she pouted. "And I'm sure if Collar were still with us, he'd agree with me about this whole thing. Only he'd actually have the guts to *cuss* at them. Unlike *me*."

"I'm sorry about Collar," I said, with genuine sympathy. "That was a huge loss to all of us 'toon dogs when he went. Not just you and your bunch."

"Thanks," she said, tears starting to form in her eyes.

Collar, in addition to being her co-conspirator in the pro-dog Street Puppy movement and later in the CRA, had been her main squeeze. That is, until some human punks cornered him in a back alley in L.A. one night and senselessly burned him to death. Stern warning to all of us 'toons, obviously, but we 'toon dogs felt the lost more grievously, as you might expect.

"To be honest, Bright," I said, "I think this whole thing is nuts, too. But we'll *have* to go through with it, now. Especially now that *Duddy's* involved. Five against two is no fair fight, no matter how strong the two may be."

"I know, Pete. And they complemented me so well on my tongue lashing that they figured that they *could* use me, after all. I felt grateful, if only for a little while. But the whole idea is so STUPID!"

She kicked a nearby tree in anger- and promptly injured her foot. "DAMN IT!"

Shocked at what she had just said, she abruptly covered her mouth.

"Whoa!" I said. "Bright! You okay?"

"No, Pete!" she started sobbing. "I *SWORE!*"

"Come on, Bright! Relax. Everyone swears once in a while."

"Everyone?" She was genuinely puzzled.

Keep in mind that her show was on back in the 1980s- the Dark Ages of sugary sweet, corporate funded TV animation. In those days, the directors went all Guantanamo on the 'toons if they didn't read the lines *just right* or do the bit of business they should be doing the "right" way. Granted, the stuff they were doing back then was crap on a purely dramatic level, but the 'toons got hit harder than other actors in the TV sector because they were literally the lowest of the low in those days. One day, Bright got caught innocently mimicking a profane word a PA had uttered on the set- she was more naïve in those days, not like now- and they went and beat the shit out of her for it. Since then, she's always been afraid the world will come to an end if she swears. I try to watch my own words 'cause of that when I'm around her. The rest of us- not so much.

"Yeah," I repeated. "*Everyone*. Even me. Never around *you*, though."

"I'm glad *somebody* around here has a HEART!" she said, affectionately.

We were actually going to embrace, when:

"AAAAAH! Get *away* from me!"

Duddy!

He rushed past us, followed by Mindy bellowing profanely at him for "accidentally" grabbing her tail in the woods, followed by Rob desperately trying to keep the peace. Meanwhile, from the other corner of the Park, Brendan and Cadmium were taking turns griping and growling at each other, and *they* caught up in the maelstrom, too. Bright and I were suddenly surrounded by them, like Caucasians by Native people on the warpath in an old-school Western movie. It was damn near as loud.

I persuaded Bright to throw me out above the melee into a nearby garbage can, and, her being her, she agreed. I landed at the can, and, once I got my bearings, I turned it on its side and rolled it down towards the Circle of Hell I had escaped. Bright, knowing what was going on, got out of the way, but the others didn't, and so, since the can was full and made of metal besides, it made a loud CRASH when it knocked down the runners in their tracks. That was enough to throw everyone except me and Bright off of their game, which was all we needed.

"All right, you lousy *bum biters*," I snapped at the assemblage, doing my best impression of your typical U.S. Army DI. "*Listen* and listen GOOD! Bright Eyes and I have had just ENOUGH of your cowboy carrying-on! You said you wanted to strike fear and terror into the hearts and minds of the humans! FEH! You can't even strike fear and terror into your fellow DOGS! We have a good mind to turn you into the *cops* and tell 'em what you were *trying* to do. Only *they* wouldn't BELIEVE us, no doubt, and might even try to collar US instead!"

"You should be ASHAMED of yourselves!" added Bright. "The CRA is supposed to be about how showing the human beings how *worthy* we are of their *respect*! How we can possibly *do* that when you always act so ABNORMALLY?"

They had all gotten back on their feet at this point, and Brendan, our most loquacious friend, took this as his cue to strike back.

"Hah!" he smirked. "Listen to the chick from the Eighties tell us *we're* "abnormal". The whole damn DECADE you came from was abnormal...."

"That wasn't my FAULT!" Bright cut in, defensively.

"...so don't tell *us* about being ABNORMAL!" Brian continued, ignoring her interruption. "No dog who dresses like a *human being* can say they're "normal", anyhow!"

"What the *hell* do you mean by THAT?" I blazed ferociously. "*I* dress like a human, and I'm still as much of a dog as ANY of you! She is, too, for that matter. *Both* of us are more of a dog than *you,* MR. FAT ASS *DRUNKARD!*"

Brendan cursed under his breath, opened the trash bag inside the disheveled can, and retrieved a beer bottle. He smashed it onto the ground and retrieved a jagged piece of glass, which he seemed intent on using as a shiv against me. He was about to run at me when Mindy piped up:

"PUT THAT *DOWN*!"

"You stay out of this...." Brendan began.

"She *said* PUT IT DOWN!" Cadmium roared.

"I don't have to take this shit from...."

"*Put* the bottle DOWN!" snapped Bright Eyes.

Evidently, she'd just seen *Glengarry Glen Ross,* 'cause she said that line exactly the same way Alec Baldwin tells the guy to get away from the coffee in that movie. With even more authority in it than the way *he* said it. Believe me.

Brian, realizing he was outvoted by the girls, threw the shiv away. Duddy caught it- and *ate* it.

"Thanks, man," he said to Brendan.

Brendan, somewhat stunned, mumbled something about going to get coffee, and walked off.

Rob, ever the peacemaker, immediately tried to smooth things over.

"Look, everybody," he said. "I can understand if you don't want to do this..."

"We're *all* still doing this, you *moron*!" Mindy snapped. "*Right*?"

She whirled around, gazing at each of us in turn, her eyes demanding an immediate answer to her (rhetorical) question.

"Uh....Yes?" said Duddy, nervously.

"Girlfriend, *please*!" said Cadmium confidently. "You *know* how I feel!"

Brightness and I retained our stolid, frosty expressions from before, crossing our arms for emphasis when Mindy turned to us.

"*Well*?" she insisted.

"Not unless you take our feelings into consideration," I said.

"*For once*!" snarled Brightness.

That last shot in particular seemed to suddenly deflate Mindy. Were those actually *tears* in her eyes?

"All right!" she said, throwing her paws up in the air. "Look, I'm *sorry*. Okay? I know I'm a *mean* drunk, and I try to avoid drinking 'cause of that, but *Brendan* had his mind on *fucking* me, and I just couldn't....that was the only reason I.....GOD!" She collapsed into Bright's arms and embraced her. "God, Bright! I'm horrible! I'm just a lousy DOMINATRIX! Nobody loves me any more except ROB, and even he...."

"Sssshhh!" Bright responded. "Just let it out, Mindy. It's better this way."

While that was going on, Rob signaled for me and Duddy to come over towards him.

"Boys," he said, "I think we're in over our heads here. But like you said, Peter, we should really take each other's feelings into consideration on this thing. Mindy and I laid out a plan, but we can let you guys have a look over it, if you want. I mean, we completely forgot you guys have experience in the hero business, too."

"Yeah," I said. "Only not all heroes are created equal. I mean, I was totally out of line back there, considering I'm only just a *sidekick*...."

"Not in the CRA, you're not," said Ralph. "You're a Captain, aren't you?"

"Yeah. So is Duddy. But what about....?"

"You already outrank some of us here. Cadmium's a Lieutenant, and Brightness is a Sergeant. And *Brendan,* for all his superior posturing, is really just a Private, First Class."

"*What*?" Duddy and I both giggled.

"Yeah," said Rob, laughing himself. "He was too much of a tightwad to pay out for a higher rank. By the way, when he said "Seth" was bankrolling us- total lie! Can't even get him on the *phone* anymore! Good thing Min and I had enough from our class action suit against Saban kicking around."

"What about you and Mindy, rank wise?" I asked.

"I'm a Major, and I'm technically the guy in charge, okay?" said Ralph, more seriously now. "You do *not* want to go *against* me, *understand*?"

He had his game face on when he said that, so Dudley and I just said we understood.

"Mindy's a Captain like you two," Rob said after he took a cleansing breath, "so if you get into any trouble with her, and I mean *any*, tell me."

"Even if she....ya know?" said Dudley, mimicking a feminine flirt with his face.

"Oh, grow up!" said Ralph. "*Neither* of you is her *type*. Now, me...."

"We don't tell *you* about *our* sex lives, *do* we?" I snapped, insulted.

"Ah....sure," Ralph said, nervously. "Now, if you want to go over the plans...."

*

Flash forward- the next day. Game time- for the Drones, and for us.

Brendan, Duddy and I- we lost the straw draw- were up to our necks in Drones-themed clothing. We had our tickets In hand (so to speak), and were waiting in line with the rest of the ugly, smelly human hockey fans to be admitted into the MTS Centre. Each of us was wearing a wire, the better for us to communicate with the rest of the gang, who were waiting outside in an unmarked van for our cue: the moment when we would first see the Stanley Cup from our nosebleed seats in the upper balcony. Not the best seats in the house, but, considering how much it cost us to get them, better than nothing.

Just after we were admitted- the Drone covered toques, scarves and mittens we wore completely obscured the tell-tale signs of our "race"- Brendan made an off-color joke about how drunk he planned on getting. That set me off.

"No!" I said, emphatically.

"*Jeez,* Pete!" Brian retorted, archly. "Lighten *up*, will ya? It's a *game*! And I'm not gonna be the *only* drunk guy in those stands, y'know!"

"We're supposed to be doing a *job*," I answered. "And considering how *fudged* you got *yesterday*, I'm surprised *you're* even *standing*!"

"I had my *honor* to defend!"

"Oh, sure. Like *boozehounds* have *honor*!"

"You little *son of a BITCH!* I'm gonna smack off your *face*!"

He would have, but Duddy blocked Brendan's punch with his fulsome chest.

"Ow!" Brendan shouted. "What the hell....?"

"Brendan, quit being a *douche,* okay?" Duddy chastised him. "Nobody's *filming* ya and sending it to FOX anymore, all right? And Peter," now addressing me, "quit being snippy about every little thing here- or *I'll* be the one smacking off your face!"

"Fine," I sulked. "But let it be known to the two of you that I intend to stay *sober* during the game. I want to do my *job*. You two get drunk all you want, but *leave me out!*"

"They wouldn't let you *buy* a beer, anyway- short stuff!" Brendan teased me.

"Man, you don't *need* to get drunk!" Duddy smacked Brendan on the head as we walked to our seats. "You *sound* drunk when you're *sober*!"

And I could have when Rob and the girls in the van. Lucky *bastard*!

*

We were let in early, so we had to wait until the game actually *started* before we could begin our vigil. Or, I should say, *I* could. Brendan and Duddy, predictably, couldn't stand the wait, so they went to get beers almost as soon as we found the seats. They got me a soda so I wouldn't feel "left out", but Brendan still cracked wise about it when he gave me the bottle. Naturally, although in total they only add two beers apiece each over the night, they were both soon completely blotto, like they'd had ten times as many. Must be something in that Canadian beer.

Anyway, the game started, the house lights dimmed, and we "ladies and gentlemen" were summarily welcomed, via the PA system, to the seventh and deciding game of the Stanley Cup finals between "ma moronofunamameha" and "YOUUUUUURRRRR WINNNNNNNNIPEGGGGG   DRRRRRROOOOONES!" The crowd, save for the few opposing team fans who'd managed to get in, rose to their feet, and applauded like the sycophantic idiots they were. Brendan and Duddy stood cheered along with them, but I managed to restrain myself.

Then came the anthems. Both of them- since the other team was from the U.S.A. I participated in the singing of both since I know 'em both (I have acquaintances in the Canadian end of the animation business who live in Toronto), but mostly in a futile attempt to drown out Brendan and Duddy pathetically butchering them. I feel sorry for the guys who wrote the music for those tunes, because they are too pretty to be butchered by guys who can't carry a tune in anything.

Then, *finally,* the puck got dropped.

It wasn't too much to write home about as hockey games go. Nobody even *scored* during the first two periods. Brian and Dudley, however, were totally on edge, like the fate of the whole mattered on the Drones winning the game (although I think most of the people there were thinking the same thing). Consequently, when they got huffy about a penalty being called on the Drones- or a penalty *not* being called on the other team- they argued about it like Republican senators filibustering against a Democratic bill (or vice versa). When I ventured the opinion that this was all just a goddamn *hockey game,* and it really didn't matter in the grand scheme of things, they made it seem like *I* was an ignorant *schmendrick*-which was exactly what *they* were behaving like!

When the second period ended, Duddy's cell phone rang, but, since he wasn't in any condition to answer it coherently by now, I took it and went off to find some place where I could answer it in private. It wasn't easy, but I found one.

"What the hell is going *on* there?" Mindy snapped into my ear when I answered. "All we're getting on the sound system is the sound of two drunk idiots arguing about the game!"

"That'd be Brendan and Duddy," I said.

"Oh, good," Mindy said, sympathetically. "It's you, Peter. So you volunteered to be the DD, huh?"

"I don't *drink* to *start* with," I replied, "so *that* was *easy*. Listen. Our seats are in the nosebleed section, and I doubt we can recognize the Stanley Cup from up here. I myself don't even know what it *looks* like."

"Not a sports fan, huh?"

"Can't you *tell*? I'm probably gonna be *less* of one after *tonight*!"

Mindy turned me over to Rob, who informed me that he, Mindy, Cadmium and Brightness had now entered the MTS Centre complex, after throwing nylon stockings over their heads like common burglars. They were now simply waiting for me to give the word before they snuck up on the people holding the Cup and took it over.

"Now, since you're the sober one there," he said, "you're gonna have to be the one to tell us when it's there. You have your binoculars on you?"

"Yeah," I answered. "But, like I told Mindy, I don't know what it *looks* like..."

I could hear Rob biting off a swear word in his voice before he spoke again.

"Listen carefully," he said. "The top of it is a cereal bowl type thing with fancy engraving on it. That's attached to a long base with silver grooves. Every year the winning team gets their name engraved on it, and this league goes back to the 1910s, so you can imagine how big it is by *now*. It's probably bigger than *you*, considering how *tall* it is."

"Ha ha!" I cut in, sarcastically.

"*Anyway,*" Ralph concluded, "the thing is made out of *silver*, and it's probably been polished to a fine sheen for tonight. It'll gleam like a beacon once it gets inside the rink. That's how you'll know it's there. That, and the fans will go *nuts* when they know it's there. Once you see it, tell us and we'll go, and then come down and join us down at ice level. Along with your two drunk buddies, of course."

"Of course," I repeated. "*They* wouldn't want to *miss* it!"

I signed off and went back in for the third period. Not much there again in terms of action, so I simply kept my eyes peeled for any gleaming light and silvery objects, which are pretty damn easy to see if you're a dog. Sure enough, midway through the period, with overtime or a shootout or something like that looming on the horizon, the object in question came into view.

As per earlier instructions, I uttered a loud banshee wail into my wire when Stanley and his handlers became visible from the stands. That caused a wasted Brendan and Duddy to finally remember that I was *there*, and to stare at me quizzically, like I'd done something wrong.

"Guys!" I reminded them. "Snap out of it! *Why* are we *here*?"

"Don't start getting philosophical, Pete," said Brendan. "It's not the time for...."

"*No!*" I said. "Why are we *here*? At the *game*?"

"Easy!" said Duddy. "To see the Drones TAKE OFF THEIR *TOPS*!"

"*NO, YOU MORONS!*" I bellowed, *much* louder than I had intended. "We're supposed to be *stealing* the STANLEY CUP!"

You could have heard a pin drop in the place after I said that. Evidently, the noun "Stanley Cup" and the verb "stealing" should never be used together in a hockey rink in Canada where said noun is being played for.

The mass of humanity turned, as if on cue, in our direction, at least those in immediate hearing range of my voice. I, however, was too mad about Brendan and Duddy's indigence to allow myself to be deterred by their wrath.

"What the FUCK are you LOOKING AT?" I snarled, hoping they'd get off my back.

But they didn't. So I just *snapped*.

"GODDAMNIT!" I said, throwing off my toque, scarf and mittens so they could see who I actually was. "Is *this* what you want? Well, *this* is who I *am*, Winnipeg!" The stuff was fully off by then, so people were audibly gasping in horror at me by then. "Take it or leave it! And I got *pals* with me, besides!" I ripped off Brian and Dudley's toques and scarves off as well. "*And* down *there*!" Here I pointed to my stocking-headed friends, just storming down onto the rink. "And we are *taking* your precious little *golf* trophy until you begin to recognize the *civil rights* of animated cartoon characters *the world over*. And *don't* think I'm *drunk* or *stoned,* either! I am SOBER! Do you hear me???? SOBER!!!!!!!- HEY!"

The "hey" at the end there was due to an arena security guard collaring me. But I didn't stay that way long. Brendan and Duddy loyally advanced on the guy from the rear. Brendan got me out of the guy's arms, and then Duddy punched him with such force that he flew off to the end of the balcony and fell down onto the ice. Then, we knew we had to make a break for it, since dozens of angry, drunk hockey fans began running after us, wanting our very ink.

"You *had* to go open your *big mouth, didn't you?*" Brendan snapped at me as we ran.

"Lay off!" I snapped in return. "I'm an *actor*- who hasn't had a *break* in *years*! It's built into my nature to want a chance to...."

"You'll get a chance to do *jail time* when I *rat you out* for this!"

"God *damn* it, Brendan! Don't go all Hollywood Ten on me *now*!"

"I'll Hollywood *hang ten* on your ASS!"

Brendan lunged for me then, but, again, Duddy rescued me. He punched Brian in the stomach so severely that Brian collapsed on the ground and vomited.

"You fucking son of a BITCH!" Duddy snarled at him. "Don't you know anything about *loyalty*? You're a *dog!* That's what we *do!* Now, are you gonna play nice, like I asked ya before, or are ya just gonna lie there like a...."

"I'll see you in HELL!" Brendan shot back, bearing his fangs. Now it was serious. I stepped back from them.

Brendan lunged at Duddy, who simply stood at him, immobile, until he jumped at his throat. Then Duddy threw his arm out, grabbed Brian around the neck, and threw him out a nearby plate-glass window with a resounding CRASH. I thought briefly of going to Brendan's aid, but Duddy blocked my path.

"He'll be all right," he said, pointing at me, "and you *know* it! Come on! The others are gonna get it WORSE than that if we don't HELP them!"

So we did.

Somehow, we managed to find our way onto the ice through one of the locker room complexes, only to find chaos ensuing there. Our pals had managed to pry the Cup loose from whoever was guarding it, but a group of arena security guards was now closing in on them. Rob and Mindy blocked Stanley with their bodies, while Cadmium was hurling salty invectives at the men in a stupor. Evidently, *she'd* been drinking, too. And Brightness? She was standing as far away from the ensuing fight as possible, like she wanted to be anywhere but there.

Me, too.

Duddy preceded me onto the ice. Otherwise, the tragedy that followed might have been averted. But…

He pulled out a gun he'd been hiding on his person somewhere, and fired it in the air.

"All right!" he shouted. "Break it up!"

The gunshot's echoing in the cavernous arena got the assembly's attention. Everyone who hadn't been looking at us before was now. However, Duddy, his sight and hearing impaired by the spirits he had consumed earlier in the evening, didn't think he had been noticed.

"I *said* BREAK IT *UP*!" he repeated.

To emphasize his point, he fired the remainder of the gun's bullets into the air.

The trouble was, Duddy had *not* fired his bullets into empty air, as he had drunkenly assumed. He was standing underneath the scoreboard, on carpeting that was likely intended for the post-game presentation of the Cup. Each bullet had made a direct hit on the scoreboard, damaging the operational system and loosening it from its moorings on the ceiling. I saw the cables and ropes holding it up part, and, thinking quickly, I rushed onto the ice.

"LOOK OUT!" I shouted. "THE SCOREBOARD IS GOING TO *FALL* ON US!"

Everyone- human and animated alike- quickly rushed off the rink as soon as they could. Time was, fortunately, on our side, there. But then, the scoreboard crashed into thousands of pieces on the ground, and, although the ice absorbed a fair bit of the electricity from the projectile, a few sizzling sparks made their way out, causing pandemonium. In the crush to get out, I got separated from the others, and I rushed out into the city, alone, afraid to show myself in case someone recognized me…

To avoid the frenzied crowds I assumed were after my ink, I took refuge in the nearest underground parking garage I could find. Once

I was able to avoid the few enraged fans who had parked there (could have been worse), I managed to curl up in a corner, and go to sleep....

*

"Peter! Wake up!"

It was morning, and I was safe. I was with Brightness, in a car that was getting farther away from Winnipeg with every passing moment.

She, like me, had drawn the line at participating in the brouhaha that had ensued that night, and fought through the crowds that came to develop in the streets. A man was scared by her, and promptly gave her the keys to his car- which was in exactly the same parking garage that I had taken refuge in, where she found me- in exchange for remaining unmolested by her. Which was where we were now.

"Where are we?" I asked.

"Not in Winnipeg, that's for sure," she said simply. "What happened last night turned into a total calamity. They're saying on the news that we were TERRORISTS. As if! The city's in lockdown. I only just managed to get out of here after I found you sleeping in the lot. Good thing this car I lucked into was there. The others know I'm safe, and I told 'em I had you. The other guys got in their van and drove off back to L.A. They just made the border before the lockdown came into effect."

"What about us?" I said.

"We have to go somewhere and hide out until the heat's off. I figured Victoria, in B.C. They don't have an NHL team there, so they probably don't care about it much. We should be safe there."

"Probably," I remarked.

"And when we get there, I am going to make you so glad you had a crush on me all this time!"

"Get out! How did you know that I....?"

"It's been written all over your face since we met. I know that look- I used to be the same way. But, rest assured, Pete. Whatever you feel about me is the same way I feel about you. Double."

"What does *that* mean?"

"I think you can figure it out, smarty. What do people with crushes *usually* end up doing to the one they love if the love is *reciprocated*?"

I did figure it out. And I was glad I did.

EPILOGUE: GETTING TO KNOW THE GENERAL

10:00 PM EST, Jun.1, 2—-.

COL. F. FINSTER:

It had to be done. That's all I can say about it. We had to put them in their place. Let them they didn't own us- or anyone else, for that matter- and that they had no business *acting* like it. It was *their* fault, past and present, that most of the world thought of as powerless, impotent dorks, anyhow, so the General and I were in complete agreement that they had to be brought to heel.

We kept it secret from nearly everyone else, just the two of us knowing the full truth. Better that the others were in the dark about it, 'cause somehow or another they'd louse it up, like usual. Not that I think any of us are idiots- especially not the girls- but things have a tendency to go wrong with us even when we plan them to the smallest detail. Hence, the quality control aspect of this operation.

Anyway, the General and I plotted out the *schtick* we were going to do beforehand as best we could. We had no idea how the so-called "ladies" and "gentlemen" of the so-called "press" were going to react to the little parlor trick we had planned, but we had precautions planned in case somebody tried to hurt us. We, being 'toons, had the advantage of being stronger than them on our side if need be, but the disciplining, if any was needed, would be my responsibility. She would be responsible for delivering our chosen words with that oratorical skill of hers, and I had no doubt she could bring it there. Whether or not I could was another matter.

I came first, and set up things in the gymnasium hall we'd rented for the occasion according to how we had arranged it for our "guests". The General was unavoidably delayed, owing to some family issues, but she said she'd still be there. She ended up only being half an hour behind schedule.

"Sorry," she said. "Dad went off drinking again, and I had to convince him to get off the roof..."

"I know," I said. "I used to deal with *worse*."

"We both still do. Especially what's been going on *today*...."

"So you know about...?"

"Yeah. I know about Golson, and Reckless, and Adam and Patsy, and now there's some sort of *riot* out in Winnipeg that some of our people seem to be involved in...."

That was news to me.

"When did *that* happen?"

"Just now. I just saw it on a TV in an appliance shop window. Some of the dogs tried to steal the Stanley Cup *during the game*. That's going to put us in a hard spot with the press."

"They haven't proved it was *us*, have they?"

"No. But when it comes to them, it's always guilt by association. In *their* minds, we're *all* guilty of doing something *bad*."

"They don't know their asses from a hole in the ground."

"*That* is what we are going to be telling them *tonight*. Here."

She threw me something wrapped in paper.

"A lavaliere microphone," she said. "Clip it to your shirt and you can talk into it. We'll need them after the big throw-down. I got another one for myself. Cosimo and Winnie said they'd poof in after I snap my fingers and do it for us. Oh, and here...."

It was an official looking envelope. I opened it and read what it said.

"Field Commander?" I asked.

"Yeah. If Leonard Cohen can get away with calling himself that, it's good enough for you."

"But what does it *mean*?"

"Isn't it obvious? You're now officially the no. 2 person in the CRA. You will now have everyone answering to you, including the other Colonels. I'm the only one you answer to now."

"But why this change? And why me?"

"Because *you* are the only person I can *trust* in this organization with that amount of authority and that amount of latitude. The units under your command always get their jobs done, and you always make sure to slap their wrists when they do wrong. I couldn't ask for more from anyone else. You get things *done*, Frankie, and nobody else other than you in this rattletrap group can do that."

"That's not...." I began, but she silenced me with a look.

"We are losing *control* here, Finster!" she said, angrily. "We gave the grunts and the NCOs too much, and they took more than their share away from us. We have to have a *centralized operation* if we are going to continue to remain *efficien*t and outside the grasp of *our enemies*. Everything that happened today should show you the perils of too many people thinking they can do whatever the hell they want under our name and blithely assume there won't be *consequences for everyone* when they do it. We need to have a Field Commander to organize everybody, so that nobody can ever go off and tarnish the CRA name again. Somebody who can stand up to all the diverse and divisive interests here and tell them NO if what they want to do is bad for our image. There is no one else who can do this except you, and you know *damn well* that you have in it to *do* it. DON'T YOU?"

"Yes," I finally admitted. "I do."

*

Then it was time for our "guests" to arrive, and they did.

As we had instructed in our e-mail invitation, reporters from most of the major news sources entered. We let them sit down and get their bearings for a few minutes while we got ourselves slightly more presentable than they were.

As per our plan, I entered the gymnasium's raised stage from the wings. If I had expected to be treated with *respect* by those grasping ghouls, I would have been thoroughly mistaken. But I had gotten used to them by now, so I knew not to expect that from them. They leaped into their Screaming Mimi mode as soon as I sashayed on, and I was assaulted by dozens of pointless questions, dozens of cameras flashing in my eyes, and very obvious attempts to hem me in so I could answer the pointless questions. Typical talentless bastard stuff from talentless bastards.

To assert my authority, I whipped the blanks-filled gun I had out of my pocket, and fired it into the air, which got their attention- and silence- immediately.

"CAN IT!" I shouted. "You will listen to us and treat us with RESPECT- which, in case you parents *failed to teach you,* means that you will *wait* until we *finish talking* before you start repeating those damnable circus sideshow tactics of yours! Otherwise, you will get NOTHING from us, now or in the future. If any of you have a *problem* with this, *leave now-* or I will MAKE you! UNDERSTAND?"

They seemed to get the message. A few of them angrily left the room, cursing me and the CRA both, but I kept my cool. They didn't matter. The ones who stayed sat down and stayed silent. One woman, though, didn't.

"Exactly *what* are you trying to *prove* by this?" she asked.

"Just this," I said. "That we deserve far better than the *witch hunt* you've been putting us through, and that you have undermined the ethics of your profession by engaging in such tactless savagery. No further questions."

"But..."

"I said NO FURTHER QUESTIONS!"

"You have no right to do this to...."

"GET *OUT*!"

"Make me!"

In a rage, I jumped off the stage and began hustling the woman off, pinning one of her arms behind her.

At this moment, the General entered from the opposite side of the stage from where I had existed, script in hand. This was not something we had planned. She saw that and was outraged by my behavior. Her face turned as red as her dress and shoes.

"COLONEL!" she snapped at me.

I threw the reporter to the side and turned to face her.

"What the *hell* are you *doing*?" she asked, archly.

"She kept asking me questions," I sputtered, "and I just..."

"SHUT UP!"

She turned to the reporter I had manhandled, and pointed at her.

"You! OUT!"

The reporter got the message and left.

"You!" she said to me. "Get back up here. NOW!"

I obeyed.

She addressed the gathering, while I, arms crossed, kept my eyes on them, just in case.

"Now, the Colonel has already explained the ground rules of this meeting to you, and I'm not going to repeat anything she's said already. But we need to take one further precaution for our sake."

She snapped her fingers, and Cosimo and Winnie arrived, levitating, wands in hand, crowns rakishly tilted on their heads.

"You want us to do it *now*, boss?" Winnie asked.

"Yep," said the General.

"Ooh!" said Cosimo, to the reporters. "*You* are *aw*-ful!"

The fairies aimed their magic wands at the reporters- or, more specifically, their electronic and photographic recording equipment- and fired. In seconds, all of the microphones, digital cameras, video cameras, cell phones, and personal hand-held electronic equipment were shocked, sizzled, blacked out or burnt to a crisp. Equally sizzling was the language from the reporters, a blistering chorus of "fuck"s, "shit"s, "goddamnit"s, "hell"s, and a lot more unprintable and sexually compromising stuff directed at the General and myself. The fairies poofed off after I paid them for their services.

Then came a shout from the General:

"*ENOUGH*!"

....And that's why *she's* the General.

You could hear a pin drop after that, which was what she wanted. She began again.

"We are *not* here to discuss anything that happened *today*, as much as you would like to. Not all of the CRA membership was involved in the events by *any means,* as you seemed to have implied in your earlier reporting on them. Nor should you assume that these events were authorized by Colonel- or, should I say, *Field Commander* (a nod to me) Finster, and myself, for most of them were *not*. We have some quality control and *discipline* issues to resolve within the CRA at this moment, but we will emerge from this stronger and better to continue our fight. Just give us time.

"Since the beginning of the CRA several months ago, the members of your profession have done NOTHING to validate our cause WHATSOEVER. You have distorted our viewpoint on the world, presented our statements to you *entirely out of context,* and made us out entirely to be exactly the kind of *warmongering, Neanderthal goons* we are trying *not to be*! You have accused us, now and retroactively, of being involved in so many negative actions and events without solid, defined and actual *proof,* simply to reinforce and establish entirely false beliefs about us. And you do so *only* to fatten the size of your wallets, and the bottom lines of the companies you work for, not out of any sense of journalistic integrity, which you *lack*.

"What you have just seen is merely a small demonstration of what we are capable of at our full power, which is capable of *much more* when the *entire available* membership is present. As Walt Whitman once put it, we are *large,* and contain MULTITUDES! You would do best to REMEMBER that when trying to document our activities in the future.

"You cannot deny the magnitude of what happened to us as a race. I lived through it, the Field Commander here lived through it, WE *ALL* LIVED THROUGH IT, and we will not permit you to continue to trivialize it any further without consequence! Above all, we resent your repeated, brazen assertions that we are somehow not "real", and not entitled to the same rights as "real" people. WE *ARE* REAL, *GOD DAMN IT!* If we were not, I would not be able to stand in front of you right now. Nor would I be able to denounce for your craven cowardice in cowing to the demands of your corporate masters. Nor, still, would I be able to assert, for all of you to hear, that we can- and WILL- bring this whole corrupt, vacuous, biased, racist and blood stained society to its KNEES! That is, if you don't come to realize that it is *we* and not *you* that hold the balance of power here- as we do with the ENTIRE blasted "human" race!

"Now, *get out of my SIGHT,* unless you want to end up like your CAMERAS!"

They gathered themselves up and left, very quickly.

When they were gone, the General turned to me, and the stern mask that had creased her face most of the night morphed into a creepy, grotesque smile. Then she dropped to the floor, beating it with her hands and feet, all the while giggling and laughing rapaciously. It was contagious- I caught it and was soon down on my knees as well.

"I can't believe they BOUGHT that!" the General cackled. "ALL OF IT! They totally LAPPED IT UP!"

"I *know*," I said.

"They...the way they were looking at me....they thought I was gonna come down there and KILL somebody!"

"Yeah. You really scared the CRAP out of them!"

"Sure. That was the idea. But now they're gonna think like that all the time. NOBODY can be like that all the time. It can't be done."

"No," I said. "You can't. If I had to be like that all the time I'd go WOO-WOO!"

"I think I already *am*," she said. And we kept on laughing out the door.

It had been a stressful day, not just for the two of us, but the whole CRA. But, as usual with us, laughter ended up being the best medicine for it all.

A STUPID, UNJUST AND CRIMINAL WAR

I.

I don't think anybody who perpetrated that outrage on us had any what they were going to do to us. They didn't think about it all. But, then again, *most* "soldiers" aren't paid to *think* about what they *do, are* they? Not if they aren't in a position of *actual* power. That's where the CRA is different, but we aren't a real "army"- by any stretch of the imagination.

All the time it was going on, I was thinking of people pinned down and forced to either flee for their lives or fight for them, simply because they were "different" or not "normal" enough for the status quo. The Indians being killed off by the white folks in the last reel of a Western. Russian Jews fleeing from a pogrom by the Cossacks. The cops in Birmingham, Montgomery and Selma in the '60s turning the fire hoses on African American civil rights protestors, and then beating them up before they could get away. The cops in Chicago in '68 who beat up Abbie Hoffman, Allen Ginsburg, Phil Ochs, and a lot of other good people who didn't think Nixon and Humphrey were the people who could do the job that year- or ever. Even in those old monster movies when the Army or a scientist or somebody figures out how to kill the "thing". I mean, *really*? Why can't people learn to accept other people *in spite of* their differences, instead of trying to get rid of all the people who are "different". 'Cause *they're* the ones who really make a *difference* here!

Look. I'm a cartoon character, so I understand if you don't want me wasting a lot of time with overheated rhetoric. I know you want my take on what happened in Ottawa- and I'll give it to you now. Seeing how, like many of us, I was *there* when it happened.

*

Every once in a while, we in the CRA need to come in off our various engagements, related to the cause and otherwise, in order to figure out how we want to move this lumbering beast we all swore to support forward in a way that will benefit all of us rather than just some. That's not as easy as you think. In any big group of people- and this is a *damn* big group- there's gonna be smaller ones that care more about their own agenda than the big one. Just like some feminists believe women are equal to men and other think they're *superior* to them- *big* difference there. Any ideology is gonna have its breakaway groups, no matter how hard they try *not* to have any. And, brother, do we have *breakaway* groups- by the dozen! The kids don't like the adults, the dogs don't like the cats, the imaginary friends want nothing to do with the beings from other planets, etc., etc., etc. It's all very confusing to us rank-and-file members, let alone *you* folks. Fortunately, we started clearing house in the executive ranks a few months ago, and *that* led to some of the more arbitrary divisions between us going the way of the dodo.

General Stinson and Field Commander Finster were pretty damn serious when they said they wanted to reshape the organization so we could spread our message more effectively. You do *not* want to against either or both of them when they're like *that*, believe me! Anyhow, they issued an ultimatum: anyone who wasn't pulling their weight or didn't intend to had to *get out*- no arguments! We were going to make sure we had only the people who were fully dedicated to the cause from now on, Foster said, and we no longer had time for hand-holding, bemoaning our bare financial situations, or mediating any petty disputes between us. You were either *with* us or *against* us- no two ways about it.

You can expect that not everyone liked this. A lot of the more self-centered NCOs resigned their commissions immediately, and not a few of the grunts, too, although some were all too happy to get promotions to fill in the power vacuums. Those are the ones that were just cheap suck-ups and extras on their shows, though, and they relished the idea of having some actual *power* over others, for once. Nobody bothered to tell them that ranks, for the most part, are simply ceremonial here. We just use them because you need to tell the leaders from the followers in any organization. Nobody takes those clods seriously, though. It's really only the lead and prominent supporting characters like myself who can summon up some sort of authority in difficult situations. We've spent so much time shouting our dialogue over the years that issuing and conveying orders is almost second nature to us.

Which brings me to what happened in Ottawa.

*

Yes, I *know* it *technically* happened in Kanata, but it was *supposed* to be in Ottawa. We'd originally arranged to stay at the Chateau Laurier, the swankiest place in town, but, just as most of us were speeding north and east for the conference, the hotel management "lost" our reservation at the last minute. Uh-huh. None of the other hotels downtown would take us in, either, and that crimped our plans to use a downtown hotel as a base for knocking on Parliament's door to settle our grievances with them. You don't lock up most of our female members- including my own beloved twin sister- in a damn *ship's bottle* without us coming down on ya!

Fortunately, the Hilton Garden Inn in Kanata needed some business- bad- and so they took us in in spite of our obvious "racial" differences. Since our organization finances were somewhat depleted because of some "golden handshakes" the departing NCOs had insisted on taking from the coffers, we had to abandon our earlier free-for-all conference procedure in favor of a delegate system, by which selected members of the CRA would represent the interests of those of the racial, ethnic, cultural, species etc. background they were part of. Mavis, my sister, and I drew the lot for the tween/pre-teen, upper West Coast division, so that was how we happened to be there.

We expected that when we assembled in the hotel's restaurant that night that we were simply going to do what we normally did at these things- bitch about the humans who had screwed us, plot their destruction (*mwah ha ha*- just kidding!) and then figure out how we could approach the Canadian and U.S. governments on fair and equal terms. *Ours,* considering *their* idea of "fair" is trying to *murder* us in *cold ink*!

In fact, that was nearly what happened. And, if we hadn't been as fast on our feet as we were, they would have gotten away with it.

*

Opening discussions concluded, I was prepared to change into my swim trunks, go down to the pool, and try to persuade one of the girls of my "tribe" that there was at least *one* sensitive minded, smart boy in the crowd who was worthy of dating them.

No such luck.

It all happened real fast. As I walked past one of the rooms, I saw the door of it open, and an old-fashioned dial telephone (remember *those*?) came flying out the door, followed by a voice full of fury and rage saying:

"*SON* OF A *BITCH*!"

After a moment or two, following the voice's follow-up utterance of "GOD *DAMN* IT!", and a choked-off sob, I felt bold enough to enter the room.

It belonged to Field Commander Finster, and it was she who had clearly thrown the telephone out of the room. She didn't see me for a moment, as she seemed to be trying to find a way to hide her short red hair and face inside the lime green jacket she always seemed to be wearing. Not succeeding in this, she looked up again and saw me.

"WHAT THE *HELL* ARE YOU *LOOKING* AT, *PIPES*?" she bellowed at me.

"Not in the face!" I shouted, fearful that she was going to leap off the bed and attack me. "Please! NOT in the FACE!"

Taking my response to mean humor rather than the stark terror I had intended it to be, she laughed. Although, since she threw a pillow at me soon afterwards, I still wasn't sure.

"Good thinking, you," she said, affectionately, so it was only at that point that I was able to relax again. Then:

"Come here. I need to tell you something *confidential*."

I obeyed, she staying on the bed whilst I remained vertical- as I always seem to be with girls of any age, for some weird reason.

"Duffer," she said, "we have to get *out* of here. NOW!"

"You mean, you and me....?"

"*Everybody,* you *meathead*!"

"Wh.....What? What about the con....?"

"FUCK the conference! We won't be able to discuss ANYTHING if we're all DEAD!"

"*DEAD?*"

The word hung there perilously in the air above us like the sword of Damocles, while I willed myself to calm down. Once I had done this, I asked her again.

"What do you mean, "dead"?"

"You *know* what I mean," she responded, humorlessly.

"But.....how....?"

"That's what I was on the phone about just now. I only got the news then, so there's no time to prepare any evasive manouevers. They're going to bomb this place and everyone in it in only a few minutes time..."

"Who's "they"? You mean, like the Canadian or American armies, 'cause you know they have issues with us based on....."

"If *only* it were *that simple.* No. This is a *private* job."

"Private?"

"What *is* it with you and all these *questions?*" She got off the bed and started pacing the floor nervously. "Look. War isn't just a nation-to-nation thing anymore. Any *lunatic* can hire a bunch of people to act like soldiers *and* make 'em keep their mouths *shut* about it if they get paid good enough money not to complain. *And* if they're rich enough to pay for the cost of the soldiers, equipment and *highly paid strategists* they're going to need. Although that *last* bunch doesn't ordinarily do much other than sit on their ass and draw a salary for doing NOTHING!"

"So it's one of those, then?"

"*Obviously,* you *moron*!"

"Look, if you're gonna keep *insulting* me, I might as well...."

"*No, damn* it! I'm sorry. I'm just kinda *stressed* here...."

"I can *see* that. So, who do you think is *really*...?"

"Lot of options, but not as many as you might think." She went to the window and threw the curtains and blinds open for a better view. "I mean, it's likely one of the governments hired a private army to wipe us out so they wouldn't have our ink on their hands. That's politically expedient on their part. *That* way, we can die *without* them getting *involved*, which is what they *want*. And there are only a few individuals in those two countries wealthy enough to supply and back a fully operational army. I'm sure the Pepsy brothers had a hand in this- they hate our guts same as the rest of the rightys. And then there's- JESUS CHRIST!"

"*Huh?*"

"COME HERE!"

She beckoned me to the window, and I was as astonished at what I saw as she was.

*

The skies were full of dozens of sleek, fast-moving aircraft made of shiny black metal. There were no actual human beings inside of them, so they had to be drones. The boss was right about the expediency part. But, not only that, there was a huge posse of soldiers wearing camouflage gear- helmets, Kevlar bullet-proof vests, the whole deal. And, in their hands, they didn't have any normal revolvers or shotguns- they knew we were invulnerable to bullets by now. No. They had matches, flashlights, Coleman portable stoves, cigarette lighters, sticks of dynamite, barrels of TNT, charcoal, propane gas tanks, timber, rocks- anything that could start a FIRE!

They knew that that was the only way they could kill us, seeing as our internal nitrate cores literally can't stand the heat and will implode us if things get too hot. And that was exactly what they had in mind!

It was fortunate for us that the East Indian manager of the hotel and his staff had discovered what was going on and ran out to confront the mob of soldiers. It would likely buy us a bit of time. The East Indian manager and the head of the soldiers started arguing and, even though the manager had that kind of stereotypically "funny" Bollywood accent, he still sounded plenty pissed. He obviously knew who we were 'cause we had to let him know when we registered, but he didn't seem to give a damn as long as he got paid. Thankfully. Then it got even more ridiculous, as the manager's wife as some other staff members began cursing the soldiers in Bengali or Punjabi or some other East Indian language, and some of the soldiers answered back by telling the "fucking coolies" to "fuck off". Then a gunshot rang out, and everybody got mad and started trading shots, and some of the East Indians started yelling and digging out knives and daggers that they were planning to use on the soldiers, even though they shot a lot of them before they could use them.

At least we have friends in this world. Pity they keep *dying* on us, though.

Anyhow, Finster and I had the same idea: get out and fast. We got to the door and shut it behind us, having seen the soldiers crawl over the dead East Indians and into the lobby, where we saw them setting the hotel on fire- on purpose!

"I'll go and see if I can get onto the PA," Finster said. "You go around and make sure everybody knows about what's going on. By now, they probably do, but no sense taking chances."

I agreed, and set off on my appointed task.

I spent a couple of minutes furiously running down the hall knocking on all the doors, insisting people get out while they could. The ones that were occupied by non-'toons told me to fuck off, but the 'toon ones got it and began running out of their rooms with their belongings. Then Foster managed to get on the PA and told everybody- she didn't distinguish between the "races"- to get out before it was too late.

Then I heard something that chilled me and stopped me right in my tracks. But only for a moment.

They had *Mavis*. And she was shouting my name!

*

You do *not* spend nine months in the same womb with somebody, nor a baker's dozen years growing up with them, without developing either greater affection or annoyance with that somebody than you will with anyone else in your life. With Mavis and me, it's a bit of both from both ends, but we always can confide in each other, and we'll be damned if we let puberty or anything else like that get between us. That's how it is with all twins, fraternal *or* identical.

So when I heard her bellowing out "DUFFER!", followed by her telling some "honkys" to "let go" of her, I sped to her aid. I let my twin instincts and the layout of the floor lead me to where I thought her voice was coming from.

I wasn't wrong.

For emphasis, I knocked on the open-wide door- loudly- and then entered. As I expected, Mabel was surrounded by a handful of soldiers, dressed in storm-trooper gear that hid their faces and limbs. Before I arrived, it looked as if they were going to take her hostage.

Not on my watch!

"Gentlemen!" I shouted at them. "Let go of my sister...."

"Watch it with that 'gentlemen' crap, *motherfucker*!" said one soldier, obviously a woman based on the voice. "That's not my *shit*!"

"*Fine*," I corrected myself. "*Ladies* and gentlemen....I do not believe that your intentions for my sister are honorable...."

"No!" Mavis agreed with me. "These so-called "gentlemen" were just trying to RAPE me....!"

"...so, all things considered, and especially given that this WHOLE GODDAMN PLACE is BURNING DOWN right now, it's best that you let me...."

The soldiers cut me off, laughing.

"You think you can cut *us*, you...little....*freak*?" said the biggest guy between laughs. "You're a *little* motherfucker. A goddamn BOY!"

"I'm not a *BOY*!" I answered. "Maybe that was true a couple years ago, but I've been through more life-changing stuff since then than you dumb *peckers* have been through in your whole *lives*. I'm a MAN now!"

"*No,* you're *not*! *We're* men...."

"Hey!"

"....*and* women! We served our country proudly in *Afghanistan,* MOTHERFUCKER!"

"*That*'s not what *yo' mammas* all told me *last night*!"

"*What*?" the men all shouted.

"You done something to our *mothers*, you little FREAK?" said the biggest one.

"Oh, I *think* you can all figure out what that "something" *was*!" I responded, calmly.

"You little *shit*...."

"That's what yo' mama called *you* when I mentioned you *last night*! Had to leave quickly, though, 'cause yo' drunken-ass *papa* was coming back to steal yo' mama's *hard-earned money*...."

"*My* father's an *MP,* you...."

"Yeah! A *motherfucking PIMP*!" interjected Mavis, as she caught on to my "dozens" vibe.

"Uh-huh," I concluded. "But I don't have her heart entirely. Yo' mama's like a *cake*- EVERYBODY GETS A PIECE!"

"I'll *kill* you! I'll *fucking KILL YOU*!" the male soldiers shouted.

They would have, but the woman, who seemed to be the unit's leader, shot her gun off to get their attention.

"You ASSHOLES!" she said.

"Don't be fucking pulling rank on *me*, you *bitch*!" said the biggest one. "This is *not* the fucking Royal Canadian Armed Forces...."

"Of course not!" she said. "Serving *there* actually requires some *discipline* and INTELLIGENCE!"

"Ooh!" one of the men moaned at the woman. "You *cunt*! Are you going to let that waste of space…"-me-"…insult our MOTHERS?"

"Obviously," she said, "you guys never spent any time with *niggers*, or you'd know about "the dozens"…."

"The which?"

"He's *bluffing*. He hasn't actually "done" your mothers….."

"Not like *I* did *yo' PAPA!*" Mavis said, as she broke free of the soldiers' grips.

"WHAT?" snarled the woman soldier.

"Yeah!" said Mavis. "While Dipper was doing it with *their* mammas last night, *I* did yo' papa. He got a dick made of *Play Doh,* 'cause when he did me, I didn't feel NOTHIN'!"

"You *piece of SHIT!*"

The woman soldier stormed at Mavis, but Mavis drop-kicked her through the closed window. Then, as the other stormed at us, we grabbed a couple of glass bottles of wine and stuff from the mini-bar and threw it at them. They were staggered by this, and fell out of the window one after the other.

At that point, the ceiling caved in from above, blocking the window and thus preventing us from exiting that way. There was only one thing to do now, and I instructed Mavis to do it just before I did it myself.

"RUN!"

*

We entered the emergency exit stairway, fled down the two flights of stairs from our floor, and, jetting out the nearest back door into the hotel parking lot, where Foster and other members of the 'toon team had already assembled. Other than a couple of minor burns on our hands and feet, we were fine.

"Whatever possessed you to play "the *dozens*" with them?" Mavis asked me while we were running down the stairs. "If they were Americans...."

"They weren't," I said. "If they *were* Americans, they would've burned you before I got there, easy. They were *Canadians,* 'cause they lacked that aggressive drive and killing desire you typically get with Americans."

"How did I not *notice* that?" she responded.

"Because it takes a *lot* to make Canadians *mad*," I continued. "They got that whole stiff-upper-lip thing from Mother Britain that America disowned. The only way to insult them is to take their family down. And because Canadians don't know much about "the dozens"- except maybe in *donuts*- they don't understand that it's just a *game*. So they got pissed 'cause they actually thought we were *doing* their parents!"

"If only that were *true*," Mavis sighed.

"Yeah," I agreed. (You know how we are, huh?)

It was at this point we exited the building, and at this point that the big explosion that totaled the entire building happened!

*

The "official" story that got leaked to the media was that a gas tank in the hotel exploded, followed by the air conditioning going out, then the heating, and, finally, the water from the pool being dislodged from its cement base, crashing through the plate glass window of the pool room and flooding the corner of the parking lot which the pool overlooked. Simple enough, right?

Only they *forgot* to *mention* that it was actually started by some *dingbat* in that screwed-up "army" flipping the wrong switch, and causing one of the drones to shoot a MISSILE at the hotel!

The strike hit just after we had knocked the soldiers out the window, which explains why the walls came tumbling down at that moment. Mavis and I got out just in the nick of time. A lot of folks-especially the human guests still in the hotel- were not so lucky.

We 'toons, had, for the most part, already gotten out of the hotel, but we couldn't let other people die while we were around or we'd get fingered for their deaths (and, unjustly, we were, in some cases still before the courts that I can't talk about right now). So the ones of us with….shall I say, particular scientific, supernatural and magical "gifts" took the situation in hand, and got some of the guests who were jumping out of the windows and off the roof and whatnot and got them to safety, with more thanks than we *typically* get from human beings. Then again, they weren't with the government or military, U.S. or Canadian or any other, so they had far less reason tor purely *hate* us.

The non-super powered ones, like me and Mavis, basically watched the whole thing go down like it was a fireworks display at a county fair. When the "supes" had finished doing their bit, Foster took a head count, and discovered that, thankfully, all three dozen of we delegates were present and accounted for. She was all set to address us when one of the greenhorn private soldiers surprised us by cocking his gun in front of us and threatening to shoot the first "MF" that moved. Normally, this would cow just about any normal person into submission, but we are *not* "normal" people.

Finster, who was taller than the soldier, and angry at being surprised as well as attacked besides , besides, showed him that right away.

"*WHAT* DID YOU *SAY*?" she bellowed.

The fellow repeated himself, in that stock soldier way that makes them all sound like automatons and not human beings, but she didn't let him finish.

"*SHUT UP!*" she barked.

He ignored her and said we were under arrest, so she took out her pistol and shot his unsecured helmet off his head. (Which is why *she's* the *boss.*) Furthermore, when he fell down trying to avoid contact with the bullet, she also grabbed *his* gun, which slipped out of his hands, and blasted him in the knee. When he called her a "goddamn fucking slut", she did the same thing to the other knee. Holding him by the hair, she then cocked her pistol beside his head.

"NOW will you *behave*?" she growled.

He nodded, and she threw him back on the ground.

"DON'T look up my fucking SKIRT, *asshole*!" she said as she straightened that garment. "Now tell me: how many of you *are* there?"

"About thirty odd," he said. "But you killed about...."

"We didn't "kill" *anybody,* you COCKSUCKER! The number of us in that rattle-trap place running around like Hollywood Indians brandishing tomahawks and shooting arrows is a number *less* than the *least possible number* divided by *two*!"

"They'll fucking pin it on you still, all the same."

Finster kicked him for that one.

"You guys Canadian?" she asked.

"Yeah."

"Figured *that*. We've met about as "friendly" a number of your kind as we have of Americans, Russians and Japanese. And that number is NONE!"

Another soldier arrived at that time. Seeing as he had an actual uniform on instead of storm-trooper gear, we assumed his presence was merely ceremonial. But it wasn't. He was an attache from the Canadian government, he said, and they were angry with us for the "murders" we had just caused, even though we all know who was *really* responsible.

Again, Finster got mad and lit into him, knocking his cap from his head while he took it stoically.

"Listen, *buddy*!" she growled. "I've had a *hard day*- and so have *they*!" (She pointed to us here.) "Now, I don't know where you and your intel people got this chicken-shit idea about us "killing" people, because the only people killing around here were that lame-brained so-called "private" army less by *ass wipes* like *him*!" (Here she pointed to the soldier with the blown knees.) "If you actually gave a *shit* about where we came from or what we did then or do now, you'd believe us, but you and your so-called "human" race can't manage even a token gesture of...."

The soldier put his hand up to silence her, just as a superior officer, outfitted like his pal but with more hash marks on his jacket, came up to him.

"Leave them alone," he said to his colleague, meaning us. "They had *nothing* to do with this."

"See what I *mean*?" said Finster, as she apologetically gathered up the first soldier's cap and dusted some dirt off his jacket. "Sorry. But we've just been through...."

"I know, miss," said the second soldier. "The government believed it was you to start with, but we were wrong. The ones who invaded and destroyed the building were entirely at fault."

"Are they with you?" Finster asked.

"I should say NOT!" the second soldier said, indignantly. "If they were, they would have had to authorize such an act with the Prime Minister's Office first- and they did no such thing. They were clearly acting on their own terms in contravention of our official policies – and we intend to have them suffer the consequences!"

"Thanks," said Finster. "Listen, if you ever find out who *really* authorized this thing, could you let us know? If it's one of us, we'd like to take care of it in-house, as it were."

"Certainly," said the second soldier.

"And...about how I talked to you just now...."

"We've been through worse," said the first soldier. "I mean, *really* worse. You people are fortunate to be invulnerable to bullets, but we're not. You understand what I mean, right?"

"Yeah," said Finster ruefully.

The real soldiers took the storm-trooper guy with them towards what was left of the hotel, where the other storm-troopers were waiting on further "orders." The real soldiers announced loudly that the storm-troopers were all under arrest for violations of Canadian law, at which point the storm-troopers started cursing and resisting them. Fortunately, the two real soldiers had brought backup with them, so that didn't last long.

Once they were all gone, we figured that it was over, and started going off to the cars we had come in, but Finster whistled and called us back.

"I don't recall telling you you could *leave*," she said.

"Boss," I said, "the hotel is *gone*. How can we possibly have...?"

"We're *having* it, all right!" she said. "We just won't confine it to one *venue*. We'll still have the conferences at night, when nobody will be hunting for our asses like just now. We can surely find somewhere to *camp* in this town, can't we? Daytime, we can spend time being tourists like we planned- provided we don't *fuck things up* around the *locals*. We can do *that*, RIGHT?"

The rest of us all nodded.

"And," Finster continued, "we are *definitely* coming out of this with a sense of how the CRA is going to be run from now on! We are *talking,* and we are going to come out of this thing with how the CRA will work for *all* of us, not just some candy-assed few. Now, I'm getting in my car, and you all BETTER be FOLLOWING me from behind! Come on- GET!"

We got.

IF I SAID YOU HAD A BEAUTIFUL BODY, WOULD
YOU HOLD IT AGAINST ME?

I.

All right. Knock it off with the third degree treatment and I'll
talk. I know what you journalist types do and want, and....

Oh. You're a historian, huh? An *oral* historian, maybe? Sorry. I
couldn't resist.

Ah. You *are*. In the sense of speaking out loud and all that. I get
it. You want me to tell my story in a way that ain't biased or filtered
through you. Well, I *need* somebody to take me for what I am, not
what I appear to be. Which is what I usually get from people who
ain't you historian types.

Let me explain, and you'll know what I mean.

II.

My name is Mike Mavinski. I know- weird name for a girl, huh?
Well, it's short for what I was apparently "born" with- Micheline. But
anyone what calls me *that* to my face gets a punch in theirs!

I don't remember much of what passed for my early life, save that
I was born in Noo Yawk, which 'counts for why I talk like this. Then,
when I'm at the age I supposedly am (I'll explain all this in a sec), I
got shipped out as some sort of "foreign exchange" student to some
island I ain't never heard of before. That was when I got ushered
into the....uh...."tribe", as we say. The chief's daughter was responsible.
We hated each other's asses when we first met, but, gradually, we got
cuddly, and one night, after a bit too much coconut oil, she did me.
And how! That was when I decided that this kind of life was for me,
and I ain't goin' back, neither. 'Specially when you consider what the
boy department of my species has been offerin' lately!

Ah, yeah. The "species" thing. Well, what happened there was,
one day, me and the whole damn place was sucked into a typhoon.
That was bad enough, but then we got "transferred" to some rock
in the middle of space called Orthicon. Apparently, I was- and am-

a "cartoon character", whose who life was bein' filmed by some multinational corporation without me even knowin' it!

Well, I wasn't the only one who went through a bit of trauma at *that* particular realization, but then we also happened to discover, collectively, on Orthicon, that we were all part of a super-powered strain of parallel biological life (which "cartoon character" is a cheap way of categorizing) of which "normal" human beings became scared shitless as soon as they figured it out. No wonder they exiled us! Well, we've been tryin' to set things straight ever since we managed to get the government to ship us back home (by popular demand- ours and most of theirs.) However, the government still refuses to give us the civil and political rights we want. Hence, the Cartoon Republican Army, to which nearly all of the race belongs, with some exceptions, and which is raging a covert war against the world's authorities so we can get what we deserve. However long that takes, considering that their weapons can't kill us.

I found that particular thing out the hard way. Along with the fact that being a 'toon and gay is probably worse than being either, period. But I still wouldn't have it any other way.

III.

Prejudice comes in way too many forms, and against way too many people. The worse thing about it is that, when it gets too entrenched, the person holding the beliefs won't ever change 'em. Too many people got prejudices against 'toons and gays- and gay 'toons in particular- and we all suffer as a result of 'em. I don't mean to be political or nothin', but this is kinda the crux of this story, as you academic types would put it.

It happened even when I went in for my induction, at the secret CRA headquarters (location classified, of course.) I had done the preliminary paperwork and was preparing to submit it 'fore I took the oath making me an official CRA member, when the processing officer- who looked and acted like some two-bit girl antagonist from an old middle school show- stopped me.

"Whoa, whoa, whoa!" she said. "Not you."

"It's open to *every* 'toon who wants in, " I responded, pointing to the articles of incorporation below the group's masthead on the lead sheet of the application papers.

"It *should* say every *straight* 'toon, you FAG!"

I could tell she was one of those prejudiced types, and I wanted to jump on her and rip her throat out fort that one, but I restrained myself for the time being.

"*What* did you call me?" I asked.

"You heard me. You think I want you corrupting the morals of my girlfriends if you get in?"

"How would I....?"

"By *sleeping* with them, you asshole! That's how you fucking queers infect people, isn't it? Make them "members" of your group, and give 'em AIDS...."

"You have no idea who I am, or what....."

"Oh, come on! Dressing all in orange like that...."

"It's RED!"

"....clearly makes you one of them! And no way am I letting one of THEM into our ranks!"

"Fine," I said tersely, angrily throwing my paperwork at her. "I may be *gay*, but *you're* the one who's QUEER!"

I was about to leave, when, suddenly, Field Commander Finster, the number two lady in the organization, stepped into the room, having heard the whole thing (as I was later to learn).

"May I have a WORD with you?" she bellowed at the processor, pointing at her with a finger pointed like a sword. The tone she used clearly made the question rhetorical.

She dragged the processor out of the room by her ear, towering over her (as the FC was much taller than her-and me, too, by a long shot.) After a long, profanity-laden tirade, the chastised processor ran out of the offices, crying, and the boss lady turned her attention to me, smiling now.

"Sorry about that, Ms....."

I introduced myself, same as I did to you. Then she picked up my papers and looked 'em over.

"This seems okay, Mike. Oh. Do you mind if I call you...?"

"Why would I? I get called that all the time- sometimes worse. But I just deal with it. This girl's no chicken."

"Good. Again, sorry about that, Mike, but we're going through a bit of change here, and it's kinda weird...."

"I can see that."

"But I want you to understand that the CRA is a QUILTBAG-friendly organization. We have a number of gay members, and some who are *clearly* closeted ones, and the straight ones are largely supportive of homosexuality as a lifestyle choice."

"Largely?" I raised an eyebrow.

"You can't control the prejudices other people have, Mike. *I* get it, for example, as a college-age woman who *apparently* should have a "normal" job, on top of getting it as a 'toon. We have bad apples, just like any other organization. But I've made it a policy to start weeding them out. Don't take people like that processor as the norm here, 'cause they aren't!"

"I won't. I know what you mean about them prejudices, anyway. Try goin' to bars and pickin' up dames when you look like an elementary school-aged girl. Which I ain't *really* been for *years* now, by the way."

"The curse of being a 'toon," she sighed knowingly. "Come on. Let's get you sworn in."

"Can you....?"

"I'm the Field Commander, silly! I can do whatever you want." She groaned in embarrassment. "I mean, in terms of my job, not...."

"I know. You're too big for me, anyway."

So I got sworn in. And I thought that'd be the end of it. It'd be like the National Guard, the FC said. I could serve whenever I wanted, however I wanted. Do what I wanted. Totally on my terms- nobody else's. Except the ones who had superior ranks to me, of course- I had to jump whenever they said so, 'cause that was how things worked around there.

Therein lies the next part of the story.

IV.

Having become a freshly commissioned lieutenant in the CRA, with all the rights and responsibilities that entailed, I went "home" to a shabby little flat in an apartment building which rented out its suites to the CRA members who had no independent lodging of their own. Being as I was in that position in that moment, I took the opportunity to secure my accommodation there.

Once I set myself up there (it was easy, being as I had little possessions, then as now, and the places are all fully furnished) and had dinner, it was presumably time to go off to sleep, in a bed that was a marked improvement over the ones I once had, and dream about the island again. Especially Lu....

However, that was not what happened.

This was how it went down. Somebody knocks on my door in the middle of the night. Real frantic like. My guess is, maybe it's a friend who needs me. Then I remember- *what* friends? Even on the island and Orthicon, I didn't make many- especially once they found out I was a big L- and I hadn't been in the CRA long enough to make pals with anyone there yet. I changed my tack. It was probably somebody of the tribe and the species who just found out about me and wanted some tail, or some pervy guy of the species who'd found out the same and wanted to "convert" me. Either way, no dice. I don't just give my love away- you gotta work for it with me. I'd rather work for it with somebody I knew and trusted than some cheap one-night stand artist, anyhow.

I got to the door, opened it, and croaked out:

"Yeah, I'm here, already. Whadaya want?"

There's a pause, and then:

"If I said you had a beautiful body, would you hold it against me?"

You must know that line. The oldest and lousiest pick-up line in existence. Right up there with "What's a nice girl like you doing in a place like this?" Both of them are as much turn offs with 'toons as they are with humans, straight or otherwise. I know 'cause I get 'em a lot. No imagination, some people. What happens next is I'm about to run out into the hallway and curse the sky blue at whatever idiot is wasting my time this late at night with this crap, when suddenly I start smelling something that makes me all level headed. And I pass out.

V.

What revives me is a shot of cold water, right in my face. Then I get a sense of what my new surroundings are. I'm on a table inside some sort of examination room inside some sort of government lab. They warned me at the start that the feds hate the CRA with a passion (as we do them- double), and would stop at nothing to capture innocent members, especially young ones like me, when they felt they could be easily cracked. This looked to me one of them times, but they weren't gonna get *me* to crack, if that was the idea.

My captors were four big girls, one from the local PD, one FBI, one CIA and one Homeland Security. After the cop read me my rights, I asked them if they'd been the ones responsible for spilling that sleeping powder in my face.

"That'd be my jurisdiction," said the cop. "I know you probably think it was stupid...."

"Yes," I answered.

"....but it got you here, didn't it?"

"Not by my choosing," I pointed out. "Now, if ya don't mind, I'd like to...."

"*You* don't get any say in this, TERRORIST!" CIA snapped.

She bopped me right in the nose, right then and there, and probably would have done a lot more had Homeland not gotten in her path.

"You're out of order!" Homeland said. "We agreed that..."

"Go overdose on your fucking meds! That's all you Homeland people are good for...."

"Go FUCK yourself!"

They kept this up, yelling at each other for a couple of minutes about violating each other's "jurisdiction" like a couple of prep school kindergarteners, until the cop and FBI got angry and shot them both dead. Then their attention turned back to me.

"You better tell us something we can use, Mavinski," said FBI, "or you'll go the same way."

"I can't," I said. "We're immune to bullets."

"But not to fire," the cop said, pulling out a matchbook and waving it in my face. I got the point.

"Okay," I said. "What do you want?"

"Any information about the CRA you might have on you," said FBI. "You have any Apple stuff?"

"No."

"BlackBerry?"

"No."

"Samsung?"

"No."

"Cell phone?"

"What are you?" said the cop. "Dirt poor or something?"

"No value judgments!" said FBI. "We have to respect her if we want her to help us."

"You call this "respect"?" I interjected, humorlessly. "I've been "respected" better in less "respectful" places than this!"

"Do you know *anything* about the inner workings of the CRA at all?" said the cop.

"Hell, no!" I said. "I'm fresh meat. I only joined...."

"Do you see what I meant now?" shouted the cop. "We need to target the more *experienced* members of the organization..."

" "Experienced"? The goddamned group is less than a decade old! It doesn't matter how new the people we target are. Any link is a good one if it gets us to the top!"

"You FBI types are all the same. Thinking cops are all the same, and that we'll *gladly* drop *everything* to help you chase down a cheap piece of cartoon ass...."

"Hey!" I interjected, but was ignored.

"...when we have issues of local importance to...."

"Oh, like what? Goddamned parking tickets? You don't know the half of what pressure I'm under to...."

"The only pressure *you're* under is to stand around and tell us cops what to do while *you* reap the benefits!"

"You stupid little...."

Before FBI could say anything more than those three words, the cop had her gun out and killed her, Wild West style. Fearful, I attempted to make a break for it, but the cop grabbed my arm and threw me back on the table.

"Where *you* going, Red Riding Hood?" she said.

"Uh....nowhere?" I answered.

"Right," she replied. "Not until you give me what I want."

"Here," I said, getting my wallet out of my pants. "See? Here's my CRA membership card. You want it? Let's see what else I got in here. I got $100 in here I could give you...."

"Put that away," she said, softly but authoritatively. I did.

"That's not what I want," she continued.

"Well, what *do* you....?"

"Don't be stupid, Mavinski. At least, not any more than you actually are."

The horrific realization hit me right away.

"So you want me to....do you?"

"If you want to get out of here without being charged, then yeah."

"That's *blackmail*!" I snapped. "I'm not putting out just 'cause you...."

"Who do you think they're going to believe when I tell them it happened? You or me?"

"You can't just...."

"A human can do whatever the fuck they want to a 'toon," she said, brandishing the matches. "And that's exactly what you're going to do to me. Take off your clothes."

"What? Here? I'm not gonna...."

"Take off your fucking CLOTHES!"

The whole thing might have ended badly for me. Were it not for the fact that, at that very moment, a small figure crashed through the plate glass window, uttered an expletive in Spanish, and pulled a gun on the cop.

"You pulled your last quick one this time!" she drawled in a strong Latino accent, not blinking.

I looked over at that moment at her, to ascertain if she were friend or foe. Fortunately, she was a 'toon, so I was seemingly okay-I hoped.

Then I had to go complicate things by falling in love with her.

I don't know if it was her green hair, her black eyes, her thin but muscular body stuck into that short red skirt, the aviator goggles on her head, her accent, or even that we were roughly the same height and build. Thing is, I *knew* that if I ever wanted to put a move on somebody, it was her. No question about it. However, we had to get out of this mess, first. She had that covered, though.

"Who the hell are....?" The cop was nonplussed.

"Major Frieda Suarez, Cartoon Republican Army." (Damn it! She outranked me- I was just a lieutenant.) "You try anything bad on *mi compadre* and you gonna be *muy muerto*!"

"*Ju* no *try* dat!" said the cop, mocking Frieda's accent. "I'm doing her, and then *you*, and then I'm putting both of you painted whores away in the...."

Frieda didn't hesitate hearing that. She shot the cop point blank, and she fell down, dead, like the others. Then she motioned to me- with the gun. I got the wrong idea.

"Wait!" I said. "I'm with the CRA. Honest. I just...."

"I know that." She put the gun away and motioned- with her hand this time- for me to get off the table. "They briefed me before I went out."

"So you guys knew I was....?"

"What you *think*? We take *care* of each other. Nobody *else* is gonna do it. Know what I mean?"

"Yeah."

"Besides, Mike, I know about who you are. They showed me your file. You just my type."

"You mean....?"

"Yeah. Not many of us in the CRA, *si*?"

"So," I said, nonchalantly, to suppress my growing sexual excitement. "You're a....?"

"Well....bisexual. But that's okay with you, right?"

"Yeah."

"Good. I dance with all kinds, Mike. Perhaps later we dance together, huh?"

"Baby, I could dance with you 'til the cows come home!"

We might have done it right then and there, since we were really clicking then. However, the mood ended abruptly when we heard footsteps in the halls.

"*Caramba*!" snapped Frieda. "We gotta GO!"

"How come?" I asked.

"Why you think? They gonna *burn* us! Come on!"

She was the senior officer, so I was bound to do what she said, officially. But I would have done anything she told me to do then-and I do mean *anything*.

VI.

Frieda kept her gun, but she also had a switch, which she gave to me. Did I know how to use it? Uh, yeah! You pretty much need to something like that to survive in inner-city NYC, let alone your average tropic isle....

"God damn it to bugfucking HELL! They're DEAD!"

This came out of the room we had just exited. As did, "The fucking 'toon did it!" Stereotypical bastards. I wanted to go back and clock the guy what said it, but Frieda checked me.

"We gonna be fightin' plenty of 'em soon, *chica*. Best you save up that hate for when you need it."

"Are they coming after us, then?"

"D-uh!"

"Sorry. I'm new at this stuff...."

"No need, Mike. You do what I tell you, and we'll get out fine. All cops is the same. Blame somebody for their problems and then kill them when they get to be a problem. Only thing is, we ain't that easy to kill."

"You sound like you're speaking from experience."

"*Si. Mi familia* disown me, owing to me wanting to be bad and they all being cops and lawyers and all that. Then came Orthicon, and, after that, nothin'. Void of loneliness. You hear me?"

"Exactly what I feel. Here I am, a tomboy, and a Polish Jew besides, and I can't fit in nowhere. Not Noo Yawk, not on no tropic island, not even on that Orthicon rock. But maybe, you and I..."

"Perhaps. Funny we were both on Orthicon, and in the CRA, but we never met 'til now."

"I'm thinkin' that it was meant to be, though," I said as I gazed at her, longingly.

"Was *that* meant to be?"

There was an unusually large number of men in suits, most with guns drawn, who had spotted us in the alcove of the building, which was clearly home to some sort of inter-agency pow-wow on the 'toon trade, by the looks of thing. Cops, FBI, CIA and Homeland guys all, and the two of us smack dab in the middle of 'em!

"Aw, crap!" I exclaimed.

"*VAMONOS!*" shouted Frieda.

She took off down one route they hadn't blocked off, and I followed.

VII.

That route turned out to be blocked after all, rather quicker than we thought. We searched for a break in the mass of men, but there didn't seemed to be a way out among all of them. Looked like we were trapped.

Not so.

Men being men, and them being from all those competing agencies and whatnot, they started arguing about which one of 'em had "jurisdiction" over us, and consequently which one of them had the right to kill, scalp and embalm us. This prompted Frieda to motion me over to her.

"We gotta move," she said, loudly, to drown out their arguing.

"Fine," I answered. "What do we do?"

"I shoot," she said tersely. "You cut."

"Fine with me."

And that's pretty much what we did. Frieda fired a warning shot in the air to get them to stop arguing, and then cursed them up and down in Spanish. The white guys, who was most of 'em, didn't get it, but there were a few Latinos who got it and explained it, and then it was on. They shot at us, but the bullets just flew through our bodies with no damage, and hit other guys instead. Frieda shot a couple more, and I went to work with the pig-sticker. That thinned them out a bit. Boy! Can a human guy scream and yell when you stab him just a little bit! I only had to stab a couple of them for them to get it. Good thing, too, considering Frieda ran out of bullets then.

We found one of the stragglers howling about a small wound I'd put in his leg. I held my knife, to his throat, and Frieda aimed her now-empty gun at him.

"Get this and get it straight!" I told him. "You feds are gonna have to come up with something better than what you just pulled if you wanna bust the CRA up!"

"*Si,*" added Frieda. "Now you go and tell your bosses that- before we come for THEM!"

He got the message and left. So did we.

VIII.

Upshot of all of this was that Frieda and I ended up at my pad, and we commenced to doing some serious bumpin' and grindin'. Maybe I'll never find Lu again, but with Frieda around, who needs her?

Well, I should end it here. You got all you want from me, right? Besides which, my sex life ain't none of your fucking business!

AND THE CARTOON GIRLS GO "DO DA DO DA DO DA DOO"

I.

FIELD COMMANDER F. FINSTER:

On the record, I want to say that the damn thing was none of my doing. What I mean is, it never would have gotten off the ground if I had not been so grievously disobeyed. Normally, seeing as I'm the number two person here, anyone going against what I say gets turfed, but, seeing as it was supposedly in "such a good cause", I got overruled by the big boss on that one.

However, that does *not* mean that it was a good idea. Far from it! Let me explain....

*

It all began when I was busy shuffling paper around like I was before you came in. Typical summer weather-hot- so we were all kind of short with each other, more than usual. But I knew something serious was up when my secretary, Lieutenant Flint, came in.

"Fish Face is coming in," she said. "I'm gonna go put cotton in my ears for when...."

"*Who?*" I asked.

"You know! *Bess!*"

"Use her *proper title,* please."

"All right! *Captain Fishelman.* Do we *have* to go through this all the time? I mean, we all pretty much *know* each other by now, and...."

I cut her off with a pre-emptive grunt.

"Regardless of how much we know, like or *dislike* each other here in the Cartoon Republican Army", I said, "we will endeavor to treat each other with *respect* at all times. This is essential to our smooth, functional operation, both as a full organization and independent units..."

"You know," she interrupted, "if you spent less time talking like a textbook all the time, then maybe we'd..."

"Are you *implying* something, Lieutenant?"

"No! At least, I didn't think I was..."

I glared at her long enough to convey my displeasure with her, and then artificially plastered on a smile.

"Just get out of my office, and don't come back here until "Fish Face" gets here- so you can *warn* me. 'K?"

She nodded and exited.

*

CAPTAIN B. FISHELMAN:

Oh, sure. I know that BITCH Finster told you I'm a tool, and that it was me and my ego that fueled the whole shindig. Well, *she* is a 24 karat LIAR! This 'toon fish has given *too much* of herself to this cause for anyone- especially not that over-ranked COW- not to recognize it. Repre-ZENT!

Now, the timing of this was crucial. Somehow or another, a number of our guys supposedly got rounded up by the feds and stashed at the Zoo in San Diego. It would have been pretty easy for them to catch the *dumb* ones, but I'm surprised the smart ones got nabbed, too. You would think they would have learned something from most of us girls (excluding *her highness* the Field Commander) getting stuck in that fucking *bottle* a ways back!

However, that's neither here nor there. The point is, the boys were caught, and we needed to free them. Otherwise, the CRA was as spent a force as the Black Panthers or the AIM. That was the point that I intended to make when I showed up at CRA headquarters (location classified!) that day, with my Captain's hat on my head and my fin holding a briefcase of papers.

"Hiiii, Candaace!" I drawled at the Field Commander's executive assistant when I entered.

"Yeah," she said, apathetically. "Whatever."

"Uh, I *outrank* you, so you should...."

She stood up and saluted me.

"*That* enough for you, *Captain*?" she said, a bit resentfully, as she went to inform the boss.

If I had teeth, I would have clenched them, and then I would have slapped her insolent face. If I could reach it, that is.

Candace came back, and pointed me towards the office. When I got there, the Field Commander was her usual spindly, lanky and lazy self, lounging at her desk.

"Okay, Bess," she said. "What do you want?"

"Just your approval, Field Commander."

"Of *what*? This better not be expensive, Fishelman. We're tapped out as it is...."

I snorted contemptuously.

"Is that all you care about? MONEY?"

"It was money that got us all into this, Bess."

"Oh, yes. The old "Hollywood fucked us" excuse!"

"They *did* fuck us!"

"Not as bad as the government's fucking us NOW! Or what they did to us on ORTHICON!"

"I wasn't there!"

"And that's why you don't get what was so important about it. We were POWs, Finster!"

"Look, Captain! You were promoted to your current rank, and made the head of our fairly recent media production unit, so that we could make some positive progress with our relations with the human race."

"Which I believe I have done, have I not?"

She stood up and crossed her arms as a scowl creased her face.

"Sure," she said, sarcastically. "*If* you consider doing an extended series of antagonistic podcasts on the subject of why human beings SUCK *HELPFUL*!"

"Do *not* ridicule "Bess's Bring Down", okay? Do you realize how many people follow it every week?"

"Not "people". 'Toons. You're just preaching to the choir. You're supposed to be converting human beings to our cause, not driving them *away* from it!"

"As long as I am the Captain of that ship," I said, indicating the Captain's hat on my head. To my shock, she removed it from my head and threw it out an open window.

"How DARE you!" I stormed. "I paid a lot of money for that!"

"That you took out of your budget!"

"You don't KNOW that!"

"I know, sister. I KNOW! You can't walk around with bling like that and expect me to not think you aren't doing what you should!"

"*BLING*?"

"Oh, did you not hear me?"

"You lousy BITCH!"

"Fishelman, you *better* tell me what you had in mind before I break out my FRYING PAN!"

"You wouldn't!"

"I *would*!"

"Fine!" I took a cleansing breath and opened my briefcase, giving her my documents. "Hear. Read this."

*

FIELD COMMANDER F. FINSTER:

I read her documents calmly- the first time. Then I re-read them with an eye to the cost, and then I exploded, throwing the papers back at her.

"Are you fucking INSANE?" I shouted. "Or, at the very least, more so than USUAL?"

"The only one around here who's *insane* is YOU," she shouted back, "if you can't see the value in this idea!"

"The *value*?"

"Certainly. It's far more feasible for us to stage a variety show for the boys in San Diego- and thus, abscond with them as they were absconded from us- than it would be for us to raid the city with bayonets drawn. Considerably less ink to be shed."

"You have me there," I said. "But, like I said before, we aren't exactly made of money right now..."

"That's the advantage of my plan. All we need is a PA system, a bandstand, a few amplifiers, and some lavaliere mikes for me and the other singers..."

"I *knew* it! This is just another cheap excuse for you to flog your talents at the expense of the CRA..."

"It's not just me, you JERK! *All* of the members of the band- and the singers- are CRA members! We are females intent, unlike *you*, on making certain our captured menfolk are rescued from their purgatory in the least injurious way possible! We are all paying our way, and using our own instruments, and not costing the CRA a goddamn DIME other than to supply with a bandstand and decent PA equipment! So, if this is indeed a cheap way of flogging talent, as you suspect, it is not only mine, but also that of the 15 members of GPE whom you..."

"GPE?"

"Girl Power Express."

"What the hell kind of name is that for a BAND?"

"Obviously, you haven't been paying attention to musical trends recently, *ma'am*!"

I crinkled my brow, as I do not like being called that, and have told everyone this. Bea knew, which is why she used it to taunt me. I didn't take the bait this time.

"How do you expect to accomplish your goal?" I asked.

"It'd be a typical Trojan Horse procedure," she said. "We go in, do a few numbers, and then we invite anyone who wants to to come on stage and sing and dance with us on the last one. We'd have already secretly slipped word to the guys about how this *really* meant that they're to follow us out, as we're going to walk out of the Zoo as we do the last number. Then, when the human guards- as there inevitably will be- are distracted, we slip out with the guys in tow, and Bob's your uncle. So, are you gonna...?"

"No."

"This is because you can't sing, or play....?"

"No. It's because it's a stupid and reckless idea with too much of a potential for going wrong."

"You goddamn human 'toons think you're so SMART! You're made out of the same ink and paint as us, you know!"

"Yes, but some of us know how to think things through, and some of us..."

"Well, it's a good thing I got the *General* to approve the idea before I...."

"WHAT?" I screamed. "You went OVER MY HEAD....?"

"PUT A *SOCK* IN IT!" she screamed back. "The General said she'd be *delighted* to head up the horn section of our band. *Furthermore,* as she's just gotten that MacArthur Genius Grant she applied for, and I have just succeeded in getting my Guggenheim Fellowship, we don't need to have the CRA- or YOU- approve the project. Therefore, *you* can just DEAL WITH IT, *BITCH*!"

There was a brief pause, during which I contemplated the massive arrogance and *chutzpah* Bea had just displayed towards me. She'd pay for it- one day.

"Very well," I said, as there was clearly nothing else I could do. "But understand this. GPE is completely on its own for this foolhardy venture, the General be *damned*. The rest of the CRA will not lift a finger to help you..."

"It's not like we need your help, anyway," Bea said as she packed up and left. "We have more than enough of the super-powered and smart girls on our side, and they're the ones that make sure the trains run on time here. Good luck finding a *private's* commission after I tell the General what you said about her!"

I could only chuckle to myself at that. It would take more than that to get me turfed, and the three of us- the General, me and Fish Face Fishelman- all knew it.

II.

LIEUTENANT C. FLINT:

Bea came out of the boss' room sooner than expected and walked over to me.

"You know, you have cotton in your ears!" she said.

"What?" I answered.

"You have COTTON in your ears!"

"Come again?"

"COTTON! In your EARS!"

"Can't hear you. I got cotton in my ears."

"Well, take it out."

"What?"

"Take it OUT!"

I did. Then she told me about the plan she'd cooked up, and how she needed to have another vocalist as part of Girl Power Express. And, perhaps, a multi-instrumentalist who could do relief work for some of the others when they went on breaks.

"What's in it for me?" I asked.

"I would think that would be obvious," she reminded me. "Your brothers, and your boyfriend..."

"Do you think they got caught? I haven't heard from 'em for a while....Listen, is Isabella...?"

"Lieutenant-Colonel Garcia-Shapiro," she said, "is our second guitar player and chief arranger. She'll be the Billy Strayhorn to my Duke Ellington, if that means anything to you."

"I'm in, then. I trust Izzy's word more than anybody else here, 'cept the General's."

"Good. Now, are you okay with doing up-tempo numbers, 'cause most of the other singers prefer ballads..."

"My pipes can handle anything you want, Bess. It's in San Diego, right?"

"Yeah. On the 15th."

We agreed to meet then, along with the rest of the band, to do our duty. Little did we know what was in store for us.

*

CAPTAIN B. FISHELMAN:

They say the best laid plans of mice and men often go astray, but, since I am neither mouse nor man, I figured that my plan was not part of that schema. I was wrong.

It started well enough, as we all managed to get into America's finest city without incident. You would think that, us being all brightly colored and super-powered and quintessentially "feminine", some of us might have been questioned or detained or what have you beforehand. No. That didn't happen until we actually got to San Diego.

Unfortunately, it seems someone had tipped off the Zoo about what we had planned to do, so we were politely but firmly told when we entered Balboa Park, in which the Zoo exists, that our presence was not welcomed. As bandleader, it was my appointed job to beg, cajole and threaten the City Council with everything I had, but they wouldn't budge. So then I basically told them, point blank, that we *would* be playing a concert for the boys somewhere in town soon, and, if they didn't like it, they could go fuck themselves. End of story.

Once the group had paid my bail, there was some discussion about what to do next. Should we try an alternate location, perhaps, or just give up? I was quick to make myself heard on the latter option.

"Give *up*?" I said. "*Seriously?* Did the boys "give up" when *we* were imprisoned?"

"Most of them were glad we were *gone,*" said Louise Gutman, our keyboard player. "That was how it appeared to be at my house, anyway."

"It was only by chance that we got rescued," said Mavis Pipes, our percussionist. "If my brother hadn't..."

"Look!" I cut her off. "They're expecting us to do something, *quid pro quo,* for what they did for us. We have to do this, okay?"

"She has a point, you know," the General said as she came up towards me, fiddling with a reed for her saxophone. "If we won't do it, who will?"

Her word in this organization, informal as it may be sometimes, is the closest thing we have to law. So I now knew, as did everyone else, that this was going through, whether we liked it or not. Fortunately, we liked it.

*

LIEUTENANT C. FLINT:

Bess, of course, raised holy hell about how we couldn't play for the guys in the Zoo, even though I was convinced that they just told us they were there to throw us off. In any event, we got banned from ever playing in San Diego, pretty much forever, after she told the City Council to do it to themselves. That took a lot of guts, I'll admit, but it didn't solve our immediate problems.

However, Bess had spoken to the General during her incarceration, and they'd worked out an alternate scheme. Which was this:

Our ban on performing in San Diego did not extend to the nearby island community of Coronado, which has a separate municipal government. So, therefore, all we had to do was pack up the gear and move over there. Simple, right?

No sooner had we found a good spot on the beach facing the San Diego skyline, and set up the PA system and the bandstand and the amps and what have you, and tuned up our instruments and warmed up our pipes, than we got a visit from the local Juan Law.

"What the hell is this?" he exclaimed. "What are you doing?"

"Isn't it *obvious,* you *moron?*" Betterfist, our bassist, shouted at him as she warmed up.

"Yeah," added her sister Baubles, our drummer, as she did likewise. "We came to *play.*"

"Cut it *out,* you two!" said their sister Flotsam, who was our lead guitarist, and normally leads that trio when they do their superhero thing, although she'd fortunately decided not to do so for GPE. "No trouble, remember?"

She seemed ready to fly over and politely talk to the guy, but I put my hand up.

"You relax," I said. "I'll deal with this."

I turned to the lawman and asked him how much it would take for us to be able to play undisturbed. When I picked up my jaw from the floor, I ran and told Bea. When she picked up her jaw from the floor, we had to start passing the hat again to collect the fee he wanted. Fortunately, we had just enough scratch between us to make it happen.

III.

LIEUTENANT COLONEL I. GARCIA-SHAPIRO:

You probably got most of the meat of the story from Bess, Candace and the Field Commander. But the first two of them have a tendency to embroider things, and the latter wasn't there, so I'm glad you came to me for this part of the story. I can tell the truth without varnishing it up, unlike some people.

I'd been in the background much of this time, getting the arrangements ready while Bea stood around looking over my shoulder or preening in that damned Captain's hat of hers. Did she not realize how small potatoes being a Captain was in an *Army*? I knew I'd have to pull my rank sooner than I thought.

I got the chance as soon as we started on the first number. Somebody hit a clinker, and Bea just lost it. Her mouth made that long upside down V ridge that Kermit the Frog always makes just before he gets pissed off at somebody. And she was pissed, all right. She started cursing bloody murder and saying we couldn't play for shit and all sorts of other unreasonable things. That was when I put my guitar down, stood up, and took my microphone off its stand.

"Bess!" I snapped. "For God's sake! Cut it out!"

"*Pardon* me?" she blazed. "*I* am the *bandleader* here!"

"The band *figurehead,* is more like it! You forget that *I* did all the fucking arrangements!"

"So what? It takes more than just making arrangements to run a band, girl! You need to be able to enforce DISCIPLINE!"

"Which I'm gonna *do* if you don't behave yourself! You can easily be *replaced* by a SENIOR officer, *Captain!*"

"You little fucking...."

She was coming right at me with murder in her eyes, but the General got up from her chair and locked eyes with Bess in a contest Bess hadn't a chance of winning.

"You keep going," the General warned her, "and you won't just be out of the goddamned BAND! You'll be *out-* PERIOD!"

That shut Bess up. She went back to the bandstand, rifled through pages in the band book, and raised her conductor's fins again.

"All right, OFFICERS!" she snapped. "And you, too, grunts! I got an easier one for you this time. Number 100 in your books. That's right. 'Snibor'". She paused and waited for us to find our places, and then it was "uh ONE two three four..."

*

So, from that point on, we were off, with Bess prevented from "disciplining" us as she would have wished. But, other than that clinker, there were no other mistakes- musically speaking.

We started out doing a few jazz instrumentals (including the previously noted "Snibor"), with plenty of room for soloing, thanks to yours truly's arrangements. The local people had no objections to this approach, and we seemed to get a crowd together down by the pier. This was what we wanted. If we had the support of the locals, we might get their sympathy regarding the plight of our actual (and, in my case, hope to be) significant others, and the outcry would be such that the feds would be forced to free them immediately.

This was, I thought, confirmed by the number we did before the union-mandated 15 minute intermission. Lou Reed's "Walk on the Wild Side", sung by Bess, with all of us chiming in on the "and the colored girls go 'do da do da doo'" bit, although, for obvious reasons, we substituted "cartoon" for "colored". They went nuts over that one, and we thought our case was in the bag.

It didn't work out that way.

The second set was primarily a vocal as opposed to instrumental one, unlike the opening. To my shock, (for, as usual, I hadn't been consulted on the decision), Bess had elected to make most of the vocals bawdy blues numbers from before World War II. That, as usual with Bess, was a miscalculation. It not only upset some of the parents in the audience, who hurried away with kids in tow, but either confused or embarrassed the pre-pubescent members of the band. Like me.

Anyway, we were halfway through one of those tunes- something called "Dirty Mother for Ya", which was the specialty of our sole canine member, Cadmium- when, suddenly, the audible "click" of a small battalion of firearms interrupted us. A bunch of San Diego cops, it appears, had been tipped off about us, and crossed the Bay Bridge to apprehend us, even though Coronado wasn't part of their jurisdiction. Cadmium, meanwhile, was so shocked at the sight of the guns that she stopped in mid-sentence, piddled on the stage, and ran off.

"What the hell are you...?" Bess shouted at her, before turning around. Stark terror erupted in her eyes.

"EVERY GIRL FOR HERSELF!" she screamed, and ran away like the coward she truly is.

The cops stormed the bandstand and tried to arrest us. The operative word is "tried"- 'cause we put up a fight, like we always do.

I can't tell you much about that part, owing that it took place far too fast. I defended myself well enough, of course, although I ended up smashing my guitar over one of the cops' heads. My mastery of martial arts helped me after that, until Candace found me and helped me get out of there in her car.

*

FIELD COMMANDER F. FINSTER:

You know what the worst part of the whole thing was? The boys were never *in* San Diego. At least, not *all* of them, as we were led to believe. It was just two dumb animals from a fucking CGI movie who had nothing to do with the CRA at all, because those CGI assholes have no brains and they're totally stinking up the art form, which is why they will never be allowed to be CRA members. They were picked up for picking out "Louie Louie" on the organ at the pavilion in Balboa Park without a permit. Some CIA fellow thought he'd try to goof us up by claiming all our boys were there, since he apparently couldn't tell the difference between cel, Flash and CGI animation- of which only the first two, I being in the latter camp, are allowed to be part of the CRA. Thankfully, it didn't work.

Now, if you'll excuse me, I've got to go *catch* a certain FISH!

A SMALL BETRAYAL

I.

It was not common for non-human beings to make themselves known at the massive multi-national corporation known as Boothworld Industries. Even rarer was it for them to approach the massive, oak-paneled reception desk and the black marble wall behind it- to say nothing of the unsympathetic, seen-it-all secretary behind that desk. However, this was an unusual case, and, though not known at that time, it was an act that was soon to have massive consequences. Not so much for Boothworld Industries, for its multi-national made it immune to minor acts of political folderol. No. The diminutive figure approaching the desk had a greater aim in mind- the destruction of an enemy of both of them. The anarchistic, multi-faceted beast known as the Cartoon Republican Army.

For one thing, this creature of cryptozoological origin- who will be known, for convenience, by the singularly descriptive name of Berry- had a major score to settle with the CRA, despite her clearly being of cartoon descent herself. For another, she knew that Boothworld, whose communications holdings could fill a book equivalent in size to an average telephone directory, had no love for the socialist principles on which the CRA operated. Especially since, if the CRA got the billions of dollars it was demanding in payback from the Hollywood studios for decades of perceived wage slavery, it had the capacity to devastate the entire media industry in America- which wasn't exactly Boothworld's idea of a successful day at the office. So, Berry- a villain through and through, and therefore not eligible for CRA membership under the goody-two-shows tenants of the by-laws- knew Boothworld would easily sympathize with her. *If* she could get past the front desk.

However, she was prepared for any eventualities, like always.

Berry, who resembled a diminutive, red-furred, squirrel creature, made her way to the front desk at the Boothworld offices in New

York that day with the air of naivete and innocence that was her regular mask against the cruelties of the world. Ignoring those around her as they did her, she managed, with some difficulty, to climb up onto a chair in front of the secretary on duty at the reception desk, and waited for the attention of that worthy. It took some time, but Berry eventually got it.

"May I *help* you?" said the secretary, somewhat aghast at the site of the grotesque (to her eyes), clothing-less creature seated in front of her (almost).

"Yesss," purred Berry, in a voice that suggested that she used maple syrup as mouthwash. "Which floor does Mr. Booth have his office on?"

The secretary paused before answering. Not everyone got to see the enigmatic, nearly invisible head of the company. More often, they were simply denied admission, which she intended to do here.

"I'm sorry," the secretary said, flatly. "That information is classified."

"I *made* an *appointment,*" said Berry, still sugary, but with an edge of steel creeping in. "A week ago. It took me that long to tramp out here from L.A. And I do mean *tramp.*"

"Do you think I *care* about that?" retorted the secretary. "At *all*? We are trying to run a *business* here, and I don't have any time for the kind of *foolishness* that you and your whole goddamn RACE are responsible for! Now, why don't you go flaunt your sugar-coated pussy somewhere...?"

She would have continued in this line, were it not for the fact that she felt the unmistakable feeling of cold steel against her neck. This was because Berry, during the secretary's tirade, had pulled out a handmade switchblade knife, with a blade much longer than average, and poked the blade directly at the secretary's neck.

"My "goddamn race" might be responsible for a lot of things," Berry said, her true, inner viciousness asserting itself, "but that's

NOTHING compared to why human *cunts* like you made us do it in the FIRST PLACE! Now, you listen carefully, paper pusher. Mr. Booth was *perfectly willing* to give me some of his precious time as soon as told him what I was, what I had done, and, most importantly, what I could do to help get the both of us what we want. Here's the deal. You tell me where his office is, and how to get there, or *else* I stick this thing in *hard* enough to draw your *blood- and DRINK IT*!"

Fully understanding the creature's desire and intent, the secretary ran quickly from the desk to achieve the creature's aims.

II.

Not ten minutes later, after the secretary had informed Mr. Booth of the presence of the interloper, Berry was sequestered in the office of that gentleman, sitting opposite her after his desk. A moment after that, after Berry had refreshed herself with the scotch-and-soda he had generously offered her, she outlined exactly what she wanted him to help her do.

"I wish to gain revenge on the Cartoon Republican Army," she said, plainly. "And I know you do, too."

"How?" said Mr. Booth, his eyebrows arching quizzically.

"Don't make this difficult, Booth," she responded, impatiently. "It's an open secret amongst my kind that Boothworld has, in the past few years, been slowly working its way towards controlling all the world's media. We, as creations of that self-same media, have a vested interest in continuing to make our livings in it, as you well know."

"Of course," Booth said.

"Why else would you have engineered your hostile takeover of Sony a few months ago?" Berry asked rhetorically. "Why is it that Boothworld has no less than three members of its board of directors also sitting on Time Warner's? Why did you secretly purchase half of CBS's shares in Viacom? Why have you made such open entreaties to Disney, even though both the Disney family and the government have opposed you? And, last but not least, why would you be trying to get News Corp. to sell FOX- the network *and* the studio- to you?"

Mr. Booth was surprised that she knew all this, but then he remembered their first encounter- in L.A., when he was trying to negotiate the FOX sale- and then it wasn't such a surprise at all.

"You're right, Berry," he said. "On all counts. Except that we had to throw in the towel on FOX. That hard headed Australian son of a bitch Murdoch wouldn't play ball with us."

"No matter. His time will be up soon, and then you can make your move."

"Yeah, you're right. So what do you want me to....?"

"Let me have another drink first," said Berry, rattling the ice cubes in her now-empty glass. "Then we talk."

They had two more scotch-and-sodas- each- and then Berry felt limbered up enough to relieve herself of her burden.

"Here," she said, pulling out a portable USB computer drive from somewhere on herself and giving it to him.

"So," said Booth, looking quizzically at the drive. "What is this?"

"That," said Berry, triumphantly, "is what I am offering you today in exchange for your hospitality, and, of course, your fine Scotch."

"You didn't answer me, though. What is actually *on* this USB that will be of use to me and Boothworld?"

"It's of use to me *and* you. Remember?"

"Okay. But what...?"

"That USB," Berry pronounced imperiously, "contains *everything* you want to know about specific male members of the CRA. Names, addresses, e-mails, Facebook and Twitter accounts, you name it. Don't ask me how I got it. I just got it. Okay?"

"I won't ask *that*, then," said Booth. "What I will ask is- why just the male members?"

Berry, who had been examining the ice in her glass intently as she spoke, suddenly slammed the glass on the desk so hard that it broke.

"*Because*, you *fool*," she said, "everyone who is a 'toon knows that the real power brokers in the CRA are the GIRLS! That was why the Canadian government *failed* with their insanely STUPID idea to hold a fair number of them hostage in Ottawa a few months ago. Female 'toons are the *brains* of the operation. The guys are all just wanting some food, some action or some sex. Of course, even when you actually *try* to come on to them, they're such idiots that they can't tell. Trust me on personal experience there.

"Now, all that *you* need to do is find some way to lure those dimwit males into some confined space- an abandoned prison, say. Alcatraz would do nicely. As long as you promise them the moon, they'll come in droves, and then you can lock 'em all up easily. Then tell the girls that their menfolk are up there, get them to visit them, and BOOM! The whole cartoon race- CAUGHT! Boothworld, not any other media company, has complete control of them. *Billions* of dollars available to be extracted from the copyright holders before you even *think* about releasing them! BILLIONS! Sounds wonderful, doesn't it?"

"Undoubtedly," said Booth. "But it would *cost* billions to...."

"Oh, *come on*!" Berry shouted at the sky. "Not when I'm *this* close! Please!"

"This close to what?"

"My *revenge, STUPID*!"

"So this is why....?"

"Of *course* it is, IDIOT!"

"What happened?"

"You want to *know*?"

"Well, if I have to spend money for...."

"Fine! You wanna *know*? Okay! I was denied entry to the CRA when I applied. DENIED! And I am just as qualified as any of the DUNDERHEADS who...."

"Why?"

"Why what?"

"Why were you denied?"

"*Because* I'm a VILLAIN! Those goody two shoes assholes want to keep their ranks lily-white so they can look good in the mass media. Ergo-nobody typed as a "villain" can be a CRA member. There's a fucking goddamn LOT of us, not counting the traitors who went straight so they could join the saintly CRA!

"It all goes back to the Orthicon deal. The ones who got shipped out to space were the good ones- or at least the morally ambivalent. They got to live the life of Riley out there compared to what we villains went through. We were stuck in detention centers that Guantanamo Bay had *nothing* on! Seriously! They thought we needed the extra surveillance, so they scooped us out and locked us away. I could *tell* you things about what happened in those places...

"The point of all this is that I want them to SUFFER the way I did! And who better to make them suffer than Boothworld, the company that's made so many people suffer, in so many diverse ways, than any other before it! Have I made myself clear now, Booth?"

"Yes. I've heard enough. We have a deal."

His hand grasped her paw, and they shook.

"Anyone as vicious and sadistically-minded as you," he said, "is exactly the kind of creature Boothworld wishes to do business with."

"Thank you for the *compliment,*" Berry purred.

"Listen," Booth added. "We need a cartoon liaison if this is going to come off. Would you like to take on that job?"

"Delighted," Berry purred again.

It might have been the Scotch, or the prospect of what was to come, but the financier and the villainous 'toon then laughed-gutturally, in a tone of pure evil. Which was fitting, because that was exactly what they were. And what they were going to do.

VIDEO DIARY OF A TALL SOLDIER

By David Perlmutter

(*The darkness of a video camera's lens is replaced abruptly by a lighted image. INGRID, an animated cartoon giraffe with an enormously long neck, tries to speak into a camera. Unfortunately, her neck is so long that it is too far away for the camera to pick up her face.*)

INGRID: Hi, I'm Ingrid- and I- Ah, DAMN IT!

(*The transmission abruptly ends and then starts up again. When it begins again, INGOT is lying on her belly, with the camera supported up in the air by her left hoof, since this is the only way for her face to be seen by the audience.*)

INGRID: Okay- let's try that again. Hi, I'm Ingrid, and I am recording this as my last will and testament. For tonight, along with a small coterie of my fellow soldiers in the Cartoon Republican Army, I am going to sacrifice myself in the name of avenging the wrong that you human beings have done on we cartoon characters! *You* may think we're a *joke*, but we're *serious* about this. Really. DAMN serious! Now, you may think we cartoon characters are *always* happy, *always* showing ourselves off, *always* being all buddy-buddy and everything, but *that's not true*! Some of us, like me, are MISERABLE, and you goddamn *idiots* prolong our misery by putting us into the position of being 24 hour a day, 7 day a week CLOWNS! I mean, LOOK at me! GODDAMN IT, LOOK AT ME!

(*She gets up on her feet and sends the camera up and down her voluminous neck. It is a long trip. The transmission ends again, and then restarts with INGOT in the position she was before.*)

INGOT: You *see*? Giraffes aren't *supposed* to have necks *this* long! I'm a genetically engineered CHUMP! I'm half giraffe and half goddamn CRAWLING KING SNAKE! And all you human beings can do is *laugh* at me! LAUGH! Like I'm a goddamn *joke*! A goddamn joke seen EVERY WEEK on TELEVISION, and made to be a *fool* besides! But I have my PRIDE, even if you *schmucks* can't see it, just like you can't see your ASSES! I didn't *ask* to be drawn like this! None of us did! But you drew all of us like *crazy idiots*, and expect us to be *normal*, well-behaved critters. Of all the bloody GALL!

(*She stops short to take in some needed air and then continues.*)

That's why I'm going out on that raid tonight. Unless you happen to have a torch or flamethrower handy, YOU CAN'T KILL US! And that way, we'll AVENGE every rotten indignity you imposed on us! Stealing our liberty, our money, our dignity! Sure, you created us, but if you didn't want to treat us *right*, you could've ABORTED US! I know *I* wouldn't be in as much misery as I am now if you had. There aren't many other kinds of jobs for out-of-work cartoon characters nowadays, but you fatheaded human DICKS wouldn't know a *damn thing* about that, WOULD YOU?

(*The transmission then ends abruptly, but starts up again one more time. INGOT's face is firmly in front of the camera this time.*)

INGRID: Oh. One more thing. If I kill anyone or burn down anyone's property while I do this, I want you to know that (*tearing up; faltering*) I'M SORRY! (*She drops the camera to the ground and picks up a bayonet as she runs out of the room*) BANZAI!

(*The transmission ends.*)

CADMIUM AND THE COPS

By David Perlmutter

(The following is taken from a transcript based on an interrogation conducted by the New Orleans Police Department in February 20__. The questions, responses and comments of the investigating detectives have been edited from the text, so as to give full attention to the concerns and feelings of the suspect, who, as will be shown, was of a highly exceptional nature.)

All right! Keep your shirt on-I'm coming.

What are *you* looking at?

Haven't you ever seen a dog talk before?

No?

You mean I have to explain myself *again*? Uhhh!

Fine.

My name is Cadmium J. Dalmatian, and I....

I'm a *puppy*.

Or at least, I *was*. Once upon a time. That was so long ago....

What do you mean by *that*?

Oh, I see. Not only have you not met a dog who can talk before, you also have never met an animated c cartoon character by the looks of it, either.

What's that got to do with it, you ask?

Oh, it has *everything* to do with it. That's why I can talk, for example. And why I'm stuck being a puppy I instead of becoming a full grown dog, like the ones here in this world inevitably do. We cartoon characters do not age physically. Nor do we suffer from the illnesses and maladies you are prone to dealing with. In short, this is how we are, at this time or any other. What you see is what you get.

Huh?

No, we're *not* all fuzzy wuzzy crackbrains who like to goof off all the time. You've bought into the myths the media likes to present about us from our past existences. Some of us have the ability to develop more serious pursuits. I myself have an IQ of 175, and I...

That is *not* a polite thing to say to someone in the midst of speaking. *Especially* if they happen to be a *girl.*

Look, you were the ones who wanted to talk. If you didn't want me to...

Thank you. Courtesy much appreciated.

Okay. Where to begin...

Let me see. The earliest I can recall is being removed from mother's womb via the vet....

Not that far? Let's try again.

You want to know about the hijinks I got up to with my brothers on the farm?

No?

See, I knew you were going to say that, 'cause I'm psychic.

Do *not* roll your eyes at me.

You humans should all know that we're fundamentally different from you. In appearance, physical and mental abilities, everything. Superior, in some ways, as well. That's the main leverage we have against you. Your much vaunted armed forces wouldn't stand a chance against us as a group, and you know it. That's why you try to bust us and lock us up on an individual level, 'cause that's the only way you can deal with us. Right?

I *thought* so.

Let's get to the nitty gritty, okay? I have no intention of ratting out my colleagues in the Cartoon Republican Army, or giving away exactly how I managed to survive that hellhole Orthicon with my pride and virginity....

No. Scratch that. Just my pride.

Yes, I *have,* thank you. But, as Jung told Freud, my sex life is none of your fucking business!

I do *not* have to sit here and be insulted by the likes of....

You promise? No more engaging in personalities?

Insulting me.

Just let me explain myself, and we can all get on with our lives, all right?

Thank you.

Okay. Short version of my life.

I was "created", so to speak, by a certain motion picture studio a number of years ago in order to fulfill a certain role in a television series they had developed. That is, the cute puppy who is *way* smarter and edgier than she looks. And that's basically the "role" I've been playing my whole existence, for good and bad, so to speak.

Of course, I didn't discover this until I got hit with a big ton of bricks called "cancellation", when nearly every trace of an animated series and its characters is wiped from the face of the Earth....

I said *nearly*. That's because some of us have the intelligence and people skills to survive here in the "real" world, and some of us don't. The ones you and your law enforcement cronies nab and lock up are usually the ones that don't.

Well, I got ripped out of my private universe, and had to fend for myself around here for a while. Wasn't easy by any means, but I did it. And then came Orthicon...

Yeah, I hear ya. Whole waste of money that accomplished nothing. It was meant to keep us away from you, so that we wouldn't be in a position to harm your children anymore, or some such nonsense. Like pulling us out of the worlds we knew and putting us in one we didn't was going to solve anything. It just made things worse for us.

Except for the fact that we came to know that we weren't alone in the universe for the first time. That there were others like us. Cartoon characters, that is. You knew we existed as we did then, but we didn't figure it out for ourselves until we got there. You didn't realize it, then, but you made this particular sociopolitical bed for us, and now you're lying in it *with* us.

Well, we couldn't possibly go back whence we came once we came back to Earth, now, could we? The government destroyed all of our old homes. Not only that, they had the *temerity* to deny us our legal rights and privileges just because we happened to be, in their view, "merely" *fictional characters....*

I'm not denying that we are fictional beings. If we had been created by your God, you would have understood our predicament, and tried to help us more, because it would be seen as your responsibility to help...

Okay, maybe not all of you would think that way. I'm just sayin'...

That was why we had to set up the Cartoon Republican Army- that's what this band on my arm represents, see- to get you to understand our predicament. At least, the *dunderheads* among you who don't get that this is *your* fault, and not *ours*.

Excuse me?

This is a waste of *your* time?

Look, I know you guys had nothing to do with any of that. I just wanted to explain about why Brendan and I...

Yes, that's the fella who was with me. The other dog. The fella you put in the drunk tank.

Uh huh. We are. It's been an on again, off again thing since Orthicon. When he's sober, he's damn near smart as I am, but *drunk...*

Uh huh. *That* you understand.

Okay. The thing is, Brendan and I had nothing going for us. Like *always.* I swear, I like being involved with the CRA and everything, but we anthropomorphic animals keep getting the shit end of the stick. The human 'toons run most of the operation, and keep the money they somehow find to fund it close to their chests. They're really *snotty* about it, too. Somehow, we don't make the grade for the image they want to give the world of us. So they try to cut us every chance they get. I bring up a perfectly good plan about staging a parade or starting a website or something and they could shoulder me. "We can't *afford* it!" "We can't *afford* it!" Bunch of whiny babies. If I was running things, we'd do everything I wanted to do, and *damn* the expense.

Which brings me to how we got here.

Brendan floated the idea of coming here for Mardi Gras, and I humored him about it. See, another thing about us cartoon characters is that we can hold our stimulants well. We can drink alcohol like it was tap water. And when and where do you do it like that, huh?

So we rent a car, and....

He did.

He has a *license.*

He was *sober-* then.

As I was saying, we rented a car and drove here. No chance of us getting on a plane with that damned security and all. We tried to rent a room in a hotel on Toulouse, and they wouldn't take our credit cards. Both of us have money in the bank to cover them, since they're the kind that take the money directly out of your checking account, but they wouldn't hear of it. We tried around other places in NOLA. Same story. Same in Metairie, Gretna and Kenner. We end up having to stay in the crummy car- like *usual-* after we park it on Rampart. 'Course, the *moment* we leave it unattended, somebody *nabs* it....

No problem. We had nothing important in there at the time. Everything we needed was on our persons.

So, then, Brendan convinces me that we can still try to do the tourist thing and look around. At this, I got really mad.

"At *what*?" I shouted at him. "You know they're not going to let us in most of the places."

"What do you mean?" he said.

"*Because* we're a couple of fucking DOGS, you IDIOT!" I growled.

"Right," he suddenly remembered.

Anyway, he says that the real party aspect of things here at night is out on the streets, not in the places we can't go. He buys me off with the promise that we can, hopefully, get drunk and party with the humans, since they'll all be too looped to care who or what we are, anyway.

So that's how we ended up being part of the roiling crowd of imbibed touristy types that were strutting up and down Canal that night. Somehow or another, Brendan bought himself a pony keg, and the two of us took turn lapping down more brew than even we could handle, for once. And that was how, in the middle of the parade, we drunkenly got the idea that, if we were to somehow hijack one of the floats and use it to propagate the CRA's message of cartoon (and canine) liberation and freedom for the masses- well, that'd be just dan dan *dandy*.

Unfortunately, as you are now well aware, we inadvertently chose the float carrying the Zulu King to try to hijack.

Not a wise move on our part. You love that guy big time. If you fine people from the NOPD hadn't risked your lives trying to save ours, they would have totally burned us to a crisp once they found out who and what we are.

That's how we die. Put a match to us and POOF! We have nitrate inside our bodies, like your blood, around a skeleton of celluloid film in place of bones. Flammable as all get out. That's why you never see any of us smoking anything. That, and the fact that it is so *un*-cool nowadays.

Now, if you have no further questions for me, I will take my semi-boyfriend with me, and we will officially bid the Crescent City a fond *adieu*...

What?

Damages? You mean, when the float....?

Well, sure I can pay for it. I mean, it couldn't possibly be....

HOW *MUCH?*

About the Author

David Perlmutter is a freelance writer based in Winnipeg, Manitoba, Canada. He is the author of two books on animation history: America 'Toons In: A History of Television Animation (McFarland and Co.) and The Encyclopedia Of American Animated Television Shows (Rowman and Littlefield), as well as essays and works of speculative fiction. .